I Remember You

Book three of the Harry Devlin series

ACORN BOOKS

Martin Edwards

First published in 1993
This revised edition published in 2021 by
Acorn Books
www.acornbooks.co.uk

Acorn Books is an imprint of
Andrews UK Limited
www.andrewsuk.com

Copyright © 1993, 2021 Martin Edwards
Introduction Copyright © 2021 Margaret Murphy

The right of Martin Edwards to be identified as the author of this work has been asserted in accordance with the Copyright, Designs and Patents Act 1988.

All rights reserved. No reproduction, copy or transmission of this publication may be made without express prior written permission. No paragraph of this publication may be reproduced, copied or transmitted except with express prior written permission or in accordance with the provisions of the Copyright Act 1956 (as amended). Any person who commits any unauthorised act in relation to this publication may be liable to criminal prosecution and civil claims for damage.

All characters appearing in this work are fictitious. Any resemblance to real persons, living or dead, is purely coincidental.

Dedicated to Jonathan

Contents

Introduction vi
Chapter One 1
Chapter Two 6
Chapter Three. 12
Chapter Four 18
Chapter Five 25
Chapter Six 32
Chapter Seven 38
Chapter Eight. 45
Chapter Nine 50
Chapter Ten. 57
Chapter Eleven 63
Chapter Twelve 70
Chapter Thirteen 78
Chapter Fourteen. 84
Chapter Fifteen 93
Chapter Sixteen. 99
Chapter Seventeen .105
Chapter Eighteen. 110
Chapter Nineteen 116
Chapter Twenty. 121
Chapter Twenty-One. 127
Chapter Twenty-Two 132
Chapter Twenty-Three. 139
Chapter Twenty-Four 146
Chapter Twenty-Five. 152
Chapter Twenty-Six 157
Chapter Twenty-Seven. 164

Yesterday's Papers – Preview 169
The Harry Devlin Series. 175

Introduction

Harry Devlin is that most traditional of detectives – the amateur sleuth – yet he is no mere dilettante. Devlin is a lawyer who defends clients in criminal cases, so he knows the law, and he knows the criminal mind. Martin Edwards has played with the genre to produce in Devlin a man who knows his stuff, and whose encounters with criminals and criminality have more plausibility than the average fictional amateur detective. Devlin is an eminently likeable character; open-hearted and kind, with a dry sense of humour. Yet he redeems himself from obnoxious perfection: he is also unlucky in love, and sometimes displays more curiosity than common sense in his investigations. He is endearing and infuriating by turns, but always sympathetic. He has seen the worst of humankind, but he is tolerant of others' foibles; worldly-wise, yes, and perhaps sometimes even a little world-weary – but he always able to see the absurdity as well as the darkness in the situations he fetches up in. Devlin wants people to want to do the right thing, rather than to impose his brand of morality on them – and you have to like a man who believes in the intrinsic goodness of humankind, but rejects entirely the temptation to preach.

I Remember You was written – and is firmly rooted – in the Liverpool of the early nineteen-nineties, when the city's elevation to Capital of Culture was still a decade-and-a-half away. European money had secured the reclamation of the Albert Dock, creating luxury apartments and quality retail units in a beautiful waterfront setting. But by 1993, the year in which I Remember You was published, Liverpool had suffered decades of decline; the manufacturing base of the city had been eroded, unemployment was high, and many of those dockside businesses did not flourish. It seemed that post-Militant Tendency, pre-regeneration Liverpool simply did not know what to do with luxury.

As a Liverpudlian, the picture I retain of the city at that time is grey, windswept and litter strewn. But it was also a landscape of opposites – and as a solicitor specialising in criminal law, Harry Devlin moves (sometimes uneasily) between the worlds of Chamber of Commerce types with their black tie dos, and low-life scallywags who drink in back street hotels where rooms can be hired by the hour.

When I think of schoolfriends, the names Sheehey and Dolan and Cusack and Donnelly come easily to mind – second generation Irish immigrants raised during the Anglo-Irish troubles. Feelings on both sides remained strong well into in the nineteen-nineties, and Edwards marks the ties as well as the sectarian divisions between Liverpool and Ireland in this story.

I Remember You is the third in the Harry Devlin series; Martin Edwards is always strong on plot, and his trademark dry humour is evident here, alongside some pithy insights into jurisprudence. Indeed, some of the subtext-told-in-monologue is reminiscent of Yes, Minister – and just as funny.

Margaret Murphy

I Remember You

Chapter One

Flames licked at the building, greedy as the tongues of teenage lovers. They curled out from the windows above the shopfront and up to the gutters, fierce in their hunger, intent on conquest.

The smell of burning filled Harry Devlin's sinuses. Smoke stung his eyes and the back of his throat.

'Don't even think of going in there.'

'For the love of Jases,' said Finbar Rogan. 'What d'you think I have for brains? I'd not try to force my way inside if the missus herself was trapped the other side of that door.' He threw back his head and laughed. 'Come to think of it, if she was – I'd be chucking in a match or two myself.'

A thunderous splintering of glass made them duck in a reflex of self-defence. Straightening up, Harry saw the first-floor panes disintegrate. He shielded his face as a thousand shards showered the paving all around.

Finbar cried out in pain and stumbled to the ground. Seeing blood trickle from a cut on the Irishman's cheek, Harry didn't hesitate. In a matter of seconds, he dragged Finbar back towards the shelter of a doorway on the other side of the street. There they leaned against each other for support, fighting for breath as the fumes leaked into their lungs.

The narrowness of Williamson Lane intensified the heat and Harry felt the skin of his face tingle. Finbar groaned and wiped the blood away with his sleeve.

'Thanks for that, mate,' he gasped. 'So now we know what we're in for when we go to Hell.'

'Speak for yourself.'

'Listen, you're a solicitor. Even I have a better chance of Heaven.'

Harry couldn't help grinning at his client. Even as his business blazed on this cold October night, Finbar showed no sign of fear or despair. He would always scoff at any unkindness of the Fates.

'Are you all right?'

'I'll live to claim the insurance, don't you fret.'

Never before had Harry witnessed at such close quarters the raging passion of a fire out of control. A dozen viewings of Mrs Danvers perishing in the ruins of Hitchcock's Manderley had not prepared him for this; nor could he have imagined that the city centre could be so claustrophobic. He had a dizzy sense of everything closing in on him.

Disaster had begun to seduce late night Liverpool's passers-by, excited by the sound and fury. 'Better than Blackpool bloody illuminations!' someone bellowed from the safety of the adjoining square.

The wail of a siren pierced the hubbub, growing louder as each second passed. Harry could hear the fire engines' roar and saw people pressing back into the shadows, making way as first one, then another of the vehicles rounded the corner and pulled up with a shriek twenty yards away.

'The cavalry,' said Finbar.

Suddenly the place was teeming with firefighters. In their yellow headgear and drip pants, navy blue tunics with silvery reflective stripes and rubber boots with steel toe-caps, they might have been storm-troopers from a distant planet. They moved to a pre-ordained routine, running the hose along the ground, connecting it to a hydrant, waving the crowd back, roping off the end of the street. Harry and Finbar were the only spectators within fifty feet of the fire. A man whose white helmet marked his seniority hurried towards them.

'Anyone left inside?' His urgent tone held no hint of panic.

'No one,' Finbar called back. 'Though I might have been in there doing my books if this feller hadn't been due to buy the next round.'

The officer spoke into a walkie-talkie, ordering help from an appliance with a turntable ladder, keeping watch all the time on the spread of the fire.

'You own the shop which sells leathers? Or the travel agents next door?'

'No, I'm up above.'

The words on the blackened signboard at first-floor level were hard to decipher. The officer peered at them. 'Tattooist's studio, is that? You're the feller I heard on Radio Liverpool this morning?'

'The one and only. Liverpool's Leonardo da Vinci.' With boozy bravado, Finbar shrugged off his jacket and ripped open his shirt. On his chest was an extravagant, multicoloured image of a naked woman astride a horse. Her modesty was not quite saved by long dark tresses, and she seemed unaware of the exophthalmic scrutiny of a caricatured Peeping Tom.

Chapter One

'I'll gladly autograph you as a souvenir,' he offered. 'And if you can salvage the electric needles I keep up there, I'll turn you into the Illustrated Man free of charge.'

The officer tipped his helmet back, a now-I've-seen-everything expression spreading across his face.

'Thanks very much, but I'm pretty as a picture as it is.'

In the distance, a second siren howled its warning.

'Here come the police,' said Harry. Ruefully, he asked himself why, earlier that evening, he hadn't refused Finbar's invitation for a quick one. He knew the folly of becoming too closely involved with his clients and their misfortunes, yet it was a mistake he could never help making. If only he'd been taught at college the knack of remaining aloof, of concentrating on rules in books, instead of becoming fascinated by the people who broke them...

'Anything combustible in there?' demanded the fire officer.

Finbar bowed his head, momentarily abashed. 'I had paint and thinners on the landing. Been planning to decorate. Early resolution for next New Year.' He gazed up at the flame-lit heavens. 'Sod's law, eh? I should have left the dirt to hold the place together.'

'What about the ceiling tiles?'

'Polystyrene.'

'Perfect. A fire trap, waiting for a spark. All right – wait here out of harm's way while I take a gander.'

As the officer re-joined his men, a police car appeared, its lights flashing. One of its occupants raced towards the blaze, the other strode towards Harry and Finbar, waving his arms like a farmer directing sheep.

'Move, will you? Don't – hey, for Chrissake, it's Harry Devlin! What are you doing here, pal? I thought you chased ambulances, not fire engines.'

Harry nodded a greeting. He knew Roy Gilfillan of old.

'Where there's a disaster, there's sure to be a solicitor. Finbar's a client. We were having a pint in the Dock Brief, putting the world to rights, when some bloke burst in and said a building in Williamson Lane had gone up in flames. We dashed over and it turns out to be—'

Another siren interrupted him and he swung round to watch the arrival of the turntable while Roy Gilfillan marched over to his colleague, who was conferring with the fire officer outside the entrance to Finbar's studio. Harry noticed the Irishman's eyes slide away from the fire to a couple of girls in the crowd behind them, blondes *en route* for a nightclub who had paused to goggle at the inferno. Finbar winked at them and was rewarded by smirks of encouragement. Even at a time like this he was incorrigible.

'Do you need to call Melissa?' asked Harry, hoping to lead Finbar away from temptation. 'Tell her what's happened?'

'No problem. She's not neurotic, not like Sinead, doesn't make a fuss when I tell her to expect me when she sees me. I'm not a train, I don't run to timetables.'

'Neither does InterCity, but at least it stays on the rails most of the time.'

Finbar chuckled. 'Truth to tell, I've a lot on my plate already, so far as the fair sex are concerned – even leaving Sinead and her bloody alimony demands aside. I bumped into a girl I used to know only this morning. A lovely lady. I reckon I might be able to persuade her to rekindle the flame – 'scuse the phrase, in present circumstances. And then there's Melissa… Jases!'

Across the street, the door which led to the tattoo parlour finally disintegrated in an explosion worthy of an Exocet. Awestruck, Harry and Finbar gazed at the wreckage. Above them, men in breathing masks were directing water jets from the top of the ladder down on to the blaze, while at ground level two more firefighters armed with axes moved towards the entrance. Safe behind the cordon, winos cheered as if on the terraces at Anfield. Oblivious to his audience, the fire chief pointed towards the building. The policemen stared obediently at something, then Gilfillan gestured for Harry and Finbar to approach. The two of them edged closer.

'What's up?' asked Finbar. 'Any closer and I'll get scorch marks on Lady Godiva.'

'Smell that!' shouted Gilfillan, pointing towards the doorway.

No mistaking the stink of petrol from close range. Harry exchanged a look with the policeman.

'And see the inside of the passageway?'

The fumes made their eyes water, but squinting through the hole Harry saw charred walls immediately beyond the space where the door had been.

Finbar pushed a hand through his unruly dark hair. He was a stocky man, barely as tall as Harry but broader in the shoulder and a few years older; yet his wonderment was that of a wide-eyed schoolboy.

'Are you telling me this wasn't an accident?'

The policeman shrugged. 'The seat of fire seems to have been the other side of your front door – the burning is worse there than further up the stairs. Add that to the smell and there's only one diagnosis.'

'Arson?' asked Harry. For all the heat, he felt a sudden chill.

'Suspected malicious ignition,' Gilfillan's colleague corrected him primly, before turning to Finbar. 'Is there anyone who might have a grudge against you?'

Finbar looked nonplussed. After a pause for thought, he allowed a guilty grin to lift the corners of his mouth. It was a moment of self-knowledge.

'Only everyone I've ever met.'

Chapter Two

Two hours later Harry was standing on the doorstep of a club listed in the phone book as the Dangerous Liaison, but known to everyone in Liverpool as the Danger. Finbar had persuaded him to come here against his better judgement. Sometimes he felt as if he spent his entire life going against his better judgement.

'It's on your way home,' Finbar had insisted while hailing a taxi.

'Not unless the cabbie's got less sense of direction than a roulette ball.'

'C'mon! I owe you a drink from earlier this evening.'

'Forget it.' Knowing it was a mistake to ask, but unable to resist, Harry added, 'Anyway, why do you want to call at a dive like the Danger?'

'Listen, it's just on the off-chance. I happened to mention to the girl I saw this morning that I'd be at the Danger tonight. It's the first place that sprang to mind. She's hooked herself up with another feller now, so ten to one she won't be able to make it anyway. But let's give it a try, eh?'

Harry had known Finbar for only a few months, but he'd soon learned that his client never took 'no' for an answer. After five years of separation from his wife and persistent demands for a divorce, Finbar was at last about to get his own way. Sinead Rogan, a strong Catholic, had withheld her consent for as long as the law allowed. Now she had no choice, she had evidently resolved to take him for every penny he had. Harry could understand her bitterness. For Finbar, adultery was a hobby – a habit, almost – rather than a vice or guilty secret. He had no more conscience than a one-armed bandit. Yet Harry could not help liking the man. He was a good companion; more than an acquaintance, if not quite a firm friend.

'Have you no shame?' he asked, already knowing the answer.

Finbar chuckled. Earlier, he'd admitted to Gilfillan that his studio was handsomely insured, almost daring the policeman to make of that what he would. He had more reason to celebrate, it seemed, than to mourn.

Chapter Two

Harry climbed with resignation into the back seat of the cab. 'And what about Melissa? You've only been going out with her a matter of weeks.'

'What the eyes don't see.'

Finbar leaned forward to tell the driver his destination, then glanced back over his shoulder and gave a devilish wink. Harry found it easy at that moment to imagine his client with cloven hooves and forked tail.

'Tell you something, Harry – I could murder a pint.'

'One of these days you'll end up murdered yourself.'

'If so, I wouldn't back your mate Gilfillan to track the culprit down. Jases, I feel like I've been through the third degree. And I'm the blessed victim!'

The police questioning had continued long after the fire was finally doused. Harry could read Gilfillan's mind. Finbar had probably tattooed half the inmates in Walton Jail in his time; it did not take too much prejudice to guess that a man who decorated villains' flesh might have made ugly enemies over the years. Yet Finbar had been adamant; no one had threatened him or sworn revenge. He couldn't think who might have wanted to burn down his studio. The fire, he maintained, must have been started by youngsters careless of the identity of the people whose property they sought to destroy.

Harry could see Gilfillan didn't believe what he was being told. But Finbar's complex love life had no doubt schooled him in the art of telling careful lies. If he had guessed who was responsible for the arson, he was keeping it to himself and no amount of nagging would make him say more than he wished. Harry wondered if a drop more alcohol might loosen his client's tongue. In any case, he always found Finbar's company exhilarating. With him around, there was always the chance that something extraordinary would happen; perhaps that was the secret of his charm. So when the taxi arrived at the Danger, Harry found himself clambering out as well.

The club occupied the cellar of a redundant mariners' hostel on the waterfront. The place looked as though it had been punished by the Luftwaffe in the Blitz and not repaired since. On the door was a giant whom Finbar introduced as Mad Max and whose handshake almost fractured Harry's arm.

'Had a lady asking after me tonight?'

'No *lady* would ever ask after you, Finbar,' grunted the giant.

'Max's brother owns this dive,' Finbar said, waving Harry down a narrow wooden staircase. 'They have to use him as a bouncer because he wouldn't fit anywhere inside.'

Harry could believe it. The Danger earned its name, if only because it transgressed every health and safety rule in the statute book. At the bottom of the stairs he and his client plunged into a mass of bodies wedged together between wooden uprights which propped up the low ceiling with an unnerving lack of conviction. Shadowy outlines of damp marks could be seen through the distemper someone had splashed haphazardly on the walls. There seemed to be more smoke than in Williamson Lane at the height of the blaze and the tuneless thud that was supposedly music made Harry's ears feel as though they were about to burst.

Whilst Finbar disappeared in search of drinks, Harry fought through the crush. A jostling girl spilt vodka and lime over his arm and legs and swore with a fluency that would have made a docker gape. In the disco, teenagers in tawdry clothes writhed as if afflicted by disease, their lips moving to form the words of meaningless lyrics, their bleary eyes staring unfocused. In one corner, a leather-clad lad had his hand up the skirt of a high-heeled brunette with a schoolgirl's figure and a harridan's smile. In another, a fat boy was being sick on matting strewn over the concrete floor.

Finbar returned and thrust a pint pot into his hand. Harry downed the beer in record time and gestured towards the exit. He had to shout to make himself heard.

'Did you find her?'

Finbar shook his head. 'Not my lucky night!' he bellowed in reply. He finished his drink and followed Harry back up the stairs. At the top, Mad Max was cuddling a coquettish blonde; Harry doubted whether her rib-cage would survive the experience.

Outside again, he gulped in a lungful of air. For all that it was tainted by factory dust and car exhaust fumes, in comparison to the atmosphere in the Danger it had the tang of a Highland breeze.

'Thank God for that! At last I've realised I'm past it.'

Finbar laughed. 'It's all in the mind. And compared to one or two places I know in Dublin, the Danger is as sober as a confessional.'

'You're welcome to them. Why did I let that taxi go?'

'You're not so far from home. Since I've been stood up, let's stroll by the riverside and I'll pick up a cab when you say goodbye at Empire Dock.'

For a while neither of them spoke as they followed the roadside path parallel to the Mersey. The temperature had dropped to freezing point, but at least the cold sharpened Harry's thoughts. He decided to seek again the answer to the question that bothered him.

'Are you sure you have no idea who may have started the fire?'

'Didn't I tell your policeman friend exactly that?'

'Yes, but...'

'Don't say you're pointing the finger too! When I told him about the insurance, I could see him sizing up my wrists for handcuffs.'

'He was only doing his job.'

'Face it,' said Finbar with sorrowful good humour, 'so far as Gilfillan is concerned, I'm uniquely qualified for a life of crime. I'm not only an Irishman, but a tattooist as well. With the busies, old prejudices die hard. They don't understand the body is a canvas and...'

'And you're a picture of innocence. Okay, okay, spare me the propaganda.'

'All right, mate, don't get the needle!'

Harry grinned. In full flow, Finbar was a formidable advocate of the tattooist's art; the Bar's loss was the saloon bar's gain. Harry had heard not once but a dozen times that illustrated skin is like a personal diary, as fitting for a businessman as for a fairground freak.

Three huge buildings loomed ahead of them: the Liver, the Cunard and the Port of Liverpool – monuments to the city's maritime traditions and its glorious past. The sight of the Pierhead, whether by day or night, always stirred Harry. For all its faults, he loved his home town. There was too much squalor for it to be a comfortable place, yet he relished the architectural reminders of the time when this had been the Empire's second city. For him, Liverpool and its people remained intensely and defiantly alive.

Finbar paused and sighed as he pointed at the floodlit Liver Building.

'See? When I first arrived here on the ferry as a kid, my ma lifted me up to look at the lights. My first sight of England. I've never forgotten it.'

A faraway expression misted his eyes. He gestured back in the direction from which they had come, towards Princes Dock. 'We used to land over there. The boats were packed with the Irish, sailing here for a weekend or a lifetime.'

As Harry's forebears had done, a hundred and fifty years ago, in the wake of the potato famine. He was the last of the line, knowing nothing of his ancestors, not sharing their faith, which the Devlin family like so many others had lost through the passage of time. Yet still he felt an affinity with those Irish people who had crossed the sea in search of a new start. Perhaps it helped to account for his liking of Finbar.

But Finbar was quick to destroy the romantic impression he had conjured up. 'I can see them now. Fellers lying on the floor in the toilet, still trying to sing along with the ceilidh music playing everywhere. Sad-faced women, travelling so they could have an abortion – I remember watching them throw up over the side of the boat.'

He stopped and stared out into the night. 'And to think that Eileen might still be alive...'

'Eileen?'

'A sweet girl I used to know. Ah, Harry, if only we could unmake the past!'

Both men became quiet, lost in their own visions of what might have been. Eventually Finbar said, 'We don't stop dreaming, you know, us Irish. When I made the trip for the last time, I still had the notion that one day I might return to Dublin.'

'And will you?'

'Are you serious? The ferry doesn't even sail from Liverpool anymore!'

A lone black cab came into view and Harry flagged it down, but shook his head when Finbar suggested he jump in for the short journey to his flat in Empire Dock.

'Thanks, but I've walked this far, I may as well keep on. Clear my head. Tell Melissa I may see her at Radio Liverpool tomorrow. And – watch yourself.'

'Stop fretting. A gang of kids torched the place, depend upon it. It was nothing personal.'

***

All the way home, Harry juggled the possibilities. Finbar's wry admission to the police about the number of his enemies had probably not been much exaggerated. He was a man who might easily drive others to fury – but arson? Perhaps Finbar was right after all.

He was glad to reach the sanctuary of his flat. The Empire Dock building was a waterfront warehouse, part of a complex transformed in recent years from dereliction into housing and leisure facilities. His neighbour was a nocturnal saxophonist, but the old walls were so thick that Harry never heard a note. Passing the jazz player's front door, he remembered the previous occupant, a lonely woman with whom he had shared a brief relationship in the aftermath of his wife's death. Shaking his head, he hurried on.

Alone in his flat, he lay on the bed fully clothed, too exhausted to undress. Yet now he had the chance to rest, sleep stubbornly refused to come. He could still see the fire's flames and smell the suffocating smoke and the cacophony from the Danger continued to pound in his ears.

At last darkness gave way to misty morning. Yawning, he set off for the magistrates' court and his daily struggle to portray wrong as right – or at least as not deserving of a custodial sentence. Five guilty pleas and a minor crimewave of offences taken into consideration made him wish that his clients displayed as much ingenuity in escaping the clutches of the law as they expected him to show in finding plausible mitigating circumstances. He returned to his firm's office in a semi-daze, his mind a blank, his imagination sucked dry.

Chapter Two

Arriving at Fenwick Court, he had a vague impression that something was missing. Picking a path through the rubble left by a gang of navvies who were renovating the block on the opposite side of the courtyard, he tried to fathom what it was. The moment he pushed open the door which led into reception at New Commodities House, an electric drill started to scream and he remembered. Sometimes he suspected they waited for his return before resuming work.

The throbbing in his head began again. It was as bad as being back in the Danger.

'Shit!'

He hadn't meant to speak out loud. In so doing he startled a young woman, whom he had not at first noticed, sitting in the corner reading a tattered copy of *Exchange Contracts*. She glanced up at him in bewilderment.

In the shabby waiting room, with its threadbare carpet and faded posters extolling the virtues of legal aid, she seemed as out of place as an orchid in a nettle patch. The subtle perfume; the Enny handbag; the sheepskin jacket; all hinted at an affluence rare among his firm's clientele. Her heart-shaped face was framed by shoulder-length dark hair and she had painted her fingernails the colour of blood.

Harry gasped, feeling a sense of shock verging on disbelief. It was not due simply to the woman's glamorous looks, but because for an instant he thought he was seeing a ghost.

Chapter Three

Of course his wife Liz had not come back from the dead. This girl's eyes were brown, not green. She lacked Liz's high cheekbones and had a snub nose; her mouth was wider and her figure fuller. Yet the way she tossed the magazine aside and concentrated her attention upon him reminded him irresistibly of the woman he had loved with a passion as fierce as it had proved futile; a woman murdered less than two years before.

The resemblance exceeded any superficial similarity of physical appearance. As he overcame his sense of shock on seeing the girl, instinct told him she had the same thirst for life as Liz, and as strong a faith that tomorrow would be better than today. Her body seemed taut with suppressed excitement, as if she were about to embark on a great adventure. In her presence, he felt clumsy and ill-at-ease, and not simply because she had heard him swear. He realised he looked haggard, a rumpled man with hair that defied any comb and a suit as shiny as his shoes. A man whom Liz had left for someone else.

The beginnings of a smile stretched her lips as she contemplated him. It untied his tongue and he blurted out the first thing that came into his head.

'Sorry... are you being attended to?'

Christ, of all the anodyne questions! Uttered, too, with a frog-in-the-throat nervousness excusable in a schoolboy, but close to absurd in a Solicitor of the Supreme Court of Judicature.

She spoke quickly, words tumbling from her in a torrent, as if she were eager to please.

'Thanks for asking. I'm here to see your Mr Crusoe about a house sale. Your receptionist,' she glanced in the direction of gum-chewing Suzanne on the switchboard, 'told me he's on the phone, but he'll be free soon.'

Her vowel sounds betrayed native Scouse origins. This was a local girl made very good.

Chapter Three

'Have we – have we asked if you'd like a coffee while you wait?' Behind him he heard a stifled cough of indignation from Suzanne. She regarded clients as a necessary evil; offering them hospitality was someone else's job.

'It's quite all right,' said the girl. 'I had a cup before I left home.'

'Fine,' he said, trying to regain his composure. 'I'm sure my partner will be here in a minute.' He wanted to think of a reason to stay, but his powers of invention hadn't recovered from their courtroom work-out and he found himself walking away into the corridor which led to his room.

Marching in the opposite direction, burly and brisk as a sergeant major, came his partner Jim Crusoe.

'For God's sake, old son, you all right? You look terrible. I've seen more blood in a banana.'

Harry was glad of the chance to shove the girl out of his mind. 'I went for a drink with Finbar Rogan in the Dock Brief last night. A hangover I might have expected – not a ringside seat at Dante's *Inferno*.'

Rapidly he recounted the events of the previous evening. No hint of surprise disturbed the contours of Jim's bearded face; Harry had often thought that he would treat the onset of Armageddon as phlegmatically as a seminar on the law of registered title.

'Arson, eh? Insurance job, do you reckon?'

'I gather that when Finbar renewed the lease, you recommended him to take out a much bigger policy.'

'If only I filled in the pools with equal foresight! Good advice, so long as he didn't see it as a short cut to a small fortune.'

'He would never be so stupid. He's the obvious suspect.'

'If all your clients were Mensa material, you'd be redundant, old son.'

'True, if unkind. All the same when we were told about the fire in the pub, I didn't think it was news he'd been expecting to hear. And when we saw the blaze he was genuinely shocked.'

'Maybe the husband of one of his fancy women decided it was time to retaliate.' Jim rubbed his beard. His amusement was tinged with disapproval; the most uxorious of men, he could never understand the impulse to promiscuity. 'Anyway, can't stop any longer. I have a client waiting.'

'So I see.'

Something in Harry's tone made Jim pause. 'You know her?'

'Not even her name. But for her, I'd gladly take up domestic conveyancing.'

'Rogan's corrupting you, old son. Keep your grubby paws off, she's a respectable married woman. At least I assume she's respectable. But she's certainly married.'

A trickle of disappointment dripped down Harry's spine.

'Who is she?'

'Name of Rosemary Graham-Brown. I love clients with double-barrelled names, they never kick up about the bill. And she's married to money. They're selling a palace, to judge by the price and the property particulars.'

'Any purchase?'

'No, they're emigrating to Spain. Never mind. If she wants a divorce, I'll put a word in for you. After all, nothing like moving house for bringing hidden tensions to the surface.'

'So people say. Personally, I've found cheaper ways of putting relationships under strain.'

Harry went to his room, a cramped cubicle overflowing with the papers he never quite got round to. His last remark had been truth spoken in jest. Since Liz's murder, he had failed to find contentment with any of the other fish in the sea. The affair with his next-door neighbour had soon petered out and earlier in the year a fling with a young barrister had ended in bitter recrimination and a mutual feeling of betrayal. Lately he had lacked a woman in his life and at times he found it hard to restrain a reluctant admiration for the carefree manner of Finbar's philandering. Part of him deplored his client's behaviour, but another part envied the luck of the Irish.

The phone trilled. 'Mr Rogan's here.'

Suzanne would have sounded bored if announcing that Elizabeth Taylor had called for matrimonial advice under the green form scheme, yet, for once, enthusiasm lightened her adenoidal tones. Finbar was incapable of speaking to a woman without trying on the charm. Although some proved immune, he had a flair for making people feel good – and for making them do his bidding. Some day he might even persuade Suzanne to make him a coffee.

'We weren't due to meet until two, outside the court door.'

'He knows that,' she said, as if explaining the obvious to a child. 'But he says he's come to take you out to lunch.' She left Harry in no doubt that she considered him undeserving of such an honour.

He swept away a sheaf of unanswered correspondence to clear a space on the spare chair and returned to reception. His client was doodling a picture of a butterfly on the back of a Law Society newsletter, seemingly unscathed by the events of the previous night.

'I can't tell a fib, mate – you look the worse for wear after all our excitement together. Fancy a bite at the Ensenada, to sharpen you up for the battle this afternoon?'

Chapter Three

'After last night, a lie-down in a darkened room might do me more good. Anyway, come through for a minute.'

Once in Harry's room, Finbar leaned back in the chair and put his feet on the desk. 'I must say that girl of yours always takes my eye. She could lose a stone or two, for sure, but never mind. More of her to love, eh? She's quite an advertisement for Crusoe and Devlin. First impressions in an office count for so much.'

'We chose her specially to project a rude, lazy and brainless image. The next step is a logo with a V-sign superimposed over the scales of justice. Anyway, we're stuck with her – no one else would take the wages we pay. So what are you doing here so bright and early, Finbar?'

'Ah well, I wanted to give you lunch to say thanks for all your support last night.'

'Don't mention it. How's your place looking?'

'Ripe for the bulldozer if you ask me, although the landlord's coming round to see what can be done. And the leather store down below is doing a roaring trade in what they call a Fire Sale. I reckon they're flogging twice as much stock as they had in the entire shop last night.'

Harry laughed. He never ceased to marvel at the entrepreneurial genius of his fellow Liverpudlians.

'How do you intend to keep the business going?'

'I'm thinking of taking a winter break. I insure with the people whose ads brag about how fast they come up with the readies when calamity strikes. If they're as good as their word, I should get a payment on account within the next few days.' Finbar rubbed his hands. They were tattooed with dragons, picked out in vivid colours. 'Tell that partner of yours I owe him a pint. It was a lucky day I followed his advice about the policy.'

'As long as you didn't give Fate a nudge.'

Finbar groaned. 'Have you no trust at all? I thought we'd settled this last night. Listen, as Jases is my judge, I didn't torch my own place. Nor did I pay anyone else to do it for me. Satisfied? Or do I need a plane to skywrite that I'm innocent?'

'Sorry.'

A magnanimous wave of the hand. 'We'll say no more about it.'

'You realise Sinead will want her slice of the insurance cake?'

'What? Ah, be buggered to that. The massed army of the saints couldn't persuade me to cut her in.'

Harry sighed. In this job, his tact and patience were tested as often as a whore's knicker elastic.

'Look, it's another reason for doing a deal on the maintenance payments at the door of the court. Why don't you let me talk to her lawyer at least? Kim Lawrence might fight each case like a personal crusade, but in the end she's usually realistic.'

The Irishman grunted. 'Let's talk about it over lunch.'

Harry led the way to the front of the building. As he stepped into the courtyard, he realised that Finbar was no longer right behind him. Glancing over his shoulder, he was startled to see the Irishman dodging back into reception and out of sight.

A sleek BMW had parked at the opposite end of the courtyard. A big dark man was leaning out of the driver's window and haranguing one of the builders. The other members of the gang had stopped work and were looking on with folded arms and mutinous faces.

Harry stared at the tableau for a moment, then hurried back into the office. Finbar was winking at Suzanne, but Harry could tell he was shaken.

'This young lady tells me there's another way out of here.'

'There's an emergency exit at the back, yes.'

'Mind if we leave that way? We can make sure the door isn't blocked off – wouldn't want you to fall foul of the fire inspector. Blazes can start when you least expect them, as I discovered last night.'

Finbar headed off in the direction Suzanne was pointing. Harry did not catch up until they were both in the street outside.

'So what was all that about?'

Finbar slowed to a stroll. 'No sweat, Harry, I simply spotted someone I'd rather not bump into. It makes no sense to spoil a meal. We have a lot to talk about, you and I. Sinead is so...'

'Who didn't you want to meet? The big feller in the BMW? Who is he?'

Finbar waved dismissively. 'An old pal of mine by the name of Dermot McCray, if you must know. We go back a long way.'

'You won't be going forward a long way if you dive for cover whenever you see him.'

'We had a spot of bother – let's leave it at that. Now, about Sinead. The truth is, I just want rid of the whole damned business. I'm beginning to wish I'd never bothered with divorce after all. I won't be making the mistake of matrimony again, believe me. It grieves me to think of that woman living the life of Riley at my expense.'

'The judge will want to be convinced she is properly provided for.'

'But she seems to want me to fund the entire bloody animal rights movement, by the sound of it. God, why ever did I get hitched to a woman crazy about all creatures great and small – except for her poor bloody husband?'

Sinead Rogan was a leading member of Free Animals Now!, better known as FAN!, a group of militant activists. Her approach to matrimonial litigation was equally bellicose.

'I agree her claims are excessive, but let's face it, what you offered originally wouldn't keep one of her cats in Whiskas.'

'I'm prepared to negotiate,' said Finbar with dignity. 'All I want is a fair settlement; surely that's not too much to ask. What's the old saying – let justice be done, though the heavens fall?'

'Forget that idea,' said Harry amiably. 'It might ruin our case.'

Chapter Four

'Women!' expostulated Finbar, stretching out his arms in an extravagant parody of despair which almost swept a strawberry pavlova from a passing dessert trolley. 'They'll be the death of me.'

Harry drained his coffee cup. The Ensenada's cuisine had left him feeling replete. Finbar had, as usual, been a generous host, and Harry didn't have the heart to say that for his client to malign the opposite sex was much the same as Billy Bunter badmouthing the school tuck shop.

'Offer a few more quid each week to keep Sinead quiet,' he advised. 'Business isn't so bad. You can afford it.'

Finbar grunted. He was too free-spending for his own good much of the time, but Sinead's admittedly exorbitant demand for maintenance pending suit had provoked a mulish refusal to compromise on a more realistic figure.

'Lord knows what I've done to deserve this,' he complained.

Persistent adultery, perhaps, reflected Harry. Spendthrift habits, general fecklessness… but clients embroiled in messy divorce proceedings were seldom open to reason. The trick was to let them convince themselves that acrimony was counter-productive.

'When marriages break down,' he said gently, 'there are only losers.'

He had first-hand knowledge of the truth of that. He and Liz had drifted apart long before she had left him for a man who promised the good life and in the end brought her nothing but disillusion and disaster.

Finbar nodded in agreement. An opportunistic waiter took the gesture as a sign that the bill was required and produced it with a conjuror's flourish. Scarcely glancing at the bottom line, Finbar opened his wallet and passed over a sheaf of notes. 'A feast fit for a king,' he said. 'Keep the change.' After much lavish gratitude, the waiter disappeared.

'You'd never believe it these days, but at one time Sinead was a fine-looking woman,' Finbar said sorrowfully. 'Yet look at her now! I've met better-dressed bag ladies.'

Harry forbore to point out that neither he nor his client were exemplars of high fashion.

Finbar scratched his nose. 'I suppose I blame myself.'

Harry leaned forward. This was more promising.

'She wasn't keen on coming over to England originally – moving away from her friends and family in Dublin. I talked her into it; the worst mistake I ever made. We hadn't been married long, but already the writing was on the wall. Mind, in those days she didn't rant and rave every single time I opened my mouth.' Finbar gave a reminiscent shake of the head. 'I should have known better. I'd always sworn I liked women too much ever to marry one. And Sinead was hardly my type. Steeped in the faith and mad about animals, while all I ever knew about was the birds and the bees. Even in those days she was into animal lib, going on demos and that kind of malarkey. I ought to have spotted the warning signs.'

Finbar mused for a few seconds. Then he grinned. 'But there's something irresistible about a passionate woman, wouldn't you agree? And she was that, all right. So I set my sights on having my wicked way with her. In the end, I managed it, but at the cost of a wedding ring. I'd have done better with her in the long run if I'd had four legs and fur.'

'There must have been good times.'

'I won't deny it. In the earliest days she even let me tattoo her boobs with flamingos – free-hand stuff. Takes guts, that, you know. You only have one chance to get it right. I hoped in time she'd agree to a complete body stocking, from her neck to her knees. A sight to make any man swoon.'

Harry winced. 'Women *like* that sort of thing?'

'Ah, you're an old chauvinist at heart. Let me promise you, some of them love it. I reckon Michelangelo would envy some of my canvases.' He smiled to himself, as if enjoying a private joke. 'At least when all the papers have been signed, Sinead will have something to remember me by. That's one of the beauties of tattooing, mate. You carry your history with you, you can't deny who or what you were.'

Finbar blinked, shook his head again and returned to the present. 'Anyway, things started to go sour between us. I had the studio, a few girlfriends, I've never exactly kept regular hours. And Sinead could never be content as a housewife. She got involved with Free Animals Now! I remember years ago she bragged to me FAN! had broken into a vivisection lab and smashed open all the cages – as if there weren't enough rats in the big bad world already.' A slow smile spread across his face as he added, 'Mind. I won't pretend it was all bad news. At least I never had to buy her a new mink coat.'

'And Melissa, what about her?'

'I'm not cut out for wedded bliss. I learned my lesson with Sinead. All the same, Melissa's been good for me. I'd been having a tough time, what with… well, it doesn't matter. We met at a party, I got talking about body art and she explained she worked on local radio and they might be interested in doing a programme about it. So I offered to draw a garland on her ankle.'

'She took you up on it?'

'The very next night. We've been together ever since.' Finbar rubbed his chin. 'Funny thing, though, Harry, she's asked me to tattoo her thigh with a heart linking her name and mine and I can't bring myself to do it. I keep making up excuses.'

'You think it would give her a special claim on you?'

'Spot on. Besides, Melissa's a funny kid. Lovely to look at, but sometimes she bothers me. She's had… well, let's call it trouble with her nerves. She's the sort who easily gets hurt.'

It was on the tip of Harry's tongue to say: *So don't hurt her*. Realism kept him quiet. Urging Finbar to settle for monogamy would be like inviting Sinead to join the Quorn.

Finbar belched pleasurably. 'By the way, are you doing anything tonight?'

'Not apart from worrying about my debut on local radio tomorrow. Why? You're surely not planning another bonfire?'

'Something completely different, I promise you. Radio Liverpool are sponsoring a talent contest at the Russian Convoy this evening. Come along and I'll introduce you to Baz Gilbert.'

Harry consulted his watch. The court hearing was due to start in fifteen minutes. He clambered to his feet.

'Okay, but we'd better move. It's time to try and tip the scales of justice.'

Outside it had grown colder and wisps of mist hung in the air. This kind of weather always made Harry think of *Bleak House*; Dickens' description of fog on the river had stuck in his mind. Fog, rolling defiled among the waterside pollution of a great and dirty city, yet never so thick as to assort with the groping and floundering condition held by that most pestilent of hoary sinners – the court.

The Divorce Registry was packed with sulky spouses, refusing to look at each other while their legal representatives haggled over the kids, the mortgage payments and the Dire Straits albums. Harry caught sight of Kim Lawrence at the end of the corridor, talking to a woman who wore dungarees the colour of mud. With a shock, he realised who she was.

Sinead Rogan had half a dozen badges pinned to her breast and grubby moccasins on her feet. Her dark hair was thick and hadn't seen shampoo for some time. But something oddly familiar about her features struck Harry. Watching her interrupt Kim Lawrence, stabbing the air with her finger to emphasise a point, he realised what she reminded him of.

'Sinead was the model for your picture of Lady Godiva,' he whispered.

Finbar tapped himself on the chest and nodded. 'In happier times, as they say in the newspapers.'

When Sinead paused for breath, Kim Lawrence nodded briskly. She turned and, noticing Harry and Finbar, loped down the corridor towards them.

'Afternoon,' she said to Harry. 'I take it this is your client?' She eyed Finbar with an ill-concealed distaste which contrasted with his admiring scrutiny of her tall and slender frame.

This is all I need, thought Harry. *Kim is up in arms on behalf of the wronged wife and miladdo is on the point of making a pass at her.*

Hastily, he asked, 'Anything doing, Kim? Mr Rogan is ready to come to an amicable agreement, if that's possible.'

'You're well aware of what my client is looking for.'

'And you must be aware that she has no chance of getting it. Ask her to be realistic, and we can wrap this up in five minutes.'

'Mrs Rogan wants her day in court. She has received dreadful treatment from your client and she expects him to start paying for it, from this moment on.'

'I realise you have your instructions and I'm not suggesting Finbar here is a boy scout. But let's talk things over. You'll see from the list we're in front of Buffalo Bill.'

'Judge Cody wouldn't have been my choice to hear this case. Nevertheless, Mrs Rogan's mind is made up. Unless her terms are met, we proceed.'

'You know as well as I do, Cody won't allow any latitude with cross-examination. Anything that might make him late for the cup-tie this evening would definitely be out of order.'

The weary scorn on Kim Lawrence's face conveyed her opinion of the old men who made up a politically incorrect judiciary. She was known in the city as a champion of the oppressed, spokesperson for an equal rights pressure group and Chair of the local branch of the Miscarriages of Justice Organisation. Harry often read in the *Echo* about her leading candle-lit vigils for the unjustly accused or running in marathons to help finance a new refuge for battered wives. Perhaps the creases of tiredness around her eyes marked the first faint signs of compassion fatigue.

'What do you have in mind?' she asked.

Harry named a figure, which fell short of the maximum Finbar was willing to pay. A margin for negotiation was always required when dealing with a formidable opponent who acted for a stubborn client.

'No chance,' said Kim Lawrence.

'Listen, darling,' said Finbar, unable to contain himself any longer, 'when a woman reaches a certain age...'

In a tone cold enough to freeze the rest of the sentence on his lips, Kim Lawrence said, 'I am not your darling, Mr Rogan. And I'll be grateful if you'll spare me your puerile pub philosophising.'

Harry was beginning to lose hope. 'Look, some allowances need to be made here. Do you know Mr Rogan's business was torched last night? As of this moment he has no trading income whatsoever. What's the wife after – blood?'

'That will do for a start,' said a husky voice.

Sinead Rogan had joined them. She sounded triumphant. For all her unkempt appearance, she exuded a raw physical energy and Harry could guess why Finbar had once found her attractive. At close range, he became aware of the smell of cats clinging to her. Her hazel eyes gleamed with hostility as she contemplated her husband.

Finbar made the mistake of addressing her.

'Ah, come on, love. I'm willing to throw in a few more quid. Can't we sort this out like reasonable human beings?'

She shrieked with laughter: a wild, uncontrolled noise, as out of place in the court building's calm as the sound of someone kicking a tin can down a church aisle. A security guard at the other end of the corridor cast a sharp glance in their direction.

'The offer we're willing to make is fair,' said Harry. 'I have Mr Rogan's authority to increase it by another ten per cent. Talk it over with your solicitor.'

Kim Lawrence opened her mouth, but before any words could come out, Sinead laughed again, the same discordant shriek.

'You will have to excuse me, Mr – Devlin, is it?' she said at last. 'Money may be what makes you tick, but not me. It's pound of flesh time, so far as I am concerned.'

'For Heaven's sake,' said Finbar. 'I don't pretend I'm an angel, but...'

'Shut up,' she said, spitting out the words. 'You've had plenty to say in the past. Now it's your turn to listen.' She paused for effect, then hissed: 'You see, you bastard, I know what happened to that wretched girl Eileen.'

Finbar's cheeks reddened. Harry had thought him incapable of blushing, but with a few words, Finbar's customary self-confidence had dissolved into uncharacteristic embarrassment. He shifted from one foot to another and cleared his throat.

'Sinead, for Heaven's sake! You don't know anything about Eileen.'

She wagged her finger at him, well aware she had struck a nerve.

'You couldn't be more wrong. I've heard the whole story.'

Finbar half-closed his eyes. 'Listen, I'm the only one who knows it.'

'You think you know it all, where women are concerned; but the truth is, you're the most despicably ignorant man I ever met.' She spat on the floor and turned away. Kim Lawrence gave the security guard a worried look, but he now had his hands full with a wailing infant, probably the subject of an access dispute.

Finbar shrugged and spoke with a soft sadness. 'Ah, but there's no reasoning with you. Come on, Harry, let the law take its course.'

So they went in before Judge Cody and in cross-examination, Kim Lawrence made her contempt for Finbar clear. Every time he prevaricated about his means, she slapped him down. 'Answer the question, please, Mr Rogan!'

'But it's like this, you see...'

'Yes or no, please, Mr Rogan.'

On another day her tactics would have worked to perfection, but today they succeeded only in infuriating Buffalo Bill, who was banking on an early dart home. Finally, he threw his pen onto the desk.

'Miss Lawrence!'

He paused deliberately, allowing the advocate a moment to fume in silence. He knew she called herself Ms, not Miss, but he had never held with that sort of nonsense.

'Miss Lawrence,' he repeated with careful emphasis. 'You have already been told that Mr Rogan's premises were burnt down last night: a traumatic experience by any standards. You are now indulging, if I may say so, in character assassination for the sake of it. And I will not have that in my court, do you hear? I will not have it!'

In the face of which even the most resilient advocate had to admit defeat. No one was surprised when Cody awarded Sinead a pittance that fell well short of what Finbar had said he was willing to pay. Harry bustled his client out of the courtroom before their luck could change.

The temperature outside had dropped and they walked along Brunswick Street through thickening mist. Finbar seemed miles away. His shoulders were hunched, his dark eyes were glazed; he didn't even notice when they passed two pretty girls whose giggling suggested they were in the mood for a little street banter.

Harry felt overwhelmed by the desire to follow up what Sinead had said. He remembered that on the way back from the Danger, Finbar had spoken of a girl called Eileen before stopping himself. Who was she and why had mention of her name induced such a guilty response?

Curiosity in a lawyer, Harry knew, can be costly. There are so many things it is better not to know. But riddles tantalised him; even to leave a crossword puzzle unfinished filled him with frustration. He always hungered to learn a little more, to help make sense of life's innumerable mysteries.

'So who was Eileen?'

Finbar halted in mid-stride. He considered Harry with care, as if wondering how much to give away.

'For once in my life, I'd rather not utter a word. All I'll say is this: at lunch I said women will be the death of me. But it was different with that poor kid Eileen. I was the death of her.'

Chapter Five

'What d'you call a Scouser in a five-bedroomed detached house?' asked the boy on the makeshift stage in the Russian Convoy's cavernous public bar. 'A burglar. What d'you call a Scouser wearing a collar and tie? The accused.'

He was a scraggy teenager wearing a dinner suit two sizes too big for him. Most of his jokes had been old long before he was born, but he told them fast out of the corner of his mouth and just about deserved the spurt of applause which greeted the end of his act.

Which was more than could be said for most of the evening's entertainers, reflected Harry. Flanked by Finbar and Melissa Keating, he'd spent the last hour and a half watching a procession of hopefuls for whom opportunity was never likely to knock. A ventriloquist with an inflatable doll; a woman who mimicked bird noises; a juggling traffic warden and a Rastafarian banjo player; together with more comedians than were members of Liverpool City Council.

He finished his pint. At least the beer was good. The Russian Convoy was a relic of days gone by, in the quality of its interior design as well as its ale. The decor was heavy, with much emphasis on red plush and gilt. The ornate plasterwork on the ceiling was supposed to be a fine example of its kind; something for customers to admire as they slid to the floor at the end of an evening. And listening to some of these acts would have driven a Rechabite to drink.

A skinny girl who rejoiced in the name of Rosie Rollings began to murder 'Memory' in a thick Scouse accent. *Rosie for remembrance*, thought Harry, closing his eyes, remembering another Rosemary. The gorgeous Mrs Graham-Brown. The brief encounter in reception earlier that day had stayed in his mind; merely to recall it roused him, made him shiver with the need to see her again.

He was a fool, he realised, to let his imagination roam. After all, he had scarcely spoken to her; moreover, she was unattainable, a married woman, about to leave Liverpool for Spain. But she reminded him of Liz, and whenever Liz had tempted, he had been sure to succumb.

Meanwhile Finbar was scarcely setting an example of restraint. In his white suit and velvet bow tie, he looked too natty for a waterfront pub less than an hour before chucking-out time: a wolf in Moss Bros clothing. Earlier in the day he had refused point blank to say any more about the mysterious Eileen, and now he was misbehaving yet again. All night the Irish eyes had been smiling at the curvy redhead producing the local radio broadcast of the event. The girl hadn't failed to notice. Every now and then she favoured him with a glance, once even a brief mock bow of acknowledgement. Harry's mind slid back to his visit to the Danger. Finbar might have met the redhead when making his own guest appearance on the breakfast radio show. Could she be the girl he had hoped to meet at the nightclub?

If Melissa was aware that Finbar's attention was wandering, she gave no hint of it. He had left a hand in hers, as if to reserve his interest while his mind was otherwise engaged. Out of the corner of one eye, Harry saw Melissa give the strong hairy fingers a squeeze. To his surprise, he found the gesture irksome. How did Finbar do it? How could someone to whom infidelity was no more important than a sneeze captivate women with such ease? It was impossible for an ordinary man not to feel a stab of jealousy.

Finbar's good fortune might have been easier to bear had Melissa not been lovely enough to have her choice of men. At first glance, she resembled a sculpture rather than a living woman. Her skin seemed too pale, too flawless, to belong to a creature made of flesh and blood. Yet once or twice during the evening Harry had sensed a tremor running through her; he could only guess at the effort of will she must have made to suppress it.

What could be bothering her? The arson attack? Or was she more aware of her boyfriend's philandering than she appeared? Finbar had said she had had trouble with nerves and looking at her, Harry was struck by the vulnerability of the thin body beneath the lycra dress, a fragility that put him in mind of a piece of porcelain. Melissa, he thought, might easily break. When he'd talked with her in the past, he'd gathered she saw Finbar as a challenge and wanted to persuade him to mend his errant ways. Mission impossible, of course; it would be easier to teach the Liver Birds to fly.

At long last the show drew to a close and the disc jockey who had been acting as compere proclaimed the scraggy teenager the winner, going on to introduce the man who would present the lad with his cheque. 'Put your hands together for the gentleman responsible for the sponsorship of this fantastic evening's entertainment. The managing director of Radio Liverpool – Mr Nick Folley!'

Taking the applause as no more than his due, Nick Folley strode on to the stage. His jowls had fleshed out and his wavy hair had thinned since his days as a rising star of local television; Harry could even discern, beneath the Italian suit, the beginnings of an executive paunch. For upwards of fifteen years Folley had been the golden boy of the Merseyside media, envied and disliked by many, but always a force to be reckoned with. It seemed that everything he touched made him money. And, for good measure, he was not only Melissa's boss but had also, until recently, been her lover.

'A boy from Bootle who wants to make the big time has three choices,' he said into the microphone. 'Music, football or comedy. Wayne here is tone deaf and has two left feet. Thank Heavens he's a born funny man.'

He pumped the lad's hand before turning to give the redhead a wink, self-satisfaction splashed over his face like ice cream. Harry had first seen that thick-lipped smirk on the small screen umpteen years ago when Folley's duties included announcing the region's weather. Even then, he could make a forecast of black ice on the M6 sound like a cause for self-congratulation.

Since then he had kept in the public eye, persistent as a piece of grit. A 'leisure industry entrepreneur', he called himself, which meant in his time he'd run a nightclub and a ritzy restaurant on the Albert Dock, besides owning a recording studio and a half share in the Sergeant Pepper theme park out in Southport. Time and again envious journalists scoffed at Folley's Follies; yet, like a termagant wife, he always managed to have the last word.

As the lights dimmed and the winner of the contest disappeared in a crowd of jubilant family and friends, Folley kissed the redhead and she responded with enthusiasm. Harry knew media folk were demonstrative, but he guessed there was more between the couple than a mere working relationship. Interesting, he thought. And it might become explosive if Finbar, having taken up with Folley's previous girlfriend, now developed too close an interest in the great man's latest dolly bird. Folley was not a man to cross; his ferocious outbursts of temper were legendary. Years ago he'd famously punched a regional newscaster on screen. Nonetheless, he had managed to get his own contract renewed; the other man was rumoured to be selling second-hand cars somewhere in the Morecambe area these days.

'I suppose we ought to mingle,' said Melissa. 'Show the Radio Liverpool flag.'

Harry gave a non-committal smile. After enduring Rosie and the juggling traffic warden, he felt a white flag would have been more appropriate.

While Finbar ordered drinks, Harry followed Melissa through the people converging on the bar, pushing past the giggly girls in Radio Liverpool sweatshirts who lavished promotional leaflets on anyone who wandered within reach of their outstretched hands. They headed towards the stage, where the musicians and engineers were packing their gear.

Melissa pointed to a handsome fair-haired man in his early to mid-thirties, deep in conversation with a girl in a clinging mini-dress.

'Look who's there! Baz Gilbert. I'll call him over and you can have a chance to rehearse for tomorrow's broadcast.'

Baz was rubbing his hand over the girl's rump and she seemed to be loving it. Her features were strong, although a diagonal scar running from the left side of her mouth to her chin robbed her of beauty. But the passion with which she gazed into Baz's eyes was shameless.

'Who's the girl with him?'

'Penny from Sales. She's been crazy about Baz ever since she joined the station.' Raising her voice, Melissa said, 'Baz! Come and meet Harry Devlin. Your guest for tomorrow.'

Ten days earlier in the Dock Brief, Finbar had urged Harry to make a guest appearance on Radio Liverpool one morning. 'No problem,' he'd said. 'Simply give me the word and I'll ask Melissa to fix it. Baz Gilbert has the most listeners, more than ever since he gave up his late-night show and moved to early mornings. You can review the newspapers, ask Baz to spin your favourite disc, give Crusoe and Devlin a plug. Go on, it'll do your image a power of good. I'm on *Pop In* myself next week – same idea, spread the word about my business. The oxygen of publicity, to coin a phrase. You can't beat it.'

Finbar was so sure he was bestowing a favour that Harry was tempted to act like a senile old judge asking what a compact disc was and demand, 'Baz who?' But he could hardly deny knowing the name. Baz Gilbert had done the rounds of the Merseyside media; after reporting on pop for the *Daily Post* and spending a couple of years with Radio City, he'd started a midnight phone-in programme on Radio Merseyside before moving back to the commercial side when Nick Folley had launched the city's third station. Like Folley, he was a local personality.

The resemblance went no further. There was no hint of self-regard in Baz's cool blue eyes or ironic smile. He didn't brawl in public to boost his ratings, though the telephone callers to his show whose mouths were bigger than their brains might have preferred a punch in the stomach to one of his sardonic put-downs. Whereas Nick Folley's aggression had fuelled a

Chapter Five

successful business career, Baz remained a nearly man. He would never be a fat cat or, Harry guessed, make it into national radio. Though he had a loyal following, after ten years on the Merseyside airwaves, he still earned his living by dedicating top ten songs to Toxteth's teenage lovers and opening grocery stores in Garston.

Nodding to Melissa, Baz said, 'Harry Devlin? Pleased to meet you. This is Penny Newland, a very good friend of mine.'

The girl said hello in a soft Irish accent and clutched at Baz's hand, pushing it towards respectability.

The disc jockey turned to her. 'Harry here is a lawyer in the city centre. He's sacrificing a couple of billable hours to appear on the show in the morning.'

'Following in Finbar's footsteps,' said Melissa.

'A hard act to follow. The guy's such a good bullshitter, he almost had me investing in a tattoo. They certainly look good on the right body. You know Melissa's fancy man, Harry?'

'Actually Finbar introduced us,' said Melissa, while the dark girl studied her fingernails. 'Harry's his brief.'

'Did you hear him on air, Harry? The bugger caused a commotion when he changed his mind at the last minute about his favourite music. Mind you, he managed to twist my producer round his little finger.'

Harry had meant to tune in to Finbar's appearance on *Pop In*, if only to pick up a few tips. But work had claimed priority, following an early morning police raid on a shopkeeper client whose stock of videos gave a new meaning to the concept of animal husbandry.

'Missed it,' he said. 'I'm sure he was good.'

'Flattery will get you everywhere, provided you don't charge me for it on your next account,' said the Irishman, returning with the drinks. 'Evening, Penny, Baz. So we haven't discovered another Ken Dodd or Cilla Black tonight? Ah, perhaps it's as well.'

Penny Newland grimaced. Harry guessed that, like Kim Lawrence, she was one of those women who found Finbar's chat easy to resist. Still irked by the redhead's encouragement of his client's ogling, Harry began to warm to her.

'Don't you think we ought to circulate, darling?' she said quietly.

'Sure,' said Baz, wrapping his arm round her shoulder. 'Nice meeting you, Harry. Till tomorrow. *Ciao*, Melissa.'

Finbar handed Harry his pint. 'Here. Help you blot out the memory of the last couple of hours.'

Melissa turned to Harry. 'Don't let Nick–'

'About to take my name in vain?'

Nick Folley's voice was a brash boom. He placed his lips against Melissa's cheek in the manner of a man exercising *droit de seigneur*. Harry saw a spasm of dislike distort her fine features and sensed the stiffening of her body in resistance. He recalled Finbar's description of the man: 'If he was a chocolate drop, he'd eat himself.'

'The name's Folley,' said the newcomer to Harry. He was holding a glass of red wine and had in tow the girl whom Finbar had been eyeing up all evening. Like each of his employees here tonight, Nick Folley wore a Radio Liverpool name badge; yet his tone made it plain that he knew self-introduction was unnecessary.

'This is Harry Devlin,' said Melissa. Harry sensed she was trying to control a shiver and her reaction intrigued him. Was it mere distaste for her boss – or fear?'

'Harry's my solicitor,' Finbar said.

Nick Folley cast a quick contemptuous glance at the Irishman, but when he spoke his voice was as smooth as ever and he wore his smile like a mask.

'I imagine you keep him busy.'

'Harry's starring on Baz's show tomorrow,' said Melissa.

'Great,' said Nick Folley, his manner making Harry feel like a first-former in the presence of the Head of School. 'In that case, er – Harry? – meet Sophie Wilkins. She produces Baz.'

'Hi,' said the redhead huskily.

She pecked Melissa on the cheek and Finbar wasted no time in kissing her hand with a flourish worthy of Errol Flynn. Sophie threw a glance of triumph at Melissa, as if to say: *See, I have the boss and your boyfriend, both dangling on a string*. As she shook Harry's hand, her freckled breasts almost bobbed free of the confines of her black velvet dress.

'It's a delight to see more of you,' said Finbar, unable to resist a double meaning.

Harry guessed now why the Irishman had been willing to spend an evening enduring a talent show in which he had no interest and it had nothing to do with lending Melissa his moral support. He must have met Sophie when appearing on *Pop In* and hoped, after the let-down of the Danger, to see her again tonight. In any case, she seemed determined to flaunt her interest in him; treating him to a ravenous smile.

'You really were wonderful yesterday morning. Poor Harry has a lot to live up to.'

'I'm sure you'll be as kind to him, darling,' said Finbar, 'as you were to me.'

'Whoops!' said Nick Folley.

'Oh God!' cried Melissa simultaneously. Sophie squealed, as if with delight.

Folley had spilt the contents of his glass over Finbar's white jacket. The stain was huge, spreading while they watched, as if the Irishman had been knifed in the heart.

'*Mea culpa*', said Nick Folley. 'Incredibly clumsy of me.'

Malicious pleasure sweetened his voice, made a mockery of the frown of concern on his face. Harry didn't believe it had been an accident.

'That's all right,' said Finbar, breathing hard and choking back anger with a visible effort, 'though you ought to get that nervous twitch under control.'

'Of course, you'll send your dry cleaning bill to me.'

'Ah, think nothing of it. In any case, it'll be a long time before I come to another do like this.'

Finbar's expression was affable, but his words were as sharp as bits of glass. Nick Folley shrugged slightly before turning away; he'd made his point. Melissa glared after her boss and Sophie stifled a snigger before slipping a hand in Folley's pocket, a deliberate gesture of intimacy intended to be seen.

The fires burning beneath the surface at Radio Liverpool, Harry thought, would take much longer to quench than the blaze at Williamson Lane.

Chapter Six

'Take this,' said Sophie Wilkins the next morning, handing Harry a razor blade.

He drew the sharp metal edge across the palm of his hand and felt a tingling. A thin red thread appeared.

'You expect me to be that bad?'

'No, no,' she laughed. 'We ask you not to take the newspapers into the studio. The rustles would have all our listeners reaching for the telephone – or, even worse, the tuning dial. So when you see a piece you want to talk about, use the blade to cut it out. Simpler than scissors. Right then, I'll see you in twenty minutes.'

She bustled out, leaving him alone in the Radio Liverpool hospitality lounge. Fish in a huge tank stared at him with a dull-eyed solemnity, in striking contrast to the ingratiating smirks of the local celebrities whose photographs lined the walls. He sank back in the voluptuous embrace of a brothel-pink leather chair and started to leaf through the morning's papers.

Sophie's welcoming manner had been effusive enough to suggest that he lent lustre to commercial radio by his very presence. The tee-shirt she wore was two sizes too small for her and no less provocative than the previous night's cocktail dress. When she kissed him on the cheek in greeting, he felt her push against him with a groupie's ardour. After she'd finally disengaged and he'd recovered his breath, he asked what he was expected to say on the show.

'Just be your normal self,' she said, with flattering faith.

'That could cost you your franchise. Come on now, what's the brief?'

'Same as every morning. You know the programme – you must be familiar with what we want.'

Well, actually, no, thought Harry. He hadn't the faintest idea what Baz Gilbert expected of him, because he seldom listened to Radio Liverpool. He'd grown up with the city's two longer-established stations and he wasn't a man who readily transferred his loyalties, but he dared not utter such blasphemy. He cast his mind back to Finbar's trumpet-blowing account of his own experience of radio stardom.

'So I pick two or three stories from the Press which catch my eye and then tell Baz about my favourite record?'

'Right.' She consulted a clipboard. '"There's Always Something There To Remind Me"? An old one, isn't it? Before my time. But no problem, we have it in the record library.'

She bustled out and he turned his attention to the papers. Flipping through the tabloids, he was rewarded with a story beginning: *A randy reverend defrocked a teenage organist five times a night, a court was told yesterday.* For slaking the Great British Public's thirst for legal cases with a little spice, the Street of Shame beat the All England Law Reports hands down.

He was cutting out the last paragraph of a snippet in *The Independent* about an Australian bigamist who wanted to plead guilty but insane when Penny Newland walked through the door.

'Hello again,' he said.

She started. 'Mr Devlin. What brings you – oh yes, you're on the programme with Baz this morning, aren't you?' She touched the mark on her face with her finger, a gesture he guessed was her habitual reaction when disconcerted.

'I hope he's going to be gentle with me.'

'You needn't worry. Baz is marvellous with all his guests, especially those who aren't experienced. Forget about his reputation for being sharp – people always exaggerate, he's never had the credit he deserves.'

'He's certainly a celebrity in this city.'

'A big fish in a tiny pool, that's all. He could have been a national name if he'd had a few more breaks, but Baz has always been unlucky.'

'In the wrong place at the wrong time?'

'I suppose so. He's known tragedy. He married young, but his wife died of leukaemia.' Her voice faltered. 'And his – his twin brother died a few years ago. People don't realise how much suffering he's been through. Yet you'll see when you get in the studio, he's always the complete professional.'

Sophie stuck her head round the door. 'Your public awaits, Harry. How are you doing?'

'Okay. You were right about the razor blade.'

He nodded to Penny and let Sophie lead him upstairs and along corridors through a labyrinth of offices, finally ushering him through a heavy door into the control room. From vast loudspeakers came the voice of a dead man – Otis Redding, being broadcast at that moment. Hunched over a control panel, a bearded engineer in jeans and a lumberjack's shirt nodded a greeting.

Thick glass separated them from Baz Gilbert, who sat on the far side of a circular table on top of which were crammed teddy bear mascots and a dozen snapshots: Baz in a band, Baz on the air, Baz through the years, changing from a lad with a guileless grin to a seen-it-all veteran of a business in which youth was the only thing that mattered. A couple of old photographs showed him with a look-alike brother, whose military short-back-and-sides made Baz resemble a refugee from sixties San Francisco in comparison. A couple of recent pictures showed him cuddling Penny Newland. In other shots, taken years back but carefully preserved, he shared a joke with Roger McGough, chatted with Paul McCartney.

Now he had his headphones on and was raising his thumbs in salutation. His mouth framed the word: 'Welcome.'

Harry realised how nervous he was. Excited, too. No big deal, he told himself, to appear on a local radio show; yet he had never done it before and his mouth was dry and his stomach unsettled. He imagined microphones picking up a thunderous rumble from his innards, causing the listeners to flinch. The stories he had chosen in the papers seemed to have fled his mind; he did not know what he could say about the Sandie Shaw song. Downstairs he had been struck by the casual atmosphere. Here, things were different. Sophie and the engineer swapped flip remarks but tension was as heavy in the air as approaching thunder. He felt the adrenalin pumping through his own system. No doubt about it, to appear on a live show was to rekindle long-forgotten childhood fears of public humiliation.

Sophie sat astride a chair at the opposite end of the control panel to the engineer and spoke into an intercom which connected her with Baz. Harry found it disconcerting to see him mouthing his replies, yet to be unable to hear what he was saying. A jingle played and a phlegmatic Lancastrian voice began to extol the virtues of a chain of launderettes, whilst in the background a chorus of voices sang that listeners would be glad of that extra sheen that left their garments squeaky clean.

'You'll be in the hot seat in five minutes,' said Sophie. 'Nothing to worry about. After all, you're used to speaking in court: not like Finbar, and he turned out to be a natural broadcaster.'

'Somehow I can't see him hosting *Desert Island Discs* or *Yesterday In Parliament*.'

'No, I mean it. He's so warm, he has so much vitality – perfect for

Chapter Six

communicating with an audience. He comes over as a very attractive personality.'

Thinking of the arson attack, of Sinead and of the man whom Finbar had been so anxious to avoid outside his office, Harry said sourly, 'He's not top of everyone's popularity charts.'

'Oh, believe me, I can see why Melissa fell for him. Though I'll admit Nick's not his number one fan.'

She giggled and added. 'Nick did it deliberately, you know. Spilling the wine over Finbar, I mean.'

Harry thought it politic to feign surprise. Sophie was not saying anything he hadn't guessed the night before. But he was interested that she was frank enough to put conjecture into words.

'Finbar got up his nose, that's what I mean.' Sophie didn't bother to hide her glee. 'Nick's a hunk and I love his bones, but he does like to be the centre of attention. And if something doesn't suit him, he's apt to fly off the handle. Maybe seeing his ex hang around a humble tattoo artist hurt his pride.'

Yes, and Sophie's egging-on of Finbar had stoked up the provocation, Harry thought. He contented himself with a wry smile.

'Not all that humble.'

'Perhaps not. Finbar can take most things in his stride, I guess. Which reminds me: I forgot to commiserate with him last night. I read in the paper about the fire at his studio. Arson, I gather.'

'The police are still investigating.'

Sophie tapped him playfully on the shoulder. 'You're so guarded, Harry! A solicitor down to your socks. But it must be worrying for Finbar – to feel someone has burnt down his place on purpose.'

'He'll survive.'

'I'm sure he will. Melissa will be in a state, all the same. I thought she looked peaky yesterday. Of course, she never has much colour, but even so she looked dreadful. And she can do without that sort of hassle after all the problems she's had.'

'What problems?'

Mischievous pleasure deepened the laughter lines round Sophie's mouth and eyes. 'Don't you know? Oh, sorry. Perhaps I'd better not say any more. I simply thought that, as a friend, you...'

A tiny girl in a pink tracksuit walked into the room, followed by a spotty young man wearing an Everton scarf. She looked to Harry as though she ought to be at school.

'Harry, this is Tracey Liggett, our weather girl,' said Sophie. 'And – Jason, isn't it? – her boyfriend. He's just here as a spectator. We keep open house on this programme, people drift in and out all the time, no wonder we call it *Pop In*. Tracey, meet Harry Devlin. Harry's a local solicitor.'

'Yeah?' The girl sniffed as if she'd been introduced to a lavatory attendant.

'Tracey's one of our rising stars,' said Sophie. 'The weather report today – who knows what tomorrow may bring?'

'The football results, most likely,' said the engineer as he lifted a cassette marked KWIKSLIM from the bank of pigeon-holes which ran across one wall of the control room. With casual efficiency, he flipped it into the machine in front of him and pressed a switch. Another silly little tune played, followed by two housewives discussing the merits of a new miracle diet.

'Okay, Harry,' said Sophie. 'You're on.'

He took a deep breath and, clutching the bits of newspaper like a passport to a new world, opened the door into the studio. Baz waved him to one of the three vacant chairs round the table.

'Welcome. I hear last night ended with a splash, so far as Finbar was concerned. Rumour has it he's not one of my lord and master's bosom buddies.'

Harry wasn't in the mood to discuss Finbar. All he wanted was to make sure the next ten minutes passed as quickly as possible and without too much embarrassment. 'I have the snippets here,' he said, fanning the bits of paper out on the table between them.

'So, this is it, eh? First broadcast to the nation, right? Don't worry. Next thing, "on your dressing room door they've hung a star", and all that crap. Now, this is simple. After the news bulletin, Tracey will tell us when the fog is going to clear and the moment I start talking about the lane closure on Runcorn Bridge, you wet your lips and get ready to speak, right, 'cause there'll only be seconds to go. Okay? Good luck.'

The local news was bad, as usual: an attempted murder in St Helens, redundancies at a printing firm, a drugs haul in the docks, a strike in local government. The weather outlook was equally grim, but Harry was past caring. His mouth was dry and he was wishing he was anywhere but behind a microphone.

Suddenly, the microphone was open and he was on air. How he actually sounded to the indifferent outside world, Harry was never sure. Against all expectations, his time on air sped by. The stories he had chosen seemed to go down well, with Baz chuckling at regular intervals, and the lead-in to his choice of song was less of an ordeal than he'd imagined.

He didn't tell the whole truth about the song, of course, describing it simply as an old favourite. It had hooked onto a peg in his mind long ago, but had acquired a special meaning since Liz had left him. Whenever he walked along the Liverpool streets he had walked along with her, he couldn't help but recall how much in love they had once been. He didn't know how to forget her when there was always so much to remind him of the past.

At last Baz was thanking him and giving a thumbs-up sign and farewell wave as he cued in the next jingle. 'Great, Harry. See you around.'

He made his way to the other side of the panel, where Sophie mimed applause. She had been joined by a young man with an anarchic haircut and John Lennon glasses; Harry recognised him as an authority on the tangled web of Liverpool politics.

'Wonderful,' she said. 'I told you it would be a success. Thanks a million, sweetie. You know your way out, don't you?'

And that was it. The show would go on and Harry's part in it was history. He wandered back alone through the labyrinth and a couple of minutes later found himself outside in North John Street where it had begun to spit with rain. He turned up his jacket collar as people hurried past on their way to work, oblivious of his presence.

His flirtation with stardom was over.

Chapter Seven

'Have you heard the news?'

Suzanne's tone as he arrived at the office was hushed, yet her eyes sparkled with excitement. The carefully contrived anxiety of her frown didn't fool Harry. Joy-in-gloom was Suzanne's speciality; the misfortunes of others were her meat and drink.

Act soft, he told himself. *Ten to one all that's happened is the temp has walked out in a huff.*

'Heard it? I was actually in the studio when it was broadcast. Sterling's at an all-time low, unemployment's on the rise. Anything else you want to know?'

A cloud of bafflement passed across her face.

'You what? Oh, you were doing your thing on Radio Liverpool! God, I forgot to listen. I always tune in to Radio City, you see – the music's better. No, I was meaning the news about Mr. Crusoe.'

'What's up? Lost a bundle of deeds, has he?'

'No, no, nothing like that. He's had an accident!'

Harry felt a sudden sickness in his stomach. 'What sort of accident?'

'A car crash.' Suzanne lingered on the words. No question, she was in her element. 'There was a pile-up in the fog last night.'

Christ, yes, he'd heard something about it on the air earlier that morning. Not paid much attention, of course; other people's tragedies seldom strike us as significant compared to our own preoccupations. Now his apprehension whilst waiting to join Baz Gilbert seemed like self-indulgence. His heart beating faster, he demanded, 'And Jim – is he all right?'

'He's alive,' said Suzanne. 'His wife phoned, she's been with him at the Royal through the night. The rescue people had to use special equipment to get him out of his Sierra, she said.'

Chapter Seven

The girl sounded sorry she'd missed the chance of sightseeing at the scene of the carnage. Harry could barely restrain himself from grabbing her by the throat.

'So what's happened? Is he badly hurt?'

'He's fractured a couple of ribs and his face was cut by the flying glass. And he's still very groggy, not able to make much sense, according to Mrs. Crusoe. The doctors say it's too early to tell how bad things are. They have to make tests.'

Harry swore. His knees felt as though they were about to buckle and he sat down hard on one of the chairs reserved for clients. Jim Crusoe was more than merely a business partner. He was Harry's anchor.

'Where is Heather? I must talk to her.'

'She said she'd call again in ten minutes.'

'Let me know as soon as she does. Never mind if I'm with a client, interrupt.'

Suzanne smiled at him. She'd had her pleasure and could afford kindliness. In a motherly tone, she said, 'So how was the show?' Before he could reply, a bleep from the switchboard distracted her.

'Crusoe and Devlin. Oh, Mrs. Crusoe… yes, he's just got back. Shall I…'

Harry snatched the receiver from her hand. 'Heather? How is he?'

'Could be worse, Harry. Could be better. He spent the night in intensive care, but he's lucky to be in one piece. Some of the others in the crash aren't.'

Stress shortened Heather Crusoe's comfortable Wigan vowels, yet her characteristic calm had not altogether deserted her and in a handful of sentences she answered Harry's agitated questions. Jim didn't remember anything about the accident, but the police thought it had been caused by a car travelling too fast round a blind corner in the opposite direction, hurtling to disaster on the wrong side of the road. Three dead and a dozen injured, by the latest count. Jim's windscreen had shattered and his face was a mess – she said it as matter-of-factly as if she were describing a cut finger – but the main concern was whether he'd suffered any internal damage. Soon the truth would be known.

'No point in panic,' she said. 'I'm sure he'll be fine. Jim's so strong – it would take more than some maniac with more horsepower than sense to finish him off.'

Harry groped for words. No one was more keenly aware than he that road disasters can change lives, as well as destroying them. His parents had been killed by a fire engine frantically responding to a 999 call which proved to be a hoax. And he had once watched as another spectacular crash, to this day etched in his mind, had helped in part to avenge the murder of his wife.

'If there's anything I can…'

'Thanks, but there's nothing at present,' said Heather.

Harry detected a tremor in her voice but in an instant it was gone. She said she was okay, the kids were okay, the hospital wouldn't welcome outside visitors until people had a clearer idea about Jim's condition. She would keep in close touch.

After hanging up, Harry went to talk to the staff. Life must go on, and so must the legal process: clients still had wills to make, houses to buy and sell, businesses to trade.

'I'll take all his property files,' offered Sylvia Reid. Traces of tears stained her cheeks. A plump and serious girl, she'd been distressed by the news about Jim. He had been her principal during her two years as an articled clerk and to the partners' surprise – and considerable relief – after qualifying as a solicitor she had stayed on instead of moving elsewhere. Given the modest level of salaries which were all Crusoe and Devlin could afford, there could be no surer sign of loyalty.

They were in Jim's room, confronting a mountain of files and must-do memo notes. Harry flipped open his partner's diary.

'You can handle both the completions this morning? Fine. And what's this appointment in the afternoon regarding a contract for Crow's Nest House?'

'That will be Mrs. Graham-Brown. A big sale, no purchase. Everything has to happen yesterday – you know the sort of thing.'

Harry's skin prickled. An opportunity to see the lovely Rosemary again was a chance too good to miss.

'As a matter of fact,' he lied, 'I know a little about the file. Leave it to me. I'll see her.'

Sylvia could not conceal her amazement. Conveyancing and Harry Devlin had as much in common as *karaoke* and Kiri te Kanawa.

'Are you sure?'

'Do me good to brush up on the non-contentious work,' he said, straight-faced. He located the file and returned to his room feeling pleased with himself, although he realised he was behaving absurdly. The woman was married to a rich man and would soon be leaving the country – the situation would challenge even Finbar Rogan's seductive wiles. Harry knew that he should not even fantasise about Rosemary. No good could come of it. And yet...

The morning flew by. At lunchtime he went out to buy a sandwich and saw the builders gathered together in a huddle, talking in low Irish voices. Their expressions were sullen and an atmosphere of suspicion hung over the courtyard. He hurried past, wondering when the construction work would be finished. He remembered that the Anglican Cathedral had taken most of the twentieth century to complete; perhaps the same firm had been hired for the job in Fenwick Court.

As he got back to his desk, the phone was ringing.

'Harry, would you mind if I speak to Finbar, please?' Melissa Keating said.

'He's not here,' Harry replied, puzzled.

'Really? He didn't keep his appointment to discuss the insurance compensation after the fire?'

'What appointment?'

Too late to keep the surprise out of his voice, Harry realised he must be letting his client down. Finbar had obviously been using him as an alibi. 'Wait a minute,' he added hastily, feeling shame at his half-hearted entry into a masculine conspiracy to mislead, 'perhaps he did mention...'

'Forget it,' said Melissa. Her voice was muffled; he sensed she was close to tears. 'I understand perfectly. And by the way, I thought you sounded good on *Pop In* this morning, Very plausible. Just like Finbar, in fact. Goodbye.

She hung up and left Harry looking angrily at the receiver. He cursed Finbar. What was the bugger up to now? He resented being dragged into the deception of Melissa. But he wasn't prepared to take it up with Finbar – he had other things to think about. He turned to the Graham-Brown file.

Conveyancing was foreign to Harry. By temperament, as well as training, he was a litigator; someone who liked to work with people rather than documents of title, preferring the quirks and inconsistencies of human beings to those of the law of real property. Yet Jim's files were organised with a neatness and method unexpected in a big, ungainly man and it did not take him long to pull together the strands of the transaction. Everything was happening at speed and contracts were almost due to be exchanged. Even he could manage that.

Suzanne buzzed him. 'Mrs. Graham-Brown to see you.'

Five minutes early. Harry was accustomed to clients who turned up late or not at all, but he reminded himself that someone selling a house confronts the legal process from a very different standpoint to that of a person facing financial ruin, divorce or jail. He pushed the wad of papers to one side. No need to lose sleep over this particular matter. It was always easier to sell than to buy: *caveat emptor* and all that. Besides, Jim had already done the hard work, juggling non-committal answers to otiose preliminary enquiries and preparing the contract. Harry did not have much left to do except renew his acquaintance with the client.

His heart beating faster, he went to reception, where Suzanne was updating her bulletin on Jim's condition with more reliance on morbid imagination than solid fact. Faint scepticism turned up the corners of Rosemary Graham-Brown's mouth; he liked her all the more for that.

'I'm glad to meet you again,' he said, and shook her hand. It was small and warm and he took ten seconds too long to release it. Rosemary gave a small pleased giggle; he could feel Suzanne's eyes boring into the back of his head as he led the way through into the corridor.

'I do appreciate your taking the time to see me,' she said. 'You must be rushed off your feet. I'm so sorry to hear about Mr. Crusoe. Your receptionist was telling me the whole ghastly story of the accident – it sounds horrific.'

Trust Suzanne to turn a pile-up into a holocaust. The truth unvarnished was bad enough.

'He'll live,' said Harry. Then he remembered Heather Crusoe's anxiety and regretted the lightness of his tone.

'I'm hardly an expert on property law,' he admitted, 'but I didn't want to hold up your transaction. I gather there's some urgency.'

'Yes, very much so. That's why I've brought the contract myself. We signed it last night and I don't want to trust to the post.'

'This is my room. Let me clear some papers off that chair. I only hope you don't suffer from claustrophobia.'

She wriggled between a filing cabinet and a mound of documents as tall as a child, her figure hugged by a white trouser suit which must have cost more than Harry's entire wardrobe.

'No problem,' she said. 'I'm quite good at getting out of tight corners.'

Her lips parted in a teasing smile. He grinned, watching her settle into the chair and enjoying the sight. Perhaps office-bound conveyancing had its compensations after all.

'Sorry to be a nuisance in the circumstances,' she said, 'but as you'll have gathered, things are moving quickly and I – that is, my husband and I – would hate to lose the momentum.'

'So I see from the file. The two of you are emigrating, then?'

She nodded, the light of excitement he had noticed on their first meeting shining from her eyes.

'To the south of Spain, that's right.'

'Sounds wonderful.'

She leaned forward, hands gripping the edge of his desk, lowering her voice as if about to confide a long-cherished secret.

'I've always longed to live in the sun. Shake the dust of Liverpool off my feet, taste a bit of the good life.'

'And your husband? What does he do?'

'Oh, he's in… er… financial services. But between you and me, I think that's a fancy name for debt collection. His company's called Merseycredit.' A confessional smile. 'To tell you the truth, all his jargon's double Dutch to me. I don't take much notice of it.'

'And you've not found anywhere to buy yet?'

'No. But his company has organised rented accommodation for us.'

'I gather they are paying our bill.'

'Yes, so you don't need to stint. They can afford it. Deduct your fee from the proceeds before you send it on – as long as that won't delay matters.'

I like this woman more and more, Harry thought to himself.

'No problem. I understand you already have a bank account over there: Puerto Banus, is that right? I know the name. One of the resorts, isn't it? A millionaires' playground or something?'

She essayed a self-deprecating shrug of the shoulders. 'We're hardly in that league, Stuart and me.'

But not on the breadline either, Harry reflected. A detached house in the best part of Formby would sell for five times the price of a flat in Empire Dock.

'You ought to take care in a place like that. You may find yourself in the same bar as some of our most famous bank robbers.'

'Just like downtown Liverpool, in fact,' she said.

They both laughed.

'You could say that only the failures stick around here,' he said. 'I had a client only last week who was arrested after leaving his wallet and all his credit cards in the building society he'd tried to hold up. Needless to say, his gun was a toy and they shooed him out empty-handed.'

She laughed again. He thought he saw a spark of interest in the brown eyes.

'You have a fascinating job,' she said. 'Selling our house must seem simple – compared with all the crime and everything. But you don't foresee any last-minute hitches, I hope?'

'No, your buyers – Mr. and Mrs. Ambrose. – are willing and they seem to have the money in place. You're not in a chain. It's the perfect situation.'

'That's what I wanted to hear.' She slid a document in a plastic folder across the desk. 'Here's the contract. Stuart and I have both scrawled our signatures where Mr. Crusoe pencilled our initials. All right?'

'Fine. I can exchange for you now, so you'll have a deal. Then we'll get the draft conveyance for approval and requisitions on title.'

She wrinkled her nose. 'Sounds complicated. Mr. Crusoe reckoned it could all be done and dusted within a week of exchange – maybe less.'

'No problem,' Harry said. 'Formalities only. I'll phone you to confirm all's going smoothly.'

'No, you can't do that. We're ex-directory. My husband – in his line of business he values his privacy, even where his professional advisers are concerned. Listen, I can call in again if you like.'

'I'll look forward to it.'

'Me too,' she said.

Harry showed her to the front door. As they shook hands again, he had the impression that this time the stronger pressure came from her. But married life had proved that, where women were concerned, he was a wishful-thinker. She might be interested in him, or simply playing a game; he did not expect he would ever find out.

Suzanne caught his eye and mouthed, 'Mr. Rogan on the line for you.'

'I'll take it here… is that you, Finbar? Where the hell are you?'

'In the Hotel Blue Moon.'

Finbar was gasping, as if someone had dropped a heavy stone onto his chest, squeezing all the breath and good humour out of him. Harry knew the Blue Moon: a no-star establishment, in a side street round the corner from Mount Pleasant.

'What are you doing there?' he demanded. 'Melissa's really on the warpath. You make the Scarlet Pimpernel look like a stick-in-the-mud. And what in God's name is the matter with you? You sound as though you're dying.'

'Harry, it's a miracle I'm not already dead.'

'What are you talking about?'

'Someone wants to murder me.'

'Does he realise he'll have to join the queue?'

'Listen, I'm serious.'

Suddenly Harry believed it. He'd never known Finbar sound so desperate. 'Go on.'

'First I had the fire. Okay, I couldn't believe someone was out to attack me personally. But now there's nothing surer.'

'What's happened?'

'There's been a bastard of an explosion here. It's a miracle I've not been carted off to the mortuary.'

'For Chrissake, how come?'

Finbar exhaled noisily.

'Some fucking maniac has only strapped a bomb to the bottom of my car.'

Chapter Eight

'See the crack in the mirror?' asked Finbar, jerking his thumb towards the dressing table at the other end of the hotel bedroom. The splintered glass distorted his features, making him seem more Mephistophelian than ever. 'It's not shoddy furnishing, though in this place you might not believe it. The blast did that. And as for the window panes…'

He ground his heel into the shards scattered across the carpet. Sitting on the unmade bed, Harry grimaced as he heard the woman being sick in the bathroom next door: a violent, prolonged retching. Through the partition walls they could hear every movement, every groan.

For the sake of something to say, he asked, 'Where were you when you heard the explosion?' As soon as the words left his mouth, he realised it was a silly question.

Finbar raised his eyes skywards in disbelief. 'Come on, Harry! You don't think I invited a lovely lady like Sophie here to give me a few tips on how to be a better radio interviewee, surely to God? We were in bed, where d'you think?'

A thought occurred to Finbar. For the first time since Harry's arrival, the mischievous grin reappeared.

'I've heard of the earth moving – but that was ridiculous.'

As he spoke, the bathroom door opened to reveal Sophie Wilkins, pale and tear-stained and wiping her nose with a tissue. Her beige silk blouse was carelessly buttoned and Harry noticed a ladder in her sexy black tights. He could scarcely recognise the self-confident media person he had met earlier that morning.

'For God's sake!' She spat out the words with a hostility that smacked both men to attention. 'What's the matter with you? Your car has been blown up by a bomb and all you can do is crack puerile jokes. Well, if that makes you feel macho, fine, but I'm not staying around here to pander to your bloody male ego.'

Finbar made a movement towards her. 'Sophie, love, don't go. At times like these, a man and a woman…'

She brushed away his hand as it rested for an instant on her shoulder. Red blotches had appeared on her cheeks.

'Spare me the words of wisdom, Finbar. They belong in a Christmas cracker, not in my life.'

'Sophie, listen to me,' said Harry. 'You've had a hell of a shock – both of you have. And how do you think Finbar feels? Neither of you is thinking straight. Why don't you stay a while? The police will want to talk to you.'

The anger that lit her eyes told him he had said the wrong thing.

'That's all I need! Having to explain to PC Plod why I was on my back beneath a tattooist with the gift of the gab and not much else when I should have been at work! Do you realise I told Nick Folley I had a migraine? I feel a thousand times worse now than if I'd been forced to spend the day in a darkened room.'

Outside a siren howled.

'I can't believe this is happening,' she said bitterly. 'And all because I was weak and let myself be blarneyed into a quick leg-over! God, I hate myself sometimes. But not half as much as I hate you, Finbar.'

'Sophie darling, be reasonable.'

'*Reasonable*? Find someone else to be reasonable with. You have too many enemies, Finbar, too many people want you dead. Well, I'm not going to share your coffin.'

'Sophie, love, you need to calm down. Do that and everything will be fine. I'll see you…'

'Not if I see you first! And don't "love" me! I'm not another Melissa, you know, neurotic and clinging. Even she must see sense after this. You're dangerous to know.'

She teetered for a second, as if her legs were about to give way, then turned and slammed the door behind her.

'Hysterical,' said Finbar. 'You can understand it. She doesn't mean what she says.' He sighed. 'Jases, Harry, what a mess.'

For once, Harry thought, his client was erring on the side of understatement. He walked over to the window to view Finbar's car which had been parked in an unmade entry on the other side of Braddock Street. A police cordon now sealed off the scene of the crime, but did not disguise the extent of the devastation. Smoke thickened the air; even up here, there was no ignoring its pungent whiff. Firefighters had been pumping water on to what was left of the car body and a river was beginning to stretch down the street, where

Chapter Eight

fragments recognisably belonging to the old red Granada had been scattered over a wide radius. Uniformed policemen had blocked off traffic at both ends of the street and were now waving away any vehicles or passers-by who stopped to linger. The hum of their walkie-talkies filled the air. Harry guessed they must be nervous, wondering if a second bomb had been planted, waiting for the Special Branch to arrive, not wanting to take any chances in the meantime. He himself had only been able to enter the Blue Moon by following Finbar's telephone directions to an unmarked basement door in an extension at the rear of the building.

Amongst the debris, Harry glimpsed something which resembled part of a steering wheel. The sight of it sickened him. No one sitting in that car when the bomb went off could have had a hope of survival – and Finbar had said he'd promised to give Sophie a lift back to work once they were done in the hotel.

'It may take more than a day or two for her to calm down. She's lucky to be alive, and so are you.'

The Irishman winced. 'Don't think I don't realise. Who would have imagined it? We were only after a little harmless fun.'

He had already explained how, working as swiftly as ever, he'd called Sophie that morning after *Pop In* came to an end and invited her to lunch at the Ensenada. During the course of wining and dining her in lavish manner he had persuaded her to accompany him here. The Blue Moon was owned by an old friend of his called Rajeshwar Sharma, to whom Finbar always referred as Reg. Reg owned a chain of hotels in Merseyside, all of which catered for guests seeking a room and a bed rather than the last word in luxury. This place was one of Finbar's favourite haunts.

'It's like a second home to me, Harry,' he said now, with a touch of mischief. 'I have so many happy memories of my stays here.'

'Most of which last around the sixty-minute mark, I suppose?'

'A couple of hours as a rule, mate. I'm not a man who cares to be rushed – far less have a bomb go off at the vital moment. Talk about stealing my thunder.'

'What exactly happened?'

'There was this almighty boom, followed by the sound of glass shattering. Then a few moments of silence, before someone somewhere started to scream.' He shivered. 'I've lived through bomb blasts before, of course, I've spent plenty of time in Belfast in days gone by. In a way that silence is the most terrifying of all. I've always dreaded the despair that churns up your guts, no matter how grand the cause the bomb was meant to help. I could never convince myself that broken bodies are a price worth paying... Anyway, I rolled off the lovely Sophie and onto the floor. Crawled to the window to have a look-see and saw bits of my motor strewn all over the place. There was a young girl, I doubt if she was sixteen – she was the one screaming, just outside the front door of the hotel. I slipped on my trousers and shirt and raced downstairs to grab hold of her and ask if she'd seen anything. She was beside herself, she'd been walking past when the bomb went off.'

Finbar closed his eyes. His voice had become hoarse. 'That's another thing no bomber ever seems to understand. It's not just those who lose their lives or their legs who suffer: everyone involved goes through their own kind of agony. I bundled the girl indoors, told Reg to take care of her. Then I phoned you. Sorry if I sounded panic-stricken – the thought that someone wants you dead is a bit of a downer. Anyway, I wanted to have your advice first before I started shooting off my mouth.'

'Advice? About what?'

'How to play it with the police.'

'I don't follow. You don't have to play at anything. Just tell them the facts.' Then light began to dawn. 'Finbar, do you have any idea who planted the bomb?'

For a second Finbar hesitated. Then he said, 'No, that's just what I'm getting at. I haven't clue who could have done this. And I don't want to start pointing the finger at anyone if they're not guilty.'

Harry grunted. He doubted the profession of ignorance, but if Finbar was determined to camouflage the truth he thought it better to let the matter rest for the present and return to the attack later.

'When did you arrive here?'

'Half past two. At least, that was when I brought Sophie. But I'd left the car here in the morning. I often do, on a hopeful day. It avoids the rip-off parking fees in the city centre and makes for a quick getaway if the need arises: say the lady I'm with gets twitchy about the kids or her old feller and wants to fly back to the nest. I like to offer a lift. Simply paying for a taxi seems so clinical.'

Resisting the temptation to explore the complex contradictions that comprised Finbar's moral code, Harry said, 'So the bomb might have been planted during the morning?'

'Put it that way and the answer must be yes.'

'You need to tell the police everything. Whoever is responsible for this has come close to committing murder. More than likely he torched your studio into the bargain. You can't afford finer feelings, your life's at stake.'

Chapter Eight

Finbar looked mulish. 'Harry, the police and me, we've never got on. They may reckon it's an insurance fiddle, anyway.'

'And is it?'

'No.' Course not. But I had a good policy on the car, and to tell you the truth it had crossed my mind that if something were to happen to the blessed thing, it was such a rust heap, I'd be quids in.'

A fierce banging on the door forestalled Harry's reply.

'Finbar,' said a voice, muffled but urgent, 'this is Reg. Let me in.'

The Irishman opened the door to admit the proprietor of the Blue Moon: a balding middle-aged man with a round face, no doubt sunny of temperament in ordinary circumstances, but now evidently frightened after a close call with serious violence.

'How's the girl, Reg?'

'She is in a poor way,' said Sharma. 'A policewoman is comforting her. They can get little sense out of her at present.'

'And what are the police up to?' asked Harry.

Sharma looked at him warily, as if he were a tax inspector.

'This is Harry Devlin,' Finbar said. 'He's my brief.'

'I am pleased to meet you, Mr. Devlin. The police, they are talking to everyone. Searching for witnesses. Taking statements. They wish to speak to everyone in the hotel. I thought you would like some advance warning – especially as they seem not to know who owned the car destroyed in the explosion.'

'Ta,' said Finbar. He turned to Harry. 'Ah well, I suppose we'd better think about putting your expert counsel to the test. You willing to be with me when I have a word with them?'

'Why else would I be here?'

Finbar winked. He was beginning to regain his composure. 'Who knows, lawyers are such devious buggers. You might see the chance of all kinds of business in this situation.'

'You're not wrong,' said Harry. 'Can I persuade you to draw up a will for starters?'

Chapter Nine

'So you have no thoughts about who may be behind this incident, who may have been responsible for placing the device under your vehicle?' asked Detective Inspector Sladdin.

Were members of the Special Branch trained, Harry wondered, in the art of neutral phrasing? Or was Sladdin's borrowing of a bureaucrat's bland vocabulary simply his way of combating the horrors he met through his job? If a bomb became a mere 'device' and a brush with death no more than an 'incident', did that make it easier to choke off all emotion and concentrate on the job in hand?

'Your guess is as good as mine,' said Finbar. He sat with his hands in his lap, a picture of bewilderment.

Sladdin raised his eyebrows, leaving Harry and Finbar in no doubt that he judged the picture a fake. But all he said was, 'I see.'

The detective was, Harry estimated, in his mid-thirties, but his hair had turned prematurely grey and his worn features might have belonged to a man old enough to be his father. Perhaps those were occupational hazards, like nights broken by telephone calls bringing bad news and files closing with justice still undone.

During the last hour, here in the police station, he had done little more than test Finbar's defences. He spoke softly and, if he carried a big stick, he was keeping it hidden for the present. Although he must be feeling under pressure to come up with a strong line of inquiry, he had the knack of remaining polite, detached, without concealing his scepticism.

And there was plenty to be sceptical about. Finbar was a victim who had enjoyed a narrow escape from annihilation rather than a suspect, but with a frown here and a puzzled query there, Sladdin conveyed the clear message that while all victims are innocent, some are distinctly less innocent than others. He could be excused a measure of mistrust, given Finbar's insistence

Chapter Nine

that Harry be allowed to sit in while he explained who and what he was and described the events leading up to the explosion.

'A solicitor, sir?' Sladdin had asked. 'Do you think you're in need of legal counsel?'

'Harry's a pal, Inspector, he's been a tower of strength. I'd like him to stay, if you don't mind.'

Finbar's initial reluctance to make the short journey to the police station had also led to some shadow boxing.

'Reg Sharma has very kindly offered to put his private rooms at your disposal, Inspector. And I'm sure you'll understand, after such a dreadful shock I'd feel more comfortable there, however well you'd look after me.'

He cleared his throat. 'I'll be honest with you,' he added.

Harry held his breath, wondering what dreadful secret was about to be revealed. But Finbar was not that naive. He did no more than state the obvious and dress it up as a heartfelt admission.

'Truth is, I'm rather embarrassed by the circumstances which brought me to the hotel. You're a man of the world, Inspector, I'm sure you'll understand. I'm going through a difficult divorce at the present time and Harry here is advising me on how not to put another foot wrong.'

Sladdin maintained weary courtesy whilst making it plain that the interview must take place on his own territory rather than in the Blue Moon. Harry nodded, signalling Finbar not to push his luck. The detective would want the questions and answers recorded on tape and, if irked, could make sure he had his way. Finbar was Irish and a bomb had gone off: easy to make out a case for detaining him under the Prevention of Terrorism Act.

Once they had arrived at the station, the interrogation had been shrewd rather than hostile. Harry recognised techniques he often employed in court when cross-examining a witness whose devotion to the truth was uncertain. Cautious probing was called for at first, with direct attack an option all the more effective for being held in reserve.

In his search for a motive for the bombing, Sladdin inevitably touched on Finbar's Irish antecedents and allowed himself a doubting smile when Finbar protested ignorance of anyone from his native land who might wish him dead. 'Thank you, Mr Rogan,' he said, for the benefit of the tape recorder operating silently on the table between them, and motioned to the constable accompanying him to switch off the machine. The gesture was obviously intended to encourage Finbar to greater frankness.

'Now, then. The tape has stopped, as you see, so let's talk man to man for a minute. We don't know yet whether the bomb was meant to kill you, and went off too early, or was simply meant to scare you rigid. Either way, it's clear that someone is seriously displeased with you. So I need you to be frank. Exactly how much contact do you have with the Republican movement?'

Harry had seen the question coming. He had seldom heard Finbar talk about the Irish troubles, but the inference to be drawn from the bomb attack could have been drawn by a Lestrade. Anyone could start a fire, even one sufficiently fierce to destroy a building. Car bombers were a rarer breed.

Finbar rubbed his nose. He was no fool; he too must have foreseen this line of enquiry.

'I won't deny I knew a few people who were that way inclined.' He might have been speaking about bashful gays. 'Same as anyone living in Liverpool might know a bloke who earns a crust selling dodgy cars. But that's as far as it went – I was never mixed up in any sectarian shenanigans. Live and let live, that's my motto.'

Harry could see his client calculate pros and cons before deciding to name names. Those he mentioned mostly sounded small-time: people who might have done a bit of fund-raising for the cause. The only one which meant anything to Harry was the last.

'And of course,' said Finbar, 'there was Pearse Cato.'

For a moment it seemed to Harry as if Sladdin had been struck by lightning. The careworn features would never betray shock, but a flickering of the eyelids was akin to a squeal of amazement from someone less self-contained. Finbar glanced at the detective uncertainly. If, by adopting a casual tone, he'd hoped to lessen the impact of his reference to Cato, he had failed. Even Harry, no student of current affairs, had heard the name in a hundred news bulletins.

'Pearse Cato?' asked Sladdin, careful not to sound too eager. 'Tell me how you happened to know him.'

'Not much to tell, really,' said Finbar. He bit his lip and Harry could see he already regretted mentioning Cato. But Sladdin would not let it go now. You couldn't claim acquaintance with Lucifer and then dismiss him as a bit of a nonentity.

'His family lived across the road from ours in Dublin,' said Finbar unhappily. 'He was maybe five years younger than me. We were never close.'

'But you were aware of his – connections?'

'From when he was a kid, he was committed to the armed struggle. His uncle had been shot in a tit-for-tat killing. All the Catos were bred to battle, but Pearse was special. No one messed him around.' Finbar shook his head. 'Everyone kowtowed to Pearse, me included. He had a mad streak. Nothing was surer than that one day he would wind up dead.'

Chapter Nine

As indeed he had. His assassination had made headline news, Harry recalled: mown down in a bar a couple of summers ago by a gang of Kalashnikov-wielding paramilitaries who called themselves loyalists. They had fired as many bullets as were necessary to destroy the face seen on so many Wanted posters. In England, the tabloid press had celebrated the killing of the man they dubbed Europe's most wanted terrorist; for Pearse Cato was notorious, an outcast from the Provos who had formed the Irish Freedom Fighters with a handful of others more concerned with murder for murder's sake than with political progress. According to rumour, he had been responsible for upwards of a dozen murders on either side of the Irish Sea: a retired brigadier in Virginia Water; a backbench MP in Great Yarmouth; a judge in Magherafelt and a motley assortment of British soldiers and suspected Army informers.

'Might someone,' suggested Sladdin, 'think you were on better terms with Cato than you describe? Perhaps now they're gunning for you.'

Finbar gave an incredulous laugh. 'I promise you, Inspector, my religion is the same as my politics. I'm a card-carrying member of the self-preservation society. Violence frightens me. It hurts people! Believe me, the closest I got to Pearse Cato was when I tattooed him.'

Sladdin pursed his lips. 'Tattooed him? With what?'

'A mailed fist flourishing the Irish Tricolour,' said Finbar, a mite shame-faced. 'It covered his chest. Not one of my more elegant creations, but Pearse liked body pictures, for his women as well as for himself. He didn't know much about the finer aspects of tattooing but he knew what he liked.'

'So you were neighbours and had a fleeting business relationship, that's all?'

'Not very business-like,' said Finbar. 'The sod didn't pay for any of the work he told me to do. And with Pearse, you didn't ask. He hated putting his hand in his pocket, unless maybe it was to impress a girl. If he'd lived till fifty, he'd have died a millionaire.'

'I see.' Sladdin returned to a topic he'd worried at earlier. 'And are you quite sure no one could have known you were coming here with Miss – er, Wilkins?'

'I didn't know myself until this lunchtime.'

'But you'd left the car parked outside the hotel earlier in the day,' Sladdin pointed out, 'so someone following you from home, say, might have had the opportunity to fix the bomb while you were in the city centre with Miss Wilkins.'

'I didn't see anyone following me.'

'Were you expecting to be followed?'

'Well, no…'

Work it out for yourself, then, Sladdin's expression insinuated. Aloud, he said, 'As I explained, we'll need to speak to Miss Wilkins.'

Harry knew why. The police needed to eliminate the possibility, however unlikely, that Finbar himself had activated the bomb by radio control.

'She'll not be able to tell you anything else,' said Finbar.

Sladdin gave a sceptical grunt.

'Look, Sophie was awful upset when she left, as Harry here will testify,' Finbar continued. 'Can't blame her, it's a nasty feeling for anyone – that someone has tried to blow you to smithereens.'

'Yes,' said Sladdin. 'And that's why, if you can think of anything further that might assist us…'

'Yeah, yeah, I've got the message.'

'Is that all, Inspector?' asked Harry. He was anxious to go. If this interview did not end soon, he would be too late for hospital visiting hours and a chance to check on Jim Crusoe's progress. And at any moment Finbar might say something rash.

So far Sladdin had given no indication that he intended to detain the Irishman; by now he must have received confirmation via New Scotland Yard that Finbar had no known links with terrorists. But the temporary legal powers that had been in force for a generation entitled the police to hold someone on the flimsiest of grounds for forty-eight hours, sometimes more. All Harry could offer in return for Sladdin releasing Finbar was the usual blather about his client being willing to surrender his passport and report to a police station whenever he blew his nose.

The detective considered Harry sombrely. In the end he said, 'Yes, Mr Devlin, at least for the time being.'

'So I'm free to go?' asked Finbar, jumping to his feet in his eagerness to be away.

A poor choice of words for a client with a clear conscience. Harry barely stifled a groan, although Sladdin remained impassive.

'Free, Mr Rogan? Why, of course. You've had a traumatic afternoon. I'm only sorry it has been necessary to keep you for so long. You will understand how anxious we are to identify the culprit as soon as possible – this is hardly a typical case of Liverpudlian car vandalism. And then there is the continuing need to preserve your own safety.'

The warning was as unambiguous as if lettered in blood on Finbar's front door. He would remain at risk until his unknown antagonist was caught.

'Have you really no idea who might have planted the bomb?' asked Harry when they got outside.

'Didn't I say so in there?'

'What you say and what you mean don't always coincide.'

'Ah well. Maybe I deserved that.'

'Too right. Look, I've been thinking – you implied yesterday you were involved in some way with the death of this girl Eileen. Have you...'

'You do too much thinking,' said Finbar. There was no mistaking his unease. 'Don't play the detective with me, Harry. This can't be anything to do with Eileen McCray. Remember, you're my brief and my pal; that's enough of a burden for any man to bear.'

'Fair enough. Let's drop the subject for now. What are you going to tell Melissa?'

Finbar relaxed into a conspiratorial smile. 'Y'know, I've been wondering the very same thing. If all else fails, I may have to fall back on the truth.'

'You must be worried.'

'Hey, whose side are you on? If I have to come clean, I'll make it clear Sophie was nothing more than a passing fancy. Going by the fuss she made earlier on, I've queered my pitch there good and proper.'

'Win a few, lose a few, eh?'

Finbar clapped him on the back. 'You took the words off the tip of my tongue. Tell you what, we'll nip round to the Dock Brief and have a quick pint. You can help me summon up the courage to face the music.'

'Sorry, I must go and see how Jim is. Besides, you go home smelling like a brewery and the music will make Wagner sound like *The Cuckoo Waltz*.'

'All right, all right. For once I'll take your advice. Jases, I pay enough for it! Give my best to Jim.'

Harry was halfway to the hospital before he remembered that the last couple of bills he had sent to Finbar were still outstanding. The last time he'd given the Irishman a reminder, he'd been fobbed off with a promise to put a cheque in the post. Credit control wasn't Harry's strong point; it was a wonder he'd never been appointed Chancellor of the Exchequer.

A Nurse Ratchet clone whose glare was sufficient to inspire any patient into an instant recovery gave Harry terse directions to Jim's ward. In the maze of white-walled corridors he soon got hopelessly lost and might have found himself attending a birth had he not been rescued by a dreadlocked porter who sent him to the other end of the building.

Harry was shocked by the sight of his partner. Jim was wired to a drip and resembled a character from a Christmas television campaign warning about danger and death on the road. He and Heather were having one of those jerky conversations about nothing in particular which seem so common at hospital bedsides. Harry noticed that Heather kept snatching glances at her husband's battered face, then looking hurriedly away with thinly veiled dismay.

'Not as bad as it looks, old son.' The voice was croaky but audible.

'It couldn't be, really, could it?' asked his wife.

'I suppose you'll be skiving off tomorrow as well, then?' said Harry.

Jim made a ghastly attempt at a grin. 'Give you a chance to do a bit of proper work for a change!'

'Conveyancing and probate? Piece of cake. In fact, if all your clients are as lovely as Mrs. Graham-Brown, I'll be putting in for a permanent transfer.'

'Oh yes? And who is Mrs. Graham-Brown?' asked Heather.

'A lady who fancies leaving Liverpool for the south of Spain,' said Jim with an effort. 'Strange, you may think, but it takes all sorts. And Crusoe and Devlin certainly has all sorts of clients.'

'Including victims of terrorist outrages,' said Harry. 'You'll never guess where I've been until now.'

He told them about the afternoon's excitement. Jim absorbed himself in the story, his craggy features darkening as Harry described Finbar's infidelity and apparent unwillingness to tell all he knew.

'The Irish connection, you suppose?'

'What else? Finbar may have upset a few husbands in his time, but the time-honoured remedy is a fight behind a pub. Same goes for discarded mistresses. I can see someone slashing his tyres; even, maybe, torching his studio. But car bombs are something else.'

'Did you know he had links with terrorists?'

'I don't even know it now. He disclaims all knowledge, except for this old acquaintance he tattooed in days gone by who was killed by the other side a couple of years back. But there must be some terrorist connection. After all...'

His voice trailed away as a thought struck him.

'Watch him,' said Jim Crusoe to Heather in a stage whisper. 'When Harry gets that inspired look, everyone around ought to dive for cover. Solved the mystery, then?'

Harry said nothing, but his mind was working frantically. He had realised that the mysterious Eileen's surname was the same as that of a man in a tough business traditionally associated with the republican movement: a man who might have access to bomb-making equipment.

Dermot McCray. The Irish builder and 'old acquaintance' whom Finbar, at Fenwick Court, had been so anxious to avoid.

Chapter Ten

The notice in the foyer of Empire Hall announced the title of the lunchtime seminar in garish purple: HOW TO ESTABLISH A SMALL COMPANY IN LIVERPOOL.

'Easy,' said Harry to his companion. 'Start with a big company, then sit back and wait.'

The man by his side chuckled, a reaction as unexpected as a snigger from a corpse. Stanley Rowe was a cadaverous individual whose pallor and mournful expression had earned him an appropriate sobriquet. But life hadn't been too hard on Death Rowe; he had sold his estate agency to an insurance company with more money than sense at the height of the property boom in the late eighties and had bought it back for half the price after the bottom fell out of the market a couple of years later.

Some bright spark on the city council had designated this as 'Liverpool Business Day' – although cynics argued that, given the state of the city's industry, twenty minutes would have sufficed. Jim had booked to attend a series of events due to be held here, ranging from a breakfast meeting to an early evening exhibition. In a moment of weakness at his partner's bedside the previous night, Harry had volunteered to act as stand-in for at least one session, with the idea of picking up a few clients and keeping their professional contacts warm.

'I see the discussion is being led by Geoffrey Willatt,' said Rowe. 'I suppose your paths seldom cross?'

'Not if I can help it,' said Harry, 'but he was once my principal.'

Rowe's skeletal features twitched and his eyes widened a fraction; it was his equivalent of registering amazement. It was as if he'd heard the Krays claiming to be on first name terms with the Queen.

'You trained with Maher and Malcolm? Good God.'

'How they ever came to offer me articles, I'll never fathom. It's not as if my family was named in *Debrett's* or I took a double first from Cambridge.

And I met Jim whilst I worked there, believe it or not. Of course, we both escaped long before there was any chance of our making our fortune. I can't say either of us ever learned much from old Geoffrey about how to run a practice funded on legal aid and house sales.'

They walked into the room where the seminar was being held and sat at the back. A glance around the audience suggested that solicitors, accountants, stockbrokers and financiers outnumbered Liverpool's would-be entrepreneurs by at least five to one.

Geoffrey Willatt had been born, Harry suspected, in a pinstripe suit. Senior partner of one of the largest legal practices outside London, he was Chairman of the Law Society's Standing Committee on Legal Etiquette and author of a racy little monograph entitled *The Property Lawyer's Vade-Mecum*. Now he spoke about investment, cash flow and debt recovery with his accustomed authority; but for Harry it was like listening to the owner of Fortnum and Mason offer advice on the running of a corner shop. As the talk shifted to terms of trading and employment costs, he closed his eyes. He did not doze – although the temptation was strong – but pondered again whether Dermot McCray might want Finbar Rogan dead.

Suppose Eileen was McCray's wife and Finbar had loved her and left her. If she had killed herself out of desperation or remorse, McCray's motive for revenge attacks could hardly be stronger. Whatever Finbar's reasons for refusing to disclose the truth about Eileen, Harry wanted him to start talking. If he did not, more room might be needed in the mortuary.

As the seminar came to an end, people began to move away. At the door, a young woman with a severe hair style and a grave manner pressed a glossy brochure into his hand. 'Do talk to us if you'd like to make a success of your business. May I ask what line you are in?'

Harry glanced at the logo on the cover of the brochure. It was a hand-out from Maher and Malcolm.

'I'm making a career out of crime,' he said.

She shot him a nervous glance and turned bright red.

Harry took pity on her. When he'd been an articled clerk, for a solicitor to advertise had been a monstrous breach of ethics. Nowadays P.R. was practically part of the finals course.

'I'm a solicitor,' he explained.

She stared in disbelief at his scuffed shoes before remembering her manners. Nervously, she cleared her throat. 'I'm afraid we only handle white-collar misdemeanours.'

Chapter Ten

Of course. Corporate fraud and insider trading: Maher and Malcolm would never become involved in anything down-market. In their austere yet elegant offices, a legal aid form would seem as out of place as a copy of *Playboy*.

Outside, Harry caught up Stanley Rowe and handed him the brochure. 'With my compliments. I'm sure you'll find it tastefully designed. But if it tells you anything worth reading, I'll buy you lunch at the Ensenada.'

The estate agent flicked through the pages. There were more photographs than lines of text, with acres of space on each page.

'Your money's safe,' he said in his funereal tone. 'I take it you are not a believer in practice development?'

'Truth is, I'm hopeless at marketing. Today's been a write-off. I left my business cards in the office and to make matters worse, over lunch I sat next to a banker who'd make the speaking clock seem like sparkling company. When I confessed I didn't know a mezzanine agreement from a junk bond he wrote me off faster than a Third World debt.'

'Honesty from a litigator? Even Jim would have bluffed a little. How is he, by the way?'

'You've heard about his smash?'

'Yes, sounds dreadful. Is he making progress? I must admit, I was particularly bothered because I'd just sent him a client. She was in a hurry to exchange and complete and it crossed my mind that Jim's accident might cause problems.'

To say nothing of delay in paying commission, thought Harry.

'Don't worry – Jim's on the road to recovery. And we've got his work under control.' A thought occurred to him. 'Who was the client?'

'Rather a lovely lady, as a matter of fact.' Rowe's sombre expression lightened for a moment. 'Name of Graham-Brown. Rosemary of that ilk.'

'She's been in to see me already,' said Harry. 'Know much about her?'

'Why do you ask?'

'Interested, that's all.'

Rowe tapped the side of his nose with solemn significance. 'Beware Mr Graham-Brown, Harry.'

'Don't worry, I'm not running off with her to Puerto Banus – though if the chance arose, I wouldn't say no. But who is Graham-Brown? Do you know him?'

'The name rang a bell when she came in to see me. I believe he's in financial services. I've never met the man or acted for either of them before.'

'How did they choose you to handle the sale of their place – personal recommendation?'

'Yellow Pages, more likely. I recall she said she and her husband preferred dealing with a smaller firm: more personal treatment, more willing to fit in with clients' special requirements than a bigger outfit. And when she asked for the name of a firm of solicitors, small yet competent at conveyancing, I mentioned Crusoe and Devlin. With emphasis on the Crusoe – no offence.'

'None taken. High finance is far from being my only area of ignorance. You say "special requirements". Did she have anything particular in mind?'

'Time was of the essence, that's the main thing that sticks in my mind. She didn't want any hassle with signboards or adverts in the Press. She was keen to know if I could use personal contacts to find out if any of our competitors had a client looking for that type of property. Some executive from outside the city looking for a company move would be ideal, she said.'

'And you soon found someone to fit the bill?'

'Came up trumps straight away, as a matter of fact.' Stanley Rowe could make even a boast sound like a prophecy of doom.

'The purchasers being the Ambroses?'

'Correct. As you know, Geoffrey acts for them. Ambrose is on the board of one of the subsidiaries of the Byzantium Line, who are clients of Maher and Malcolm. He's being redeployed here from Hull and wanted to find somewhere fast. Even though he haggled, our Rosemary was willing to drop the asking price; I said I thought she could get full whack if she held out for it. But no, Graham-Brown is keen to wrap up his affairs in the UK as soon as he can, it seems. So keen that despite my strong advice to the contrary, they agreed to knock thirty thousand off.' He shook his head, the gesture of a man who has given up trying to understand human folly.

Harry whistled. 'A lot of money. I wasn't aware of that.'

'No reason why you should be. As soon as the offer was accepted, I told her to give Jim a ring.'

'Thanks for that. Perhaps I will buy you lunch sometime, after all. I glanced at the particulars you'd drafted in the file. Is the house as impressive as it sounds?'

Stanley Rowe quirked his lips – his equivalent of a mischievous smile. 'I hope you're not suggesting I'm one of those estate agents who exaggerates the merits of a property?'

'Is there any other kind?'

'How cynical you are. As it happens, I can assure you that it's a palace. The Ambroses are getting a bargain.'

'Any idea why Graham-Brown should want to up and leave for the Costa del Crime in such a rush?'

Chapter Ten

'I really don't have the foggiest notion. Perhaps he's a crook who has pulled off his last heist and wants to while away the rest of his days in the Spanish sunshine with the pulchritudinous Rosemary.'

Many a true word, thought Harry. His interest in the woman was beginning to be matched by his curiosity about her husband. Where did his money come from and what made the couple's departure to Puerto Banus so urgent as to justify accepting far less for their home than it was worth?

'You have a dreamer's look in your eyes, Harry. Don't keep thinking about the lady. Graham-Brown may be in his dotage and as ugly as sin, for all I know, but my impression is that she wouldn't worry as long as he keeps her in the style to which she's become accustomed. With that kind of competition, even a worthy chap like you doesn't stand a chance.'

Harry grinned at Death Rowe. 'Where women are concerned, I've learned to expect the unexpected.'

They shook hands and Harry made his way back through Chavasse Park to his office, trying to scrub Rosemary Graham-Brown from his mind. The noise from Fenwick Court did the trick. At a distance of a hundred yards, the scream of a single electric drill assaulted his ears and as he turned the corner into the courtyard the cacophony would have made the dancers at the Danger dive for cover.

Parked in front of the entrance to Crusoe and Devlin was the BMW he had seen before. A short distance away stood its owner, Dermot McCray, talking to a couple of his workmen; from the faces of all three Harry could tell that it was heated debate. The drilling stopped, but other members of the gang kept their eyes averted, as if afraid to get involved. He watched as McCray wagged a thick forefinger at the men and, with a parting angry word, stalked back to his car.

Without thinking, Harry hailed him.

'McCray!'

The name echoed around the courtyard and its owner froze in the act of opening the driver's door.

McCray's features might themselves have been put together by a Jerry-builder doing things on the cheap. His cheeks bore the red marks of broken blood vessels and his nose had probably gained its kink in a bar-room brawl. A Rolex glinted from his wrist, but money had not smoothed him. His fists were tightly clenched.

'Who wants him?'

The hissed words carried a promise of danger. Too late, it occurred to Harry that if McCray was bent on murdering Finbar Rogan, an unrehearsed confrontation was scarcely a prudent way of tackling him. Harry sensed the labourers staring at him. He felt like an unarmed deputy who had chosen the wrong moment to go sightseeing at the OK Corral.

'My name's Devlin.'

A good Catholic name, but it did not seem to impress McCray. He slammed the car door shut and took a couple of paces towards Harry. 'So?'

'I'm a solicitor.' Harry jerked a thumb towards his front door. 'That's my office.'

McCray glanced at the rusting nameplate.

'Crusoe and Devlin? Never heard of 'em.'

'One of my clients is Finbar Rogan.'

McCray spat on the ground. When, after a few moments, he spoke again, he did so slowly, as if straining to keep himself under control.

'You ought to be more choosy about the company you keep.'

'Someone's trying to kill him,' said Harry.

McCray gave him a long, hard look.

'Good. Save me the trouble.'

'Listen. You must…'

With two strides McCray was standing in front of Harry. He dropped a palm as big as a navvy's shovel on Harry's shoulder.

'No, you listen to me, Mr Devlin.' The voice was guttural. At close quarters, McCray's face was even more ravaged; deep lines cut into the skin around his eyes and mouth.

'Tell your client this. He ought to get out of this city and stay out. Because if he crosses my path once more, he's a dead man. Understand?'

He gave the shoulder a powerful final squeeze, then released his grip, causing Harry to stagger like a punch-drunk boxer before tumbling to the ground. McCray gazed at him scornfully before getting into his car. It revved fiercely then swung back in reverse, coming within inches of Harry's toes before accelerating out of the courtyard.

One of the workmen laughed, breaking the silence. Someone else joined in, then another. Their derision stung Harry, yet he thought he detected in it relief that McCray had not directed his wrath at them. He clambered to his feet and dusted himself down. Self-esteem damaged more than his scapula, he turned into the office and banged the door, angry with himself for succumbing to impulse. Challenging McCray had achieved nothing and Finbar would not thank him for it. Perhaps he should have opted for the soft life all those years ago and stayed safe and secure with Maher and Malcolm. He might even have learned how to make crime pay.

Chapter Eleven

The phone was ringing as Harry reached his desk. He wasn't in the mood for more confrontation, whether with clients, opposing solicitors or barristers' clerks chasing payment of inflated fees, and at first he paid no attention, hoping the call would go away. No chance. Suzanne had seen him slink in and, irked by his failure to check on calls received in his absence, would let him have no hiding place. Finally he surrendered.

'Who is it?'

'Mr Rogan,' the girl said and put Finbar through before Harry could tell her to take a message.

'Harry, at last! This is the third time I've called since midday. The lovely Suzanne said you'd gone to some lecture, but this is no time for swotting. Your clients need help.'

'What can I do for you?' asked Harry, not finding it difficult to restrain his enthusiasm.

'Listen, that bloody Sladdin, you know what he's done? He's got a couple of fellers in a car down the road keeping an eye on me. When I went out to the newsagent to see what the *Daily Post* had to say about the bomb, they followed me down the road. Trying to be discreet, like, but I could tell what they were up to.'

After his humiliating encounter with Dermot McCray, Harry didn't feel inclined to offer his shoulder for crying on. 'What do you expect? You're a Dubliner, there was a bomb under your car, you gave Sladdin the impression you were telling less than the whole truth…'

'I'm a bloody *victim*! The bomb was meant for me!'

'Look, you're not dealing with a fool. Sladdin would be negligent if he didn't set up some form of surveillance.'

At the other end of the line Finbar sighed. 'Fat lot of comfort you are. How long is this likely to go on?'

'Till Sladdin finds out who has it in for you. You could speed things up by coming clean.'

'What d'you mean?'

'Come on, Finbar, let's not play games. People don't have their premises burned down and their cars bombed simply for dropping litter in the street. Until you take me into your confidence, there isn't much I can do to save your skin from Dermot McCray.'

'What?' Finbar sounded taken aback. 'Why do you mention him?'

'I had a brief encounter with him outside the office a couple of minutes ago. He's not your number one fan. And if he's mixed up with terrorists...'

'Harry, for God's sake, don't keep on about bloody terrorists, will you? You're as bad as Sladdin.'

'You seriously expect me to believe it's got nothing to do with that? I wasn't born yesterday. Okay, I realise it isn't policy to cross the people back in Ireland, far less go bleating to the boys in blue. I can see why you're keeping mum while you try to straighten things out with someone who might be able to rein in McCray. But if you're not prepared to let me into the secret...'

'Ah, I told you not to act the detective. I know it's your favourite game and you've had your successes, but leave this one alone, mate, for your sake as well as mine. I need a live Perry Mason, not a dead Sam Spade.'

'All Perry's clients were innocent. I should be so lucky.'

Down the line came Finbar's familiar burst of laughter. He could never be out of temper for long.

'Never mind. Even he would have had his work cut out if he'd practised in Liverpool. Listen, are you going to the exhibition in the Empire Hall tonight?'

'I was meaning to avoid it. Jim had offered to take a turn at the local Legal Group's stand, but I've had as much as I can take of Liverpool Business Day after listening to my old boss pontificate about Boom or Bust this lunchtime.'

'Oh ye of little faith. It's only a couple of minutes from your flat. Why don't you show up, even if only to have a drink with me and Melissa? She'll be on the Radio Liverpool stand for half an hour this evening.'

'Are you two still together?'

'Of course. Why ever not?'

'I don't know how you do it,' Harry said, half grudging, half amused.

'Well, she doesn't know Sophie was with me in the Blue Moon. As far as she's concerned, I'd just called for a chat with my old mate Reg when my car was blown to bits outside.'

'Finbar, you're less trustworthy than half the criminals I've ever met.'

'Listen, I'm only a lad with a liking for the ladies. And you know what they say about sex in Dublin, don't you? There it is, the loveliest little thing in the world and they had to go and make a sin out of it.'

'So when does the lad finally get to grow up?'

'Harry, I'm starting to think that at my age, I'm too old to grow up. So shall I see you tonight?'

'If your enemies don't beat me to it.'

As Harry rang off, his secretary came in bearing a thick brown envelope. 'Hand delivery from Maher and Malcolm.'

'Thanks.' He slit it open and scanned the contents. 'Can you fetch me the Graham-Brown sale file from Jim's room, please?'

'Conveyancing?' Lucy's expression of bewilderment made him feel like Dracula asking her to pass the garlic. 'Wouldn't you like Sylvia to handle it?'

'No need,' he said with dignity. 'I'm beginning to think I have hidden talents as a property lawyer.'

Lucy turned on her way out. 'I'd feel safer having the Boston Strangler give me a neck massage!'

After she had shut the door, Harry studied Geoffrey Willatt's letter. The problem which the Ambroses had raised seemed a simple one: the rear garden of the Graham-Browns' house appeared to dog-leg around a couple of old horse chestnut trees. The plans with the deeds – which Harry had copied and attached to the contract – indicated that the trees fell inside the boundaries of the property. Actual observation, however, suggested the contrary and there was no fence, hedge or other dividing line at that spot to put the matter beyond doubt. It was the kind of discrepancy which would prove a fertile source of future dispute if not sorted out now.

Harry's first instinct was to yawn, but after a moment he brightened. There was only one way to wrap the matter up with the speed which both buyers and sellers demanded.

He would have to pay Rosemary a visit.

It would need to be a surprise visit, too, given that he did not have her ex-directory number and that if the transaction was to proceed as promptly as required, he couldn't afford to write her a letter or wait for her to telephone him. He took one look at the pile of correspondence plaintively hoping for attention and decided there was no time like the present – for calling on Rosemary Graham-Brown, that was, rather than getting stuck in to the tedium of deskwork. He buzzed Lucy and announced his intentions.

'But what about...'

'One has to prioritise,' he said, recalling a bit of jargon from a practice management article he had once read in *The Law Society's Gazette*. 'This is a private-paying client, an urgent matter. Let Suzanne know I've gone out the back way.' He didn't relish braving the switchboard girl's wrath again. Restored to good humour, he added, 'I may be some time.'

***

The drive to Formby did not take long. It was a crisp afternoon and he felt excited at the prospect of seeing Rosemary again. Presumably her husband would now be at his office: there might be an opportunity for a chat over a cuppa once the business of the boundary was out of the way. Moreover, he would have the chance to satisfy his curiosity whilst enjoying her company.

Crow's Nest House stood on a wooded slope, commanding a view of the Irish Sea. Set back from the road and reached via an unmade track which the council had never adopted, it conformed to the odd principle that the better the property, the worse the access. As his MG bumped from pothole to pothole he began to wish he had walked up from the main road. Rounding the last tree-lined corner, he passed through open wrought-iron entrance gates and took his first look at the home Stuart and Rosemary Graham-Brown were in such a hurry to sell.

For once Death Rowe's eulogistic description in the property particulars coincided with reality. The house was a double-fronted building in white stucco with smart green shutters at every window. Koi carp swam in an ornamental pond; beyond the triple garage Harry could see a summer-house in the style of a Swiss chalet. The tranquillity of the place made it hard to believe that the city's clamour was only a short drive away.

He parked and pressed the doorbell. Musical chimes sounded. Somewhere inside a small child began to bleat.

The crying startled him. He had expected Rosemary to be alone. And yet – of course! – the particulars had spoken of a nursery. He had not realised, however, that it was in active use; she had not mentioned a child. He felt a stab of dismay before the absurdity of his instinctive response dawned on him. If it was okay to fancy a married woman, why did it bother him that she was a mother too?

Unsure of himself, he stared at the door. Coming here had seemed a good idea; now he was having second thoughts. He stood there for a full minute before he pulled himself together and rang again. The child renewed its howl of protest but soon he heard approaching footsteps. He sensed someone studying him through the spyhole cut into the oak before at last the door was opened.

Chapter Eleven

Rosemary was simply dressed, in white tee-shirt and scruffy jeans, and she had tied her hair back with an orange ribbon. Without the elegant clothes she'd worn when calling at the office, somehow she did not seem so unattainable.

'Harry.'

Her tone, like her face, was questioning and lacked any trace of welcome. It was almost as if she found his unannounced arrival alarming.

'Hello, Rosemary,' he said, disconcerted. 'There's something I need to check with you.'

She glanced at her watch. When she spoke again, her sharpness startled him.

'Couldn't you have phoned?'

'You told me you were ex-directory.'

She looked at him steadily. He could tell her mind was working rapidly, but to what purpose, he could not guess.

'Of course. I'm sorry. It's just – you've caught me at a bad time, that's all. Won't you come in?'

He followed her past a glass cabinet full of porcelain. He knew no more about *objects d'art* than he did about the law of corporate acquisitions, but he suspected that the insurance premium on the Graham-Browns' household contents would be enough to finance the purchase of the whole of Fenwick Court, with something to spare. She led him into a living room larger than the average courtroom. Through a wall of picture windows he could see a paved area equipped with lighting and a barbecue. Herbaceous borders edged a lawn which was separated by a narrow stream from the rougher grassland stretching towards the horse chestnuts Mr and Mrs Ambrose were so anxious to own.

'Take a seat,' she said, motioning him towards a chesterfield covered with skilfully patchworked cushions. The clocks, paintings and bits of china dotted here and there were straight out of a Sotheby's catalogue; enough to delight the choosiest of his burglar-clients.

'I hope you've not come to break the news that there's a hold-up on the sale,' she said.

Lacking the make-up she'd worn on their previous encounters, her face was pale. He sensed that not far beneath the surface bubbled anxiety verging on desperation. Again he wondered why the Graham-Browns were so keen to get away from one of the smartest homes in north Merseyside.

'A minor snag, that's all. I'm confident we can sort it out.'

Her whole body relaxed visibly and her expression brightened. Ridiculously pleased that he could produce even this slight change in her emotions, Harry felt his heart beat a little faster. He launched into his explanation and was halfway through describing the problem raised by the Ambroses when, in another room, the child howled once more.

'Oh God, don't tell me the baby's getting bored with the playpen,' Rosemary muttered. She raised her voice and called out, 'Coming!'

'Boy or girl?' he asked as she got up to do her duty.

'Girl. And a little madam she certainly is.'

'Called?'

'Rainbow – if you can believe that.'

He groped for a diplomatic reply and finally managed, 'Unusual.'

'You could say that. Personally, I think she'll suffer for it at school. But it wasn't my idea.'

'Stuart's?'

'Er… yes.'

The unseen Rainbow began to sob and Rosemary said quickly, 'Excuse me a minute while I go and see what her ladyship wants.'

Whilst she was gone he absorbed his surroundings. Some of the antiques – the ebony-framed sampler dated 1762 and an extravagantly-carved grandfather clock – might be heirlooms. If so, he had no doubt that they came from Stuart's side of the family. Nothing he had seen had made him revise his initial opinion that her roots were in the shabby Liverpool streets. Every now and then, she gave herself away: as with the barely concealed disdain for the ludicrous name her husband had foisted upon her daughter.

He could not help but be intrigued by the hint of discord between husband and wife. Was Stuart a much older man on the brink of retirement and Rosemary an increasingly discontented mother and housewife? Did she see in their departure for Spain an opportunity for romance and adventure?

'I love children,' she said, returning so quietly as to startle him with the sound of her voice, 'but coping with them all day every day is a test of anyone's devotion. Now, you were saying?'

Harry finished describing the query about the deeds and suggested that she let him see for himself the area of land between the Graham-Browns' property and the open ground which belonged to a farm on the other side of the slope.

'Good idea. Let's sort it out right away, if we can.'

Outside, they took a path which led to a couple of stepping stones in the stream, then strolled up to the dilapidated picket fence which formed the boundary of the grassland. While Rosemary watched, Harry followed the fence's winding progress until he arrived at its end thirty yards away from the horse chestnuts. Feeling like a Red Indian scout from the pages of Fenimore Cooper, he knelt in the undergrowth and searched around for several minutes.

'Problem solved,' he said to Rosemary as they walked back to the house. 'The pickets haven't vanished, they're buried in that tangle of nettles. But you can make out the original course of the fence and it certainly runs around the outside of the trees. Do you remember when it began to collapse? I see from the land certificate you've been here a number of years.'

'Eight, I think,' said Rosemary. She smiled at him. 'I was a child bride, you understand. So can we get the Ambroses' knickers out of their twist?'

'Leave it to me.'

'Marvellous. The least I can do in the circumstances is offer you tea. I'm sure you're very busy, but can you spare the time?'

He paused as they reached the back door. 'I can't think of a better way to spend an afternoon.'

Her hand brushed against his. 'You know, you're not my idea of a solicitor. Thank God. I'm lucky to have you.' And she kissed him quickly on the cheek before disappearing in the direction of the kitchen.

As he listened to the kettle come to the boil, he felt lust warring with common sense. It occurred to him that this encounter had echoes of scenes in movies he loved: the glamorous lady of the house charming an eager admirer in the absence of her husband. He thought of Barbara Stanwyck tempting Fred McMurray in *Double Indemnity*. Was it possible, he asked himself, that when she came back into the room Rosemary would be in seductive mood? Did she see in him a means of escape from a tiresome husband, elderly but rich?

Might she even have murder on her mind?

He became aware that his mouth was dry, his body tense with expectation. Of course, it was ridiculous to let his imaginings take hold – but he could not help himself. She was not a woman he could easily resist.

'Thinking about the law?' she asked, making another soft-soled return to the living room.

'About breaking it,' he said.

She laid the tray of tea things down on a small mahogany table and, tilting her head to one side, considered him with care, as if in an attempt to make up her mind. Harry waited for her response.

'I don't see you as a law-breaker,' she said.

And the note of regret in her voice told him more plainly than any words that he was not going to be seduced today.

Chapter Twelve

Half an hour later Harry was on his way back to the office. Waiting at traffic lights in Waterloo, he cast his mind back to the small talk he and Rosemary had exchanged while sipping their tea. No conversation between solicitor and client could have been more innocuous. She had neither made love to him nor sought to incite him to murder.

And all too soon she would be sunning herself in her husband's company at Puerto Banus. Accelerating as the lights turned to green, he instructed himself to blot Rosemary's face from his mind and treat her as no more than a name on a buff legal file.

On arriving at Fenwick Court his first thought was to ring Heather Crusoe for the latest about Jim.

'Much better,' she assured him. 'It's amazing what a good night's sleep can do. He's off the drip and they're already talking about the chances of him going home soon. Oh, and he wanted me to remind you specially that he expects you to do your duty at the exhibition. No sudden call-outs to some grotty police cell to get yourself off the hook and he said you weren't to slope off home until you have a diary-full of new clients.'

'I think I liked him better when he could hardly speak. Okay, just this once.'

An hour later, as bidden, he made his way to Empire Hall, his gloom at the prospect of having to glad-hand the city's businessmen more than offset by his relief at the news of Jim's recovery.

The exhibition was being held in The Atrium, a glass-roofed annexe to the recently renovated main building which boasted more foliage than Kew and waterfalls as noisy as the Niagara. Near the entrance a huge magenta poster urged the city's businessmen to borrow money from The Bank That Cares. Harry knew it also as the bank that spent much of its time suing debtors, repossessing houses and sending in receivers. He smiled nervously at the under-manager responsible for Crusoe and Devlin's office account and scuttled away before he could be buttonholed for a chat about extending the partners' personal guarantees. His progress slowed as someone tugged at his arm.

'Excuse me, sir, but do you know who wrote *The Decameron*? Are you familiar with the secret of nuclear fission? Don't you long for a better understanding of the world in which we live?'

The encyclopaedia salesman who had accosted him was as clean-cut as a Mormon missionary and no less enthusiastic. Harry was tempted to say the answers to the mysteries haunting him could not be found in any of the twenty-four luxuriously bound volumes the man was trying to flog. As he moved away, his eyes fell on the crowded corner bar, where Stanley Rowe was waving at him vigorously. The estate agent's skeletal features were flushed and at close quarters his breath left Harry in no doubt that he had been sampling the Special Exhibition Tankard.

'Done any business this afternoon, Stan?'

'The only joy I've had was when an old dear approached me at half four. I supposed she was a widow who wanted to sell the family home, move into sheltered housing perhaps.' Rowe shook his head mournfully. 'Turned out she'd wandered in by mistake, expecting to find an all-in-wrestling bout. When I told her that was next week, she swore herself hoarse and stamped off to complain to someone in authority.'

'Never mind, at least you should be cashing in on the Graham-Brown sale soon. The boundary—'

'And that's another thing. Have you spoken to Geoffrey Willatt yet? There's a hitch.'

'About the trees? But it's—'

'Nothing to do with trees, Harry. You need to see the wood, don't worry about the bloody trees. The whole deal may fall through.'

'That's impossible! Contracts have been exchanged.'

Stanley Rowe snorted. 'Speak to him yourself. He's on the legal stand.'

On the other side of the aisle, an exhibition floor plan was pinned to a pillar alongside a local government stand mothballed as a result of industrial action on the part of the community's servants. Looking for the Liverpool Legal Group's stand, Harry spotted a name he had not expected to see.

Merseycredit. Stuart Graham-Brown's business.

Unable to contain his curiosity, he hurried over to the Merseycredit stand. There was no sign of Rosemary's husband, but standing behind the table was a rosy-cheeked brunette in a tracksuit a size too small for her. She greeted him with so much fervour he guessed she was paid by commission only.

'Care for some literature, sir?'

He thumbed through the glossy clutcher she pressed into his hand. It was full of pictures of happy, beaming people, supposed beneficiaries of Merseycredit's financial advice. Arriving at the small print on the inside back page, he read that the firm was a partnership. And the only partners named were Stuart Graham-Brown and Rosemary Graham-Brown.

Well, well, well. So Rosemary had a direct share in the profits…

'Let me arrange an interview for you, sir,' urged the brunette. 'Free of charge, no obligation. Discretion assured.' She made it sound like a dating agency.

'This would be with Mr Graham-Brown, presumably?'

'Our senior partner? You'll understand, sir, he does have very many commitments and it's normally our assistant executives who see new clients. But if you particularly wanted to see Mr Graham-Brown, I'm sure we could fix something up next month. Unfortunately, I don't have his diary here. Perhaps I could take your telephone number?'

'No need,' said Harry. 'I'll give him a ring myself.'

'Wait a minute!' She was desperate not to let a prospect slip away. 'I can see him over there, talking to one of our clients. Do hang on for a moment, I'm sure he won't be long.'

She pointed to a man with greying hair further down the aisle. Stuart Graham-Brown was tall, with a suave manner and immaculate dress sense. He was, Harry judged, a good twenty years older than his wife. And he was deep in discussion with someone instantly recognisable – Nick Folley, of all people.

Harry made a quick decision. If Merseycredit's staff were unaware of the Graham-Browns' imminent flight to the sun, this wasn't the right time or place to introduce himself to the man responsible for their fate.

'Sorry, but I can't wait. But you can tell him my name's Harry Devlin and I'll be in touch.' He walked briskly over to the adjoining aisle, where the Liverpool Legal Group was trying to convince an indifferent public of its urgent need for skilled professional advice. Most of the men passed quickly on to the next pitch, where a blonde wearing a low-cut top and tight leopardskin pants was encouraging the belief that an impulse buy of a Turkish time-share would prove their virility.

'Harry, my dear fellow. Good of you to come.' Geoffrey Willatt greeted him from behind a counter which bore a placard saying CONTACT MAHER AND MALCOLM FOR PROFESSIONAL SERVICES IN COMPLETE CONFIDENCE.

Chapter Twelve

'Hello, Geoffrey. Sure you're not using your legal business as a front for a brothel with a slogan like that?'

Willatt chortled his appreciation. 'One of the things I always liked about you, Harry – splendid sense of humour.'

'What's up?' Harry asked, suspicious of the excessive bonhomie. 'Don't say you need me to do an extra stint?'

'No, no, no. Glad to see you at all, good heavens. Appreciate your coming along at short notice. Partner sick, busy man, damn good show. Here, take some leaflets. To be frank, we're a little quiet at present; people don't seem yet to appreciate how much we can help. So you won't find your task too arduous.'

'Fine. Now, about Crow's Nest House. The tree trouble has been resolved, you'll be glad to hear, so when can we complete?'

'Ah,' said Willatt. He invested the syllable with a wealth of meaning, as if to convey brave hope dashed by life's vicissitudes.

'Come on, then. Spit it out.'

Willatt's pained expression made it clear that he had never spat anything out in all his days. When he spoke his words were emollient.

'We have a slight problem with the Ambroses, I fear. Namely, the Byzantium Line have announced their half-yearly results today. Rather poor, as you'll have seen if you keep in touch with the stock market. No? Well, anyway, they have found it necessary to impose cutbacks. The Liverpool office is to be slimmed down and there's going to be no room in it for Mr Ambrose, poor chap. Apparently they need to rationalise, concentrate on major international business and as a result, they want him out in Nigeria instead.'

'So a house in darkest Formby won't be too much use to him, then?'

'I'm afraid that's about the size of it. But if any of your clients are looking to rent out an air-conditioned penthouse flat in Lagos, we'd be happy to look at it.' Willatt's blustery guffaw did not disguise his apprehension as he awaited a reaction.

'Not good enough, Geoffrey – you know that. Contracts have already been exchanged.' Harry said this as though the deal had been cast in tablets of stone, but as he spoke he tried to reach back into the past and his days as a baffled student of the law of real property. Couldn't the Graham-Browns issue to the Ambroses something called a notice to complete? But what would be its legal effect?

Willatt allowed himself a superior smile. Harry realised that his former principal was, for all his professional embarrassment, relishing the sight of a defector from Maher and Malcolm groping in vain for a basic bit of legal know-how.

'I think you'll find that my people are willing to make an offer to forestall the need for any unpleasantness.'

Willatt never soiled his hands with court work; he let colleagues do the dirty work associated with lucrative disputes. In lectures and after-dinner speeches he invariably described litigation as a necessary evil, rather like a Middle East arms dealer deploring the outbreak of war.

'You're well aware of the urgency. My clients need the sale so they can move abroad themselves in the very near future.'

'Tax exile, is it? I didn't know your firm made a habit of acting for the well-heeled, Harry. Or are these people simply aiming to get beyond the reach of the extradition laws?'

As Willatt chuckled, Harry wondered if it was a case of truth being spoken in jest. He decided to tough it out. 'I'm afraid you'll find,' he said, 'that my people regard this as a matter of principle.' Lawyers' code for *they'll drive a ruthless bargain.*

'I can assure you,' said Willatt, responding in the same language, 'the Ambroses are prepared to be reasonable.'

In other words, he'd advised them they didn't have a leg to stand on. Money was therefore unlikely to be a barrier to a deal, but Harry was sure that would not satisfy the Graham-Browns.

He shrugged. 'I'll take instructions.' Meaning *God knows what they'll say.* Geoffrey Willatt beamed and bade him farewell.

Harry's half hour of marketing would have turned into less a test of his P.R. skills than of his ability in staying awake, had Geoffrey Willatt's news not intervened. A few feet away, the leopardskin girl was attracting much attention, but the pamphlets Geoffrey had left him, entitled *Let a Lawyer Look at your Lease* and *Speak to a Solicitor when you want to sell a Shop*, failed to divert a single passer-by. Even so, he had plenty to think about.

He turned his mind to the Ambroses' impending default. What would Rosemary make of it? She seemed so keen to emigrate. But why was that? Was she the anxious one, or merely acting on her husband's strict instructions? Until now Harry had typecast Stuart Graham-Brown as an older man with money to burn, ready to indulge his wife's fantasies. Was that a mistake? Was Graham-Brown the one desperate to flee to his hideaway on the Spanish coast? 'Financial services' covered sins ranging from dodgy investment advice to wheeler-dealing on the futures market. Plenty of people in that line of business must have something to hide – was he one of them? He tried to think of an honest reason why Graham-Brown should allow his staff to talk about booking him for appointments he would never keep. For once, imagination failed him.

No wonder it was so important to complete the house sale quickly. No wonder the Graham-Browns were willing to drop the asking price. The financial prize of their scam – whatever it might be, a confidence trick played on investors, perhaps – must be huge to warrant leaving the business behind.

How much did Rosemary know? The idea she might be ignorant of her husband's duplicity appealed to Harry. But he recalled her air of excitement at their first meeting in New Commodities House and how nervous she had been earlier at her home. With hindsight, her behaviour seemed far from innocent. And it was not as if Graham-Brown was intending to skip to Spain with his secretary, instead of his wife. Why should he, when Rosemary put the average bimbo to shame? She might have reservations about him and his choice of their daughter's name, but she was a woman who luxuriated in the leisured life that money could bring. Harry had little doubt they were in it together.

'You look as though someone's let you down,' said an ironic female voice. 'What's up? Has Rogan done a runner without paying your bill?'

Kim Lawrence had arrived to take her turn on duty. Harry thought it unlikely that the posters she was carrying about the need to fight to safeguard legal aid would tempt many middle-aged captains of industry away from the leopardskin lady.

'It's all yours,' he said. 'And as for Finbar, he's around here somewhere if you're in the mood for a little Irish levity.'

She winced. 'With any luck, I'll avoid him. I simply don't believe that man is as naive as he makes out. I've met his kind before: totally self-centred. All hail-fellow-well-met until you cross them. Then, when you do, God help you.'

Harry guessed that Finbar would meet his match in Kim Lawrence. For the first time it occurred to him that his client did not attract such a wide range of women as he had always enviously supposed. To fall for the blarney, they had to be vulnerable – as Harry sensed Melissa to be – or simply keen on sex, like Sophie.

'You'll be telling me next that what happened in chambers the other day was a miscarriage of justice to rival the Guildford Four.'

'A travesty,' said Kim Lawrence, although the sardonic glint in her eyes robbed her words of priggishness. Her face darkened. 'And though I'll live to fight another day, my client was deeply distressed.'

'You win some, you lose some.'

'I don't think Sinead Rogan is so philosophical. I've never seen anyone as furious as she was after Cody's ruling.'

Harry was about to ask Kim if Sinead had said anything to her about Eileen McCray when someone tapped him on the shoulder.

'Harry! It's a small world.'

Baz Gilbert and Penny Newland, hand in hand, had come up behind him. The disc jockey gestured at the crowd surrounding the timeshare stand and gave a crooked smile. 'Legal business doesn't seem so brisk. Competition too hot?'

'There wasn't much hope for us once Ms Lawrence here banned us from touting for new clients under the slogan "Drop Your Old Briefs".' He dodged out of reach of feminist retribution and asked, 'And you two? Has Nick Folley insisted that you go on parade?'

'With such a small staff, everyone has to do their share,' said Penny. 'Even Sophie's graced us with her presence. Perhaps she hasn't found anyone to share a hotel room with this evening.'

Her bitchiness came as a surprise to Harry. He sensed she took personal offence at her colleague's philandering. Obviously news of Sophie's misadventures at the Blue Moon had not taken long to reach the Radio Liverpool grapevine.

'Thanks again for inviting me on to *Pop In*,' he said, hastily changing the subject. 'Until yesterday morning, all I knew about local radio was what I'd gleaned from *Play Misty For Me*.'

'I'm no Clint Eastwood,' said Baz.

'You're not so bad,' his girlfriend said, squeezing his arm as the three of them walked down the aisle.

'At least I don't have as much trouble as Clint did, fending off the psychopaths.'

'I don't know, you've had your share of nutcases to contend with. Especially on the phone-ins.'

'A hazard of the job?' asked Harry.

'Too right,' said Penny. Her expression was troubled. 'There are some very unhappy people out there. And some very disturbed ones.'

'Someone's got to support Tranmere Rovers,' said Baz.

'That reminds me! What about the man who would only make love wearing Liverpool football kit?'

'He once scored at Anfield,' said Baz drily.

'But he's had some sad cases, Harry. In the end, it began to get to him, that's why he asked Nick to let him move to the morning show. He takes his work so seriously, always gives it one hundred per cent. But it's no fun at two a.m., trying to talk sense to someone at the end of their tether.'

Chapter Twelve

Harry was struck again by Penny's fierce devotion to her lover. He wondered whether the disc jockey found it hard living on a pedestal.

'No wonder they talk about the desperate hours,' said Baz. 'The straw that broke my back was a couple of months or so ago. A young girl called, threatening to commit suicide. I tried to persuade her things weren't so bad, but it was like soft-soaping a speak-your-weight machine. She just kept repeating her life was in ruins, she was no good, she'd let her family down.'

'What was the problem?'

'The usual. A young Catholic girl who got pregnant. She wanted an abortion, but felt she could never live with herself afterwards. I'm not one for religion, never have been, and I kept arguing with her, off the air and on. A bundle of clichés, but true all the same. She was only a kid, she had everything good ahead of her, why ruin her life for one silly mistake?'

'So what happened?'

Baz's face was ashen as he cast his mind back; Penny had her head bowed. 'She took my advice, but there was a problem with the anaesthetic. She had a bad reaction to it – a chance in ten thousand. She died without regaining consciousness. I threw up when I heard the news. Couldn't help reproaching myself.'

'It wasn't your fault,' said Penny urgently. 'You'd done everything in your power to help young Eileen. She simply couldn't—'

'Eileen?' interrupted Harry. In the overheated room he felt suddenly cold. 'What was her second name?'

Baz and Penny exchanged puzzled glances.

'McCray,' said the disc jockey. 'She was called Eileen McCray. Why do you ask?'

Chapter Thirteen

'Life's riddled with uncertainties, sir!'
A fresh-faced youth in a blue polyester blazer called to Harry from an insurance company's stand.

'You take chances every single day! But don't despair! Help is at hand.' The salesman spoke with the evangelistic fervour of an aspiring Billy Graham. Having captured his prospect's attention, he allowed his mouth to relax into a smile as broad as the get-out clauses in the small print of the policies he sold.

'We offer our clients real peace of mind – about their lives, their property, their possessions...'

'Sorry,' said Harry, brushing away the proffered literature. 'Never mind hang-gliding and unsafe sex. If you knew the people I mix with, you'd declare me uninsurable.'

He'd said goodbye to Baz and Penny at the Radio Liverpool stand. Finbar wasn't there and neither was Melissa. The engineer from *Pop In* said the Irishman had gone to the bar whilst his girlfriend went to the loo. That suited Harry, who wanted the chance of a private word with his client. He was after confirmation that Finbar was the father of the unborn child Eileen McCray had decided to abort.

As for insurance, Finbar had to be the ultimate bad risk, with two attempts on his life in swift succession. Would McCray – assuming he was the culprit – try again, or would the police investigation scare him off? Harry doubted whether the builder frightened easily. Finbar's best hope of saving his skin was to put aside his guilt about Eileen McCray's death and tell Sladdin about it. But if he did not, what could be done to help him?

Two people. Rosemary and Finbar. Both fools to themselves, yet both clients for whom Harry couldn't help caring. He felt an unwanted sense of responsibility for their fates, as if they were silly kids blind to the danger of what they were doing and therefore unable to protect themselves.

Chapter Thirteen

He became aware that his head was aching, perhaps in protest against having too much to think about. Preoccupied, not looking where he was going, he almost collided with a woman heading in the opposite direction.

'Sorry,' he said. 'Oh – it's you.'

Since her tearful departure from the Blue Moon, Sophie had conquered the shock of the bomb blast and her skilfully made-up face had regained its customary composure. He detected no trace of pleasure to see him. In her mind he had obviously become a lost cause: a friend of Finbar Rogan.

'The police insisted on talking to me,' she said, as if it were Harry's fault.

'Inevitable, Sophie. Nothing more than a routine check.'

She wagged a long finger at him. Whilst she would not admit it, he guessed she was glad of the opportunity to vent her anger about her disastrous afternoon affair.

'I never dreamed when I agreed to go with Finbar bloody Rogan how things would finish up.'

'Surely with Finbar you didn't expect to live happily ever after?'

'I expect you think I deserved what I got, missing death by a whisker and having to suffer the third degree, do you? But remember, he's your client and you've always known he's bad news. I just thought he was a good-looking feller with a gift of the gab – not that he was some kind of terrorist.'

'Come on now, Sophie. Finbar has many faults, but he's not mixed up with terrorism. You must realise that.'

She uttered a sharp bark of laughter. 'Oh yes? Do you have many clients who have their businesses burned down and their cars bombed? Wake up, Harry. The man's made serious enemies, and you can add me to the list. It's taken me years to get where I am now with Radio Liverpool. And if Nick sacks me because he finds out I was screwing a tattooist when I should have been at work, Finbar will be safer with the I.R. bloody A. than with me. I'll murder him myself.'

'Folley is bound to find out sooner or later. People are already talking about you and Finbar.'

'Shit! I only told Penny, and that was in confidence when I got back to the station. I was only looking for a shoulder to cry on – just goes to show you can't trust anyone these days.'

'If you'll take my advice, you'll tell Folley fast, before someone else does. Limit the damage.'

She stared at him. 'Take *your* advice? You must be joking. Save your words of wisdom for Finbar. He'll certainly need something if he's planning to stay alive.' And with a vigorous shake of her red mane, she stalked off. Looking back, Harry saw her pause when she reached the radio station's stand and slip her arm in that of someone whose back was turned to him.

'Was that the lovely Sophie I saw you chatting up?'

Harry spun round. 'Finbar! I want a word with you. Did you realise Sophie's gunning for you now, like everyone else? I was trying to persuade her to confess to Folley about her fling with you, before Penny Newland lets the cat well and truly out of the bag.'

'Penny?' Finbar frowned. 'What does she know?'

'Sophie told her she was with you at the Blue Moon.'

Finbar swore. 'She's a darling girl, is Penny, but she ought to know the value of discretion. Don't fret, I'll have a word with her. Make sure she buttons her mouth.'

'You'll be lucky. She only has eyes for Baz and I don't think she's susceptible to anyone else's silver tongue. In any case, you can't hope to contain gossip so easily. Let me see if I have more luck getting you to listen to me than Sophie. Are you listening? Tell Melissa about the Blue Moon right now. Explain it was a one-off. Promise it won't happen again – especially if you mean it.'

'Ah, Harry,' said Finbar with a sigh, 'you really think everyone is as straight as you. But women aren't like that. They like their truth in soft focus. It's the romantic glow they go for, not the hard details.'

'You underestimate Melissa. I'm sure she's a realist.'

'Oh, sweet Jases, you really believe that, don't you? Harry, you could hardly be more wrong. Mel's a lovely girl, I care for her deeply, but compared to her Walter Mitty had his feet on the ground. She's had treatment, don't you know, for the troubles she's been through.'

'Treatment?'

'Wipe off your worried frown, it's bad for business, specially in the midst of all these well-heeled folk, they're potential clients. Yeah, the poor girl – suffers with her nerves, let's say. She had a spell in hospital and she's been on drugs and stuff. Now do you understand why she takes a fancy to me? You always reckoned a woman must need her head examined to swallow my chat – well, for once you were right.' He gave a bleak smile. 'Folley ditched her soon enough. I didn't steal her from him, he was more than ready and willing to step aside. You could say I'm a sort of social service. Y'know, I think there's something about the neurotic types that appeals to me. Maybe it's because they're so anxious to be good in the sack.'

Harry grimaced. Finbar's candour was repellent, though he was sublimely unaware of the fact. He genuinely believed himself to be misunderstood, a kind of sensual do-gooder who didn't get the appreciation he deserved.

Chapter Thirteen

'So you see, mate, there's naught to be gained by telling the lady what she doesn't want to hear. Too much honesty is bad for the soul. Come on, why don't you come over and say hello?'

He walked off towards the Radio Liverpool stand. Harry hesitated for a moment, then chased after him.

'Listen, you bugger, I need to talk to you about the bomb. I've heard about Eileen...'

Finbar kept going but a shadow passed across his face. 'For Heaven's sake, this isn't the time or the place,' he said under his breath. 'I told you I don't want to talk about Eileen. Leave it alone, can't you?'

They could both see Melissa now. She had turned up at the stand and was on the edge of the group of people standing around it, talking idly to Tracey Liggett and the engineer.

Raising his voice as he approached, Finbar called out, 'Melissa, look who we've got here! Our very own legal eagle! A professional bird of prey, come to pay us a visit!'

Melissa moved towards them. 'You bastard, Finbar,' she said in a soft but distinct murmur. 'You fucking bastard.'

Two businessmen close by heard what she said. One of them, to judge by his breath and bloodshot eyes, had spent all evening at the bar, and he whistled derisively at Finbar. 'Upset the little lady have you, pal?' he whooped. 'Oh, dearie me!'

Heads began to turn. Harry looked round in despair for the exit.

Finbar ignored the drunk. 'Don't listen to tittle-tattle, darling,' he said to Melissa. 'Let's have a talk about things, just you and—'

'Talk!' she hissed. 'You do nothing but! Except when you're carrying on with that bloody red-haired prostitute...'

'Who are you calling a prostitute?'

Sophie's voice came loud and clear. The drunk seemed to appreciate her intervention; he uttered a long, 'Oooooooh!' before stumbling over his own feet and having to clutch at his embarrassed companion for support.

Suddenly, Harry became aware of someone elbowing past him.

'Stop it! Both of you! Or you're both finished!'

Nick Folley's face was crimson with fury. Harry could tell he was about to let his temper rip.

'Oh shit!' said Sophie.

Melissa spat at her, but Folley prevented retaliation by grabbing hold of Sophie's arm and thrusting her to one side.

'That's enough, Melissa. You're fired. Instant dismissal for gross misconduct, do you hear me? Now sod off home. Your P45 and the money we owe you will come through the post.'

The words hit her with more force than a slap in the face. She blanched and clutched at Folley's sleeve.

'Nick! You can't mean that! You know how much I need...'

Folley pushed her arm away. 'You should have thought about that before making a scene.'

'Now wait a minute,' said Finbar. He sounded moderate: the voice of reason, keeping a cool head when all around were losing theirs. But as the words passed his lips, Harry glanced at Folley and realised his client's timing could not have been worse.

Folley spoke quietly, so quietly that the drunken businessman had to lean forward to hear. But there was no mistaking his venom. 'This is all down to you, Rogan. All down to your having your balls where your fucking brains should be. Do you understand what I want to do to you? This!'

He lunged forward, put his hands round Finbar's throat and began to squeeze.

Harry and the drunk's companion caught Folley's arms and tried to drag him off the Irishman. It wasn't easy. Rage gave Folley the brute power of a back-street brawler and he gripped Finbar's neck as if his own life depended on it.

The sudden onslaught had knocked Finbar backwards, but within seconds he was clawing at Folley, trying desperately to breathe. As the drunk cheered the combatants with incoherent delight, the strength of numbers began to tell and Harry forced Folley to release his hold. Losing his balance, Folley toppled on to the floor, where he lay panting as if on the brink of a coronary.

Finbar stood up gingerly and rubbed his neck. The flesh bore livid red marks where Folley had tried to throttle him, but he seemed more shocked by the ferocity of the attack than by the pain.

'I was only trying to conciliate,' he croaked.

Dusting himself down, Harry realised his exasperation was tinged with grim amusement. Despite all recent evidence, Finbar seemed unable to accept that anyone could wish to do him harm. There was something oddly irresistible about someone so thick-skinned. For Harry, Finbar was becoming a bad habit.

'Come on,' he said, nodding thanks to the drunk's companion. 'Let's go before you destroy what's left of Liverpool's business community.'

He led his hobbling client away. Halfway down the aisle, he glanced over his shoulder to see Nick Folley following their progress, crouched on his haunches, breathing heavily and looking as if he had murder on his mind. Behind Folley stood Sophie Wilkins. She put a tentative hand on her lover's shoulder, but he shrugged it off. Melissa was nowhere to be seen; during the rumpus she had disappeared.

Near the exit a pretty girl stopped them. 'Excuse me, do you realise the importance of corporate hospitality? Taking the people who give you business to Wimbledon or Lord's?'

Before Finbar could recover sufficiently to embark on a chat-up line, Harry intervened. 'Wouldn't suit my firm, love. Except if you're offering an Away Day to Wormwood Scrubs so my clients can visit their loved ones.'

Once out in the cold night air, Finbar rubbed his nose pensively. 'Listen – any chance you could do me a favour? Your place is only round the corner. Could I spend the night on your couch? Melissa may have gone back to the flat and I don't think she's in the mood yet to kiss and make up.'

Harry's heart sank but he reminded himself that Finbar had seen his business burnt down and his car blown up within the space of a couple of days. He couldn't say no.

'Just for one night?'

'That's all I need. Thanks, Harry, you're very good to me. Not just a lawyer, but a pal. I know I shouldn't have asked.'

Part of Harry wished Finbar hadn't. But he made up his mind to exact a price for his hospitality. He was determined to satisfy his own urgent need to know. Never would he have a better chance than tonight to discover his client's guilty secrets.

Chapter Fourteen

'Look,' said Finbar, draining his glass of Johnnie Walker, 'I don't come out of this very well.'

'That's the story of your life,' said Harry unsympathetically. 'You're twenty years too late for worrying about your image. So tell me about Eileen. The truth, mind – the whole truth and nothing but.'

They were in Harry's flat, far from the madding crowd of the Liverpool Business Day exhibition. Through the thick lined curtains they could hear the wind wailing down the Mersey: a wild, elemental sound. Harry could easily have believed there wasn't another living soul within a hundred miles.

Finbar cleared his throat. 'In the old days, back in Ireland, I knew a feller called Dermot McCray. A big bugger, muscles in his spit. He worked in the building trade, which is no place for Little Lord Fauntleroys. As young fellers we were pals, we'd drink together from time to time. To this day he has a line of dot tattoos I drew on the knuckles of each hand. I was only a lad then – hadn't mastered the finer points of my craft.

'At first, Dermot was one for the ladies himself, but he soon hooked up with a girl called Oonagh, a lovely creature with the most marvellous chestnut hair. They got married, she had a child and I didn't see much of him after that. The last time we met in Dublin he told me he fancied coming over to England and setting up on his own. A few months later, I heard he'd crossed to Liverpool and done just that.'

Finbar paused and scratched his chin. He had the raconteur's gift of spinning out any story, keeping his listener anxious for the next instalment.

'The McCrays came back to Dublin from time to time. They kept in close touch with family and friends, but I hardly ever saw them until Sinead and I moved over here. I used to bump into him every now and then in the De Valera.'

'The Irish club off Solvay Street?'

'Right. Noted for good beer and bad company. By that time, Dermot had started making money and formed his own company. As you've gathered, Eileen was his daughter. He brought Oonagh and her to the De Valera one night and introduced me. Oonagh had put on weight; the *dolce vita* had got to her and no mistake. But Eileen was a different proposition altogether. Sweet sixteen and with the same chestnut hair her mother had in her prime. From the moment I saw her I was smitten.'

'A bit young, even by your standards.'

'Harry, don't I know it? But there, you never know where Cupid's dart may land. And Eileen was so perfect. Looked like a virgin and loved like her life depended on it.' He coughed and became contrite. 'Sorry. A poor choice of phrase, as things turned out.'

'You started seeing her?'

'She'd lately left school and taken a job in a travel agency. I used to tell her she deserved better. Anyway, she managed to sneak off from work two or three times a week. The boss had the hots for her too – he let her get away with murder.'

'Did Dermot and Oonagh cotton on to what you were up to?'

'Give me some credit. I've had years of experience in covering my tracks. Besides, I didn't want to get on the wrong side of Dermot. He was a pal from way back and, anyway, it doesn't pay to antagonise a tough man in the building trade. I didn't fancy finishing up in a concrete overcoat as part of the foundations of a new supermarket or motorway flyover.'

'So what happened?'

'Eileen got herself pregnant, that's what happened. Ah yes, you'll say it takes two to tango, but she'd promised me she was on the Pill. She didn't set out to trap me, that's for sure. Maybe she simply forgot to take it one night. Ah, all this time and I'd never been caught before!'

'I take it you didn't offer to do what people used to call the decent thing?'

'Harry, there was no future in marriage between Eileen and me. I've been through that malarkey once and I'm not for making the same mistake twice. She was a slip of a kid, less than half my age. We were good for each other, but neither of us wanted a lifetime commitment. That left only one solution.'

Finbar pulled a face at the memory. Harry said nothing.

'I didn't force the issue. She decided for herself that it was best to have an abortion. Dermot and Oonagh had brought her up to be a good Catholic girl, but Eileen didn't want to be tied down too young.'

Baz had told the story differently, Harry recalled.

'Did either of you discuss it with her parents?'

'No way. We agreed they mustn't be told. Dermot's as devout as any man I know and the very idea of abortion would be enough to send him for his shotgun. To tell him I'd put his daughter up the spout would be like autographing a suicide note.'

'If he's as devout as all that, there shouldn't have been any danger of physical violence.'

'Harry, where have you been the last twenty-five years? Haven't you seen what people from my part of the world can do in the name of religion? If they can blow bits off the bodies of folk they don't even know, who never did them a single injury, what chance is there for me if someone like Dermot decides I need to be taught a lesson?'

'So what happened?'

'She booked into a private clinic. It was my idea, I let her have a little nest egg of mine.' Finbar closed his eyes. 'Anyway, there were problems with the anaesthetic. God knows what went wrong, but she never came round again.'

'She died in the clinic?'

'With all the pricey medical expertise at hand,' said Finbar bitterly. 'Eileen, who'd never had a day's illness in her life, who had so much left to look forward to, killed undergoing an operation that was all my fault.'

'Shit,' said Harry. 'What did you tell the McCrays?'

Finbar shifted from foot to foot. 'Fact is, Harry, I didn't tell them anything. There was no point. I couldn't bring her back. They had plenty to grieve about without knowing their daughter had been seduced by a man old enough to be her dad.'

'And you didn't relish the prospect of Dermot taking revenge?'

Finbar's expression was grim. 'There's no telling what a bereaved father might do. Specially a hard man like Dermot McCray.'

'So how did he find out you were Eileen's boyfriend?' Harry had already described his brief encounter with McCray at Fenwick Court. 'From the clinic?'

'They never knew who I was. I gave her the money, but she made all the arrangements. And not from Baz, either. Eileen told me she'd been talking to him on the bloody air, said she rang him when she was feeling low. Jases, with all those people listening! That sent me into a panic. But she swore she'd never mentioned my name to anyone.'

'Yet Dermot and Sinead obviously know. They must have found out from someone.'

'There's only one explanation. A week or two ago, I was drinking in the De Valera. I've not seen Dermot there since Eileen died. Anyway, I'd had one over the eight. Melissa was away visiting some sick relation, so I was on my own. Maybe I got a bit maudlin and the booze began to talk... late in the night I was chatting to this old pal of mine, Liam Keogh. You've met him yourself, I introduced you once in the Dock Brief, remember? I started telling him about Eileen, and before I knew what I was saying, I'd spilled the whole bag of beans.'

'Do you think he would have told Sinead? Or McCray?'

'More than likely. Not out of devilment, but he couldn't keep his mouth shut to save his life. Still, who am I to talk? Liam's a decent feller, I should've kept my own counsel. After all, I've never said a word to anyone else. Except yourself.'

'It's time for you to tell the police. Unless you want Dermot to succeed with his next attack.'

'So you think he's the one who has it in for me?'

'He has the opportunity as well as the motive. Who else do you know who is likely to be hand in glove with Irish terrorists, people with access to bomb-making equipment?'

'Maybe you're right. I must admit I've been mulling over the notion. Yet there's one thing I can't understand. Dermot never had anything to do with terrorism while I knew him. And this is a private grudge, nothing more.'

Harry leaned forward. 'Leave Sladdin to ferret out the evidence,' he urged. 'Will you speak to him tomorrow?'

'Maybe I will.' Finbar exhaled. 'Now, is there any chance of another glass of your excellent whisky?'

Harry passed the bottle and slumped back into his chair. He felt exhausted. It had been a long day and his headache had worsened. The story of Eileen's death had dismayed him; although he realised the dangers of moral judgments, he felt he could never regard Finbar in the same way again. There would always be a barrier between them, built of his repugnance for the way his client used the women in his life. But at least it seemed the riddle of the attacks on Finbar had been solved. Harry began to yearn for nothing other than a darkened room and deep sleep.

Finbar kept him up late all the same, supping his booze and telling tall stories of tattoos he had drawn and the people who had worn them. As he dozed, Harry was vaguely aware of his guest illustrating an anecdote with pictures swiftly drawn on paper torn from a Counsel's notebook he found in the hall, admiring his own handiwork then crumpling the sheets up and tossing them aside. Eventually Harry dropped off and began to dream. Strange creatures, come to life from Finbar's tattoos, were menacing him: a furious phoenix and a blood-spitting dragon, hate filled tigers and a black butterfly which flapped vast intimidating wings.

***

When he awoke he became fuzzily aware that it was morning and he was lying on the couch in the living room. His neck was sore and at first he wondered if perhaps he, rather than his client, had been the victim of attempted strangulation. Finally he realised it was simply the result of lying in an uncomfortable position. He stretched complaining limbs and tried to ignore a roaring in his head reminiscent of the noise made by McCray's navvies.

Finbar, wearing only his trousers, wandered into the living room. From his bare chest, Lady Godiva squinted at Harry with disdain. Her creator seemed well rested and in jovial mood.

'Don't you dare utter one cheerful word,' mumbled Harry, 'or I'll finish the job Folley started.'

'Not in the best of humours, are we? Shame, but the drink does have an effect. And as for Nick – well, we all get overexcited from time to time.'

'So you're in a forgiving mood?'

'I've never been a man to hold grudges. It's not as if it was a serious attempt to kill me, not slap-bang in the middle of a public exhibition.' Finbar scratched himself under the arms. 'And after the events of the last day or two, Nick Folley is the least of my worries. Now, can I get you an aspirin?'

'Never mind the aspirin – why didn't you put me to bed?'

'Ah, you looked so peaceful it seemed wrong to disturb you! And since you'd taken my billet on the couch I thought the sensible thing was for me to borrow your bed for the night. No problem about the old sheets, I'm not that pernickety.' He retuned Harry's transistor to Radio Liverpool and switched on *Pop In*, where Baz was dedicating 'This Guy's In Love With You' to Penny Newland. Finbar sang along with tuneless gusto.

Harry crawled off the couch and made himself a coffee. He responded to Finbar's attempts at conversation with monosyllables which became emphatic only when Finbar said wistfully that he couldn't expect to impose on Harry's hospitality for another night. 'No,' Harry agreed.

'Ah well,' said Finbar with a sigh, 'I suppose I'd better try and make my peace with Melissa.'

'You'll be lucky.'

'That little – contretemps, shall we say? – last evening was unfortunate, I'll agree. She was upset, it's only natural. But she'll get over it. Women do.'

'And if not?'

'Plenty more fish in the sea, Harry.'

There was no arguing with him. Harry finished his coffee. 'I'll be off now,' he said. 'I have a date in the police cells this morning. Stay here a while if you want. Slam the door behind you when you go. And for God's sake talk to Sladdin.'

'Thanks again, mate. I appreciate what you've done.'

'Keep in touch,' said Harry, unsure whether he meant it.

***

Harry spent the morning at court representing a couple of scoundrels who regarded arrest as a way of life. When he returned to Fenwick Court, the construction work had stopped, but a couple of McCray's men were there, talking in low, angry voices. As Harry walked across the courtyard, the atmosphere seemed to him heavy with unspoken menace. He wondered whether he ought to ring the police himself if Finbar reneged on his promise to tell all to Sladdin.

Sylvia Reid greeted him in reception. He could tell from the curve of her smile that she'd heard good news.

'Heather called. Jim is due to be discharged later today.'

'Seriously? That's wonderful. Though with the National Health Service in its present state, all it means is he's not in immediate need of intensive care.'

Nevertheless, the message delighted him. As he worked through the urgent post in his own room, he reflected that, but for his partner's accident, he would never have laid a finger on the Graham-Brown file, and would thus have been spared the dilemmas that now faced him. How was he to tell Rosemary that the Ambroses were unable to complete? And what was he to do about his suspicion that her husband was engaged in some kind of fraud?

He decided against paying another visit to Crow's Nest House. It might be better, he told himself, to draw her out. He dictated a terse letter to her and her husband, passing on Geoffrey Willatt's message and asking them to contact him to discuss its implications. Having signed it and asked his secretary to send it first class, he tried to concentrate on the misadventures of the more commonplace crooks he acted for in the criminal courts. But it was no good. Even when the envelope had been entrusted to the Royal Mail, he kept harking back to Rosemary. No point in fooling himself; he hadn't wanted to take the chance of seeing her again. There was too great a risk that, in her presence, he would let his heart rule his head.

Yet his instinct was, as ever, for action. Sitting on the side-lines could never satisfy him for long. By the end of the afternoon he had decided on a different kind of direct approach; it was time to introduce himself to Stuart Graham-Brown. He would tell his client face to face that the house sale had fallen through, see for himself the reaction his news evoked. Caught off guard, Graham-Brown might be tempted to give his game away.

A glance at the phone book confirmed that Merseycredit's office was to be found in Tobacco Court and he strolled there through the evening twilight by way of Dale Street, uncertain what his next move should be on arrival. His destination was one of the warrens of passageways which had once been Liverpool's mercantile heartland; a place for trading cotton, crops and animal skins. These days most of the buildings were vacant and in a state of disrepair; the courtyard was home only to Merseycredit, a sex shop, a wine lodge and a greasy spoon cafe. Perhaps, Harry reflected, Tobacco Court should carry a government health warning.

The name of Merseycredit was picked out in gold leaf on a first-floor window above the sex shop. An entrance door led to a flight of stairs. Harry hesitated at the bottom, but when he heard people talking upstairs, he dodged out again and studied the card in the sex shop window which warned him not to be shocked if he found 'adult goods' on sale inside.

Stuart Graham-Brown, another man and a woman came out into the street and walked past Harry without a glance. They were engrossed in their discussion and made straight for the wine lodge. Harry saw their reflections clearly, despite the dirt and finger-mark smudges on the shop window. Graham-Brown's female companion was a hard-faced blonde in her late thirties and she had her arm wrapped around him. It was clear they were more than just good friends. The other man was Dermot McCray.

Startled, Harry abandoned his idea of confronting his client; whilst Dermot McCray was about, it made sense to steer clear. But why was McCray here? And who was the woman with Graham-Brown?

Bewildered, he retreated to a nearby pub called the Plimsoll Line. It was a new place which occupied the basement of Exchange Precinct, a whimsical architect's pastiche of a pyramid, funded by grants from the Pharaohs of the European Community. Here, ground-floor shops offered holograms, Japanese wall coverings and cruelty-free cosmetics to a public which preferred to look rather than buy, while most of the offices up above were unlet. According to Stanley Rowe, the rents here were as high as the St John's Beacon. The mediaeval traders who had once swarmed around Leather Lane, Hackins Hey and Tobacco Court must be turning in their graves.

Chapter Fourteen

Over a pint as cloudy as a Merseyside morning, he asked himself why Graham-Brown would plan a flit to Spain with his wife whilst conducting an affair with another woman. Did he intend to ditch Rosemary? And could there be some extraordinary connection between Merseycredit and the attacks on Finbar? None of it made sense.

He finished his drink and went back to the wine lodge. Standing in an alcove just inside the door, he could see McCray arguing with Graham-Brown. As he watched, the quarrel reached its climax. Graham-Brown folded his arms, an elegant but decisive gesture; he had spoken his last word. McCray's face was purple with rage. He turned on his heel and marched out, passing within a couple of feet of Harry, who had pressed himself against the wall.

Graham-Brown smiled at the blonde and put his hand on her knee. She straightened his tie. Harry toyed with the idea of confronting his client. But what could he say? *I know you're on the fiddle? I've discovered you're deceiving Rosemary, though for the life of me I can't understand why you prefer a woman with a face as sharp as the edge of an axe?*

Lost in thought, he walked home through the city, his progress slowed by a crowd outside the Town Hall protesting to councillors arriving for an emergency evening meeting, called in a hopeless effort to balance the books. These days demonstrators campaigned for the right to work: not so many years ago, they had been fighting for the right to strike.

Back in the flat there was, to his relief, no sign of Finbar. He spent the evening working his way through a six-pack and watching a tape of *Vertigo*. The way his head was spinning, the choice of movie seemed peculiarly apposite.

Shortly before eleven, the telephone shrilled. Harry suspected it might be the police, calling him in on behalf of a car thief or house burglar – or, even worse, bloody Finbar, wanting a roof over his head for one more night. He poured himself another drink and did not move. But the phone persisted and eventually his resistance crumbled.

'Hello?'

'Harry! Thank God you're there. I was about to give up hope.'

'Is that you, Melissa? What's bothering you at his late hour?'

'I need you here urgently. In my flat.'

'Melissa! This is so sudden.'

'Listen, I'm not joking. I wouldn't disturb you if it wasn't desperate, but you're the only lawyer I know.'

'And why do you need a lawyer at this time of night?'

'It's about Finbar.'

Who else?

'What's he done now?'

'I have the police here. They've told me he's been found dead. And they think I killed him.'

Chapter Fifteen

'I'm not accusing you of anything,' said Sladdin.

Sitting next to Harry on the sofa in the lounge of her flat in Mossley Hill, Melissa began to shake. She buried her head in her hands and made muffled sobs.

For his part, Harry felt groggy, as if he'd taken a punch full in the face. Finbar's life had always seemed charmed; it was impossible to believe it was suddenly over. The Irishman had survived so much, he'd come to seem indestructible, and his death had shocked Harry profoundly; it gave him a chill reminder of every man's mortality. Despite his daze, he had been trying to listen to Melissa's disjointed answers as intently as the detective, in an effort to chart the course of Finbar's last day of life. But he was hazily aware that, for the girl's sake, the time had come for him to intervene.

'Look, Inspector, Miss Keating has told you all she knows. She's made it clear that Finbar Rogan was alive and well when he left here this afternoon. And from what you say, I gather he was killed after darkness fell but no later than six.'

'That is broadly correct,' said Sladdin in a guarded tone.

Harry sensed the detective was far from certain whether he was interviewing a lover tragically bereaved or a callous murderess; he certainly wasn't giving more away than was necessary. And the timing was critical. For if Finbar had been dead by six o'clock, Dermot McCray could not have killed him, on the evidence of Harry's own eyes. It must have been twenty past six when the builder had stormed out of the wine lodge and into the night. Harry could remember checking his watch against the Town Hall clock when he passed the demonstrators five minutes later.

The alarm had, according to Sladdin, been raised by a teenage courting couple, who had come across Finbar lying in the middle of a road running alongside the derelict site of Colonial Dock, a place long abandoned by shipping and nowadays frequented by lovers rather than stevedores. They had walked down the road an hour earlier, on their way to the disused hut where they used to make love each evening after school, and the body had not been there then. The sight of it as they headed back for home was one they would never forget.

A car had run over Finbar. Not once, but several times. Even described in Sladdin's clipped tone, the picture that formed in Harry's mind was dark with horror. But he knew he must banish the image of the crushed corpse from his thoughts; it was the stuff of nightmares. With a huge effort, he dragged himself back to the here and now.

'I still don't see why you're not treating Finbar's death as a straightforward accident.'

'We're not ruling any possibility out as yet. Nonetheless, the circumstances are suspicious.'

Harry bit his lip. He desperately wanted to hear that Finbar had not been killed on purpose. For if the death was not mischance, and McCray was not responsible, he scarcely dared contemplate an alternative explanation.

'Remember,' he insisted, 'it must have been difficult to see anything at Colonial Dock when the car struck him. I've not been that way for years, but as far as I can recall there's no street lighting there. And the world's full of hit-and-run joyriders.'

'Very true,' said Sladdin, 'but this particular driver was at the wheel of the car Mr Rogan himself hired earlier today. And as I explained before, having run over him once, the same person reversed and repeated the job a couple of times for good measure. Scarcely an innocent mistake, or even a careless one.'

Melissa lifted her head. Harry sensed she was finding it almost impossible to maintain a semblance of self-control.

'So Finbar must have been murdered?'

'As I say, we have to consider everything. And that's why I asked you if you could think of any reason for Mr Rogan to be visiting Colonial Dock this evening.'

'None – none whatsoever,' said Melissa edgily. 'It's hardly surprising. There were so many things he kept from me.'

Harry felt the conversation was drifting into dangerous waters. 'Can we leave it there for the moment, please?' he said to Sladdin. 'This news has obviously come as a great shock to Miss Keating. And whilst she's anxious to assist your enquiries, she's suffered enough for the present.'

Sladdin looked at the silent WPC sitting opposite him, as if to gauge another woman's reaction to his questioning. After a pause he clambered to his feet, seeming glad of the opportunity to escape from his low rattan chair. Harry sensed the room as a whole would not meet with police approval; it was too arty, with its French posters, studio cushions and kilim rug on the floor. During his brief relationship with Melissa, Finbar had spent a good deal of time in this flat; the attic conversion above his studio which he used as a bedsitting room was poky and unappealing even before the fire had rendered it uninhabitable. But the place bore Melissa's imprint, not his.

'Very well, Mr Devlin. You'll understand I have to pursue my investigations urgently. We'll be back in the morning; there will be a statement for your client to sign.'

Harry accompanied Sladdin and the WPC to the door of Melissa's flat. 'I'm not saying she is my client, Inspector. At present I'm here as a friend rather than a solicitor.'

Sladdin allowed himself a sceptical smile. 'Afraid of a conflict of interests, Mr Devlin?'

'You can see the girl's shocked, Inspector. That's not put on for your benefit. The thought of her harming Finbar is inconceivable.'

Sladdin pursed his lips. 'We'll be in touch.'

With the police gone, Harry returned to the living room. Melissa was blowing her nose; her cheeks were pale, her eyes puffy. She seemed as disorientated as a drunk, but he could smell no alcohol on her breath. He sat beside her on the sofa and patted her hand: not a sexual gesture, but one of support. Yet he could not remain silent.

'Melissa, is there anything you want to tell me? Anything you didn't feel able to say to Sladdin?'

Choking back another sob, she shook her head. 'It was as I described. Finbar came here about one o'clock. He was full of himself, since he'd spent the morning persuading his insurers to let him hire a new car far better than the Granada he lost in the bomb blast. He'd stopped on the way for a couple of drinks, getting up Dutch courage, he said, for apologising to me over his fling with Sophie. It was as if he thought the past could be rubbed out overnight.'

Harry could imagine. With Finbar, every day was a fresh start: an endearing quality in some circumstances, but maddening for those who found it less easy to forget.

'I–I cried myself to sleep last night. First over losing him, then on top of that the job… my mind was muddled, I blamed Finbar for everything. When he blithely assumed he could walk straight back into my life, I wanted to lash out and hurt him. A pair of scissors was lying on the table over there.'

Harry closed his eyes. It was hard enough to grasp that Finbar was dead, let alone that Melissa, rather than Dermot McCray, might have been his killer. 'So you lunged at him?'

Melissa fiddled with a bracelet she wore. 'I admitted it to the policeman, didn't I? You should have seen the shock on Finbar's face as I swung the scissors at him. I was screaming abuse, I'm not sure what I said. He wiped the back of his hand across his cheeks and saw the blood. A surface cut, nothing more, but it must have stung.'

'Did he fight back?'

'Grabbed my wrist, made me drop the scissors, nothing more. He was never a physically vicious man. The roughest thing I ever knew him do was nibble my neck.'

The Great Lover would not be doing that again. Harry felt sick in his stomach, but something prompted him to keep on with the questions.

'What did he say to you?'

'I don't think he could believe I might want to hurt him, cause him pain. Finbar always had a blind spot – he could never conceive that, deep down, whatever was said and whatever was done, people might not capitulate to his charm. He saved himself by instinct, but once the immediate shock passed, he seemed sad. He told me I wasn't myself and I screamed back at him. I said that was exactly what I was, I was myself and I belonged to me, not him. I'd never forgive him for how he'd behaved, humiliating me with Sophie, costing me a job I cared about. Never!'

Harry could picture the scene. Even when confronted by all Sinead's bitterness, Finbar had failed to grasp why she felt so badly let down. With Melissa, it would have been exactly the same: impossible for the Irishman to understand why a woman who loved him might not be able to tolerate his sneaking her colleague off to a hotel for a little afternoon delight.

'He kept repeating he was sorry, he'd never meant to make me unhappy, far less get the sack. He was so sure we could go back to where we'd been before he betrayed me.'

'And you put him right on that score?'

'Of course. I was furious!'

Harry studied her, trying to see beyond the emotional words and the nervous mannerisms. How angry had Melissa been? Furious enough to kill?

'So you told him to go?'

'As I told the policeman. I said he should fuck off back to his fancy woman.'

On her lips, the obscenity sounded shocking. It gave him a clue to her depth of feeling. He needed to be careful how far he pushed her.

Chapter Fifteen

'You mean Sophie?'

'Who else? I'd gone through enough with Finbar, I wasn't prepared to take any more. I decided she could have him.'

'What made you think he still had a chance with her? They seemed at daggers drawn during the argy-bargy last night in Empire Hall.'

'Oh yes, she's volatile enough. But I could tell he had something – or should I say some*one*? – up his sleeve. As soon as he realised he'd get no more change out of me, it was as if he'd written me off his conquest list, for the time being at least, and was ready to move on. No reason why he shouldn't try his luck with Sophie again. She's as hungry for sex as Finbar was. It's common knowledge in the office that she's got a season ticket to the VD clinic.'

She was saying much more than she had earlier, in answer to Sladdin's probing. The initial shock of learning that her lover was dead had rendered her almost incoherent; on Harry's arrival she'd been weeping copiously, with the WPC trying in vain to comfort her. He sensed she was starting to gain strength once more. Might she also be seizing any opportunity to embarrass Sophie and make things difficult for her? Was she taking revenge over her rival regardless of the truth – or was her real motive to divert attention from herself? After all, she lacked an alibi. Sladdin had established that she was unable to prove she had not left Mossley Hill during the afternoon and travelled to the city centre or the dock area, either alone or in Finbar's company. She said she'd stayed at home all day, too depressed to leave this flat. No one had called and she admitted that none of the neighbours would be able to verify her movements. Most of them worked all day and of the two pensioners in the building, one was stone deaf and the other was living it up on an over-60s trip to Madeira.

'What sort of mood was Finbar in when he left?'

Melissa gnawed at her fingernails. 'I don't know why you're asking me so many questions. I wanted you here to protect me from an inquisition, not start one of your own.'

'Sorry,' he said untruthfully. Was she buying time while she thought up a credible reply? 'I won't bother you much longer, but I'm as keen as anyone to make sure the facts come out, to pinpoint anything which will help the police to find Finbar's murderer.'

'Why concern yourself?' she asked, her tone harsh. 'He's dead now. He won't be paying any more of your bills.'

'He hardly kept me in luxury whilst he was alive. I seem to have spent most of the past few days defending him from people who had good cause to despise him.'

'The truth is, you can't resist poking your nose into other people's business, can you? This detection thing – it's a kind of game where you're concerned.'

Harry felt himself flushing. He was honest enough to accept there was a grain of truth in the slur.

'Finbar didn't deserve to die.'

'That's a matter of opinion. To answer your question, when he left here he was still in one piece. You'll have to take my word for it. Knowing him as I do – as I do *now*, I should say – I expect he was thinking: easy come, easy go.'

Harry winced. Finbar himself had used exactly that phrase.

'I didn't ask him for a lift into town, if that's what you're hinting. Or arrange to meet him later.'

'I just wondered – if there was anything else you wanted to say to me, something you might have forgotten to mention to Sladdin in the aftermath of the shock. Or something – it might be entirely innocent – you felt you'd rather not disclose.'

'You never give up, do you? We're not in court, Harry, and I'm not on the witness stand.'

'Look, Melissa I realise things have been tough lately and your emotions...'

'*Emotions*! Where Finbar is concerned, I only have one emotion. I'm glad. Not glad he'd dead, so much, simply glad he's out of my life for ever, and won't be coming back to treat me like shit ever again.' For a moment her expression froze in defiance, before dissolving into tears.

Harry hesitated, then put an arm around her shoulder. He expected resistance, but all she did was sob. 'Cry as much as you like,' he said. 'It will do you good.'

She brushed at her damp face with a hand. 'Oh God, Harry, what a fucking mess. Finbar's dead and I'm alone and out of work and the world seems to have stopped moving.'

Neither of them said anything for a minute or so. Finally he withdrew his arm.

'Thanks for coming over,' she said. 'I panicked when the police called, didn't know what else to do but call you.'

'No problem.'

'I appreciate it. After all, you were Finbar's friend, not mine.' She compressed her lips and gave him a look full of challenge. 'So – do you think I murdered him?'

He considered Melissa, white-faced and desperate. It was tempting to tell a soothing lie. But in the end he opted for the truth.

'I really don't know,' he said.

Chapter Sixteen

Chewing a slice of cold toast the next morning, Harry asked himself if he really believed Melissa to be capable of murdering Finbar.

A premeditated assassination would surely be beyond her. He could imagine her committing a crime of passion – but not a pre-planned, cold-blooded killing. Her attack on Finbar with the scissors showed she had a dangerous streak; yet she had admitted to it, despite knowing the only other witness was dead. A good defence lawyer could make capital out of that, even though her frankness might be motivated by something other than an innocent devotion to the truth.

What had been the purpose of Finbar's nocturnal visit to deserted Colonial Dock, whence no ships had sailed in years? He must have known his killer. Harry could not believe that this was a case of accidental death, nor that Finbar would have made his hire car available for a perfect stranger to climb in, seize the wheel and mow him down.

He could still hardly credit that Finbar was dead. All night he'd found it impossible to sleep but now he was up he felt physically drained. Time after time he stole a glance at the telephone, half expecting it to ring. How he would love to pick up the receiver and hear the Irishman announce, like a modern Mark Twain, that reports of his demise were an exaggeration. But for once the phone remained silent.

Strange to think that never again would he be deafened by a burst of Finbar's exuberant laughter. No more invitations to sink a pint or three at the Dock Brief; no more tall stories about life in Dublin; no more boozy philosophising about why people should want their bodies disfigured by elaborate tattoos. Over the past few days Harry had discovered the selfishness underneath Finbar's charm. But he couldn't help mourning the man, all the same.

It was almost half past eight: time for a news bulletin. Harry reached across the breakfast bar and switched on his transistor radio, curious to learn how Radio Liverpool would announce Finbar's death.

The Who were singing about their generation – they hoped they would die before they got old. It might have been Finbar's theme song. Harry remembered his client's rueful confession to the police on the night of the fire: that he had made too many enemies to have any prospect of ever drawing his pension. With hindsight Finbar's throwaway remark seemed tragically prophetic.

A jingle played and Baz Gilbert said, 'And in the newsroom, it's Clive Sheron.'

A young man's solemn voice said, 'Merseyside police are treating the death of a well-known local tattoo artist as suspicious. Mr Finbar Rogan, whose body was found at Colonial Dock yesterday evening, had apparently been run over by a motor vehicle, but the driver failed to report the incident. A police spokesman told us that enquiries are continuing.' Further items followed – about lay-offs at a Halewood factory and Everton's injury worries in the lead-up to Saturday's derby game – as Harry pondered Sladdin's role in the enquiry.

If Special Branch continued to be involved, a terrorist connection with the crime could not have been ruled out. Did that point the finger back at Dermot McCray? Might McCray have been an associate of Pearse Cato back in Ireland in days gone by? Harry thought it possible, despite Finbar's denial. Yet how could McCray have killed Finbar and drunk with Graham-Brown and his blonde bit-on-the-side at one and the same time?

Of course, McCray might have slipped out of the wine lodge whilst Harry was supping in the Plimsoll Line. However, the idea that he might have done so, quickly taken his revenge on Finbar and then raced back simply to conclude his argument with Graham-Brown stretched credulity to breaking point. Harry suspected that McCray had given Finbar a fright with the fire and the bomb; but someone else had managed to finish him off before the builder had the chance.

All this speculation was, Harry knew, idle; the police were in charge of the investigation and the sensible course – and the soft option – was to leave them to it. But sensible courses and soft options held no appeal for him. Finbar, for all his faults, was entitled to justice. Harry owed it to him to find out what had happened. All his training in the legal process, his learning to see it as trial by combat, adversarial rather than inquisitorial, had never succeeded in smothering his urge to discover the truth. He could feel now the physical signs of the hunger which had in the past cost him dear. The churning in his stomach was familiar, so too the dryness in his throat: no point in pretending otherwise. He couldn't be satisfied, wouldn't find peace, while the puzzle remained unsolved.

Chapter Sixteen

'Time for a song from the latest Luther Vandross album,' said Baz in the background. He sounded relaxed, unaffected by doom and gloom from the newsroom. It was as if he had never met the man whose death had just been reported. 'Luther's a special favourite of my lovely producer, Sophie Wilkins, so you can expect to hear plenty more from him for the rest of this week.'

Harry considered Sophie. Last night he'd paid little heed to Melissa's suggestion that, on leaving her flat, Finbar could have headed straight for Sophie's arms, because it had seemed so unlikely. Harry's reading of the row at Empire Hall had been that Sophie's priority was to re-establish herself in Nick Folley's affections; she wouldn't see any long-term future for herself as one of Finbar's fancy women. Harry guessed her visit to the Blue Moon had been prompted by a fleeting lust rather than any desire for a more lasting relationship. On the other hand, Finbar was ever the optimist. If anyone had a skin thick enough to turn up again on Sophie's doorstep, he was the man.

A visit to Radio Liverpool was called for, Harry decided. But before he went there he would need to work out exactly what he intended to do – there must be no more cocked-up confrontations. The humiliating encounter with Dermot McCray in Fenwick Court still burned in his memory.

As he stepped out of the Empire Dock buildings, he felt the morning's cold bite. Fog shrouded both the river and the city streets. It gave everything an eerie feel, with cars and people suddenly looming from nowhere. As he walked towards the front door of his office, he was struck by the calm of Fenwick Court. It took him a moment to realise the reason for it: there was no sign of McCray's workers. He peered through the gloom to left and right. It didn't require a site agent to tell him that the job was barely half done, yet the courtyard was deserted.

'Where's the building gang?' he asked as he entered reception.

Suzanne shrugged. 'Your guess is as good as mine.'

Finbar's death should have been mystery enough for him to worry over without the distraction of wondering what had happened to McCray's men. But their disappearance bothered him and, as he picked up his post and wandered to his room, he began to wonder if it might be connected with their boss's activities the previous evening. A call from Suzanne interrupted his conjectures.

'Mrs Graham-Brown's arrived. She says she must see you. She's just received your letter about her house sale falling through.' The girl paused and then added, in a complacent whisper, 'She seems very upset.'

The shock of Finbar's death had almost made him forget how much he wanted to see Rosemary again. Although he didn't kid himself that she had come here to do anything more than discuss the Ambroses' default, he was glad she had risen to his bait, and the sight of her husband with the hard-faced blonde had made him wonder again about the state of the Graham-Browns' marriage. Was she unaware Stuart was playing away from home – and if he told her, how would she react?

He went out to greet her. She was perched on the edge of her chair, as if she didn't feel she had the right to be there. He was shocked to see how pale she looked; in her haste to get out that morning, she hadn't bothered with make-up. Her face looked younger than ever – and pinched with anxiety.

'I got your letter,' she said. 'This is dreadful news. How can people behave like this? I had to come over to see you straight away.'

He took her to his room. 'I'm sorry you've been upset. Snags like these do occur from time to time. Of course, you will be wanting to press the Ambroses for compensation for your inconvenience.'

'The money's not important,' she said.

How many times had Harry heard clients utter that sentiment? It was the regular refrain of the obsessive litigants who talked a lot about principles and kept lawyers in business. Almost invariably it was untrue. Yet when Rosemary wore that earnest expression, he could not help believing her. She seemed to have been shattered by his news.

'You have a fine property,' he said. 'You'll find another buyer, sooner or later.'

She waved the suggestion away with an angry jerk of her hand. 'That might take ages and we can't afford to hang around. You don't understand, it's so important that this sale goes through. Surely you can do something?'

She had a beseeching look that he found hard to resist. He was a fool to be flattered by her faith in him, he knew, but he could not help it. In a gentler tone, he said, 'I'm sorry. You do have various rights. But you can't force the Ambroses to buy at the point of a gun.'

She closed her eyes and he moved his chair close to hers. Greatly daring, he took her hand in his.

'Why is it so important, Rosemary? Surely a few weeks don't make any difference.' He paused. 'Especially when Stuart hasn't even got round yet to telling his staff that he's leaving town for good.'

She stared at him and withdrew her hand. 'What? You don't have any connection with Merseycredit!'

'The firm had a stand at an exhibition I was attending. I came across it quite by chance.'

'Have you – have you spoken to Stuart?'

She was stunned by what he was saying, no question about it. He determined to press home his advantage.

'No, not yet. But I've seen him and, though it's none of my business, I can't say I like the company he keeps.'

'What do you mean?'

She seemed genuinely puzzled by his remark. He had to make a split-second decision whether to tell her about her husband's fancy woman. He chose to leave that to one side; his first concern was to ask after Dermot. Even as they talked, an idea had been forming in his mind which would explain why the builder and financier had got together.

'There's a man called Dermot McCray, a local builder – I believe he may have links with an Irish terrorist organisation. I've seen him drinking with Stuart and I've wondered what they had in common. The answer may be that McCray has funds he needs to launder: illicit money, to be sent back to Ireland perhaps. A company like Merseycredit might be able to help.'

It was a long shot, of course. He had no hard facts to support his theory. And yet if McCray was involved with terrorists it would explain a good deal: not only the bomb, but perhaps also the odd behaviour of the building workers.

Rosemary gazed at him in bewilderment, apparently lost for words. He was thinking furiously. If some of McCray's gang were members of, say, an active service unit, using the Fenwick Court contract as a cover which had somehow been blown, no wonder there was no sign of them outside this morning. For all he knew, they might be back in the Emerald Isle by now.

'You're crazy,' she said. 'Stuart would never get mixed up with anything like that. Terrorists? I can't believe I'm hearing this.'

'Stuart may not know who or what he's dealing with. Where there's money, there's often muck. It's wise not to ask too many questions.' The same could be said of work in the legal profession, he knew, but he resisted the comparison.

Rosemary cradled her chin in her hand. She too seemed to be thinking fast.

'I don't want you talking to Stuart about this, do you hear? You're imagining things. It's bad enough that you haven't managed to sell our bloody house. If he even dreamed you'd said these things, he'd raise blue murder.'

'I want to help you,' said Harry. 'Believe me, I'm not sure what Stuart's up to, and I suppose it's none of my business, but I'd hate to see you getting into any kind of trouble.'

She snatched up her handbag and rushed to the door. When she turned to face him again, there were high spots of colour on her cheeks. 'I'm not in any kind of trouble, do you hear? You mean well, I do see that, but you have the wrong idea about Stuart and me. Take my word for it. I'm not in any kind of trouble!'

The door slammed behind her. Harry thought for a moment about following her but at once realised to do so would be folly: let her think things over alone and make her own decision about whether to accept his help. For he was sure she was protesting too much. When she denied being in trouble, Rosemary was desperately trying to reassure herself.

Chapter Seventeen

'Why in God's name are you scaring away one of our best clients? I should have known leaving you to run the practice would be like putting Charles Manson in charge of a crèche.'

Harry looked up from his desk with a start. Jim Crusoe was framed in the doorway, leaning on a stick for support and jabbing an accusatory finger. Anger had brought a flush of colour to his bruised and battered face.

'Morning, Lazarus! It's good to see you, but what do you think you're doing here? You're supposed to be recuperating.'

'I heard the news about Finbar on the radio, so I thought I'd better catch a cab and come in to see if we've still got a business left. And what do I find? Those of our clients who haven't been murdered are racing past me without a second glance, looking so terrified I can only assume you've been showing them our balance sheet.'

'You saw Rosemary Graham-Brown?'

'Just a foggy blur, she was moving so fast. What have you been doing to her? I know today's Hallowe'en – don't tell me you offered her a trick or treat.'

'It's a long story.'

'With you,' said Jim through gritted teeth, 'it usually is.' He hobbled painfully to a chair. 'You can start by telling me where we are with the sale of Crow's Nest House.'

'The good news is,' said Harry wryly, 'we've exchanged contracts.'

'I know I'm going to regret asking this, but what's the bad news?'

'The buyers have pulled out. Byzantium are relocating Ambrose to West Africa.'

'Then serve a notice to complete. Sylvia will prepare the paperwork we need.' Unspoken was the suggestion that she should have been allowed to handle the whole file in Jim's absence.

'I don't think legal orthodoxy will give the Graham-Browns what they want.'

'Which is?'

'A quick sale and a flight to the sun. Beyond that, I can only guess at what they have in mind. One thing is definite: you and I haven't been told the whole truth.'

'God forbid I should discover the whole truth about any of my clients! I'm sure it would shatter every last shred of my faith in human nature. It's not our job to unravel the mysteries of their lives.'

'Sometimes there's no alternative.'

Jim groaned. 'Typical Harry Devlin. If you ever called at the Law Society Library, I'm sure you'd find a body in it. Go on, then, what have the Graham-Browns been up to?'

Harry described the sequence of events leading up to Rosemary's anguished departure from the office a few minutes earlier and Jim listened closely, his displeasure fading into bewilderment.

'So what do you make of all that, Sherlock?'

'Wish I knew.'

Jim made a scoffing noise. 'Time you donated your deerstalker to Oxfam.'

Provoked, Harry said, 'Maybe Rosemary got wind of Stuart's affair with the blonde. Although she must be bitter, she won't want to give up the good life she's accustomed to. It's not as if she's a free agent; she has a small child to care for. So she's desperate to pack them all off to Spain before Stuart changes his mind, sues for divorce and does a bunk with his fancy woman instead.'

'And how come the office doesn't know he's about to disappear?'

'I imagine his mistress works there and he hasn't summoned the courage to tell her he's on his way to warmer climes.'

'But you said the business is a one-man band – Rosemary's obviously no more than a sleeping partner. The moment Stuart emigrates, Merseycredit is bound to collapse.'

'So perhaps he's been creaming a few bob off for himself along the way. He might not be going to Spain simply to improve his tan. They say it's easier to extract beer from blotting paper than to extradite a crook from his exile in the sun.'

Jim frowned. Harry sensed his partner succumbing to the urge to speculate.

'You think his scam may involve McCray? That might be another reason why he's keeping quiet about the flit and why it's so urgent to sell the house.'

'Could be, though he'd have to be truly tired of life to try pulling a fast one with money earmarked for terrorists. Those people have long memories and they won't worry about the niceties of Spanish extradition law. If he defrauds them now, sooner or later he'll finish up with a bullet through his brain.'

Deep in thought, Jim tugged at his beard. 'Tell me this. How can you be sure McCray *is* hand in glove with terrorists? I know we have a fine tradition in this country of convicting Irishmen on dodgy evidence, but it seems to me you haven't actually got anything on the man at all. The same goes for Graham-Brown: what if Rosemary flies straight from here to Tobacco Court and tells Stuart we suspect Merseycredit of moving around money for murderers?'

'It could be the end of a beautiful friendship,' admitted Harry.

'It could be the end of your practising certificate, if the Graham-Browns complain to the Law Society. I know we're encouraged to provide client care, but tipping Rosemary off that her husband's guilty of criminal conspiracy when you don't have a shred of proof is taking things to extremes. I reckon you've been hanging around with Finbar Rogan too long. He's taught you there's no difference between the truth and a tall story.'

'Finbar won't be pulling the wool over any more eyes,' said Harry softly.

Jim bowed his head. 'Yes, well, perhaps I've become tactless too. It's bloody awful news. I know you liked him.'

'He was good company, though the more I found out about him, the less harmless he seemed. He was so full of life, it was easy to be blind to his shortcomings when you were with him.'

'At least you don't suspect McCray of doing him in.'

'Some people might not blame him if he had – Eileen was his only daughter. No wonder he hated Finbar and set fire to his studio, blew up his car.'

'You're sure that was McCray?'

'You missed your way in life, you ought to have become a defence counsel. I suppose the honest answer is, I'm not sure about anything. He had the motive, of course.'

'So did plenty of others.'

'True, but how many of them had access to bomb-making equipment? Not Melissa, not Sophie, not...' His voice trailed away as a thought occurred to him.

Jim narrowed his eyes. 'I can see the great detective has had an idea. Come on, spit it out.'

'Perhaps I've been on the wrong track all along.'

'It wouldn't be the first time.'

'Thanks very much. But look, what if the Irish connection is totally irrelevant?'

'A green herring?'

'With your sense of humour, you ought to be appearing in one of Nick Folley's talent contests. No, there is someone else who had cause to hate Finbar, who could have planted the bomb in his car: someone who might be off-balance and behaving more dangerously with each day that passes. Someone who failed to kill Finbar by fire or explosion and finally settled for running him down.'

Jim had given up all pretence of disdain for amateur sleuthing. He leaned forward in his chair, his damaged face alive with interest. 'Who do you have in mind?'

'The woman Finbar cheated on more than any other, of course. His wife.'

'*Sinead*?'

'Don't sound so surprised. She's an obvious suspect, if you think about it. Remember she's a member of an extremist group of animal rights campaigners – presumably they wouldn't be averse to bombing labs where experiments are carried out. The republican movement don't have a monopoly on terror, you know.'

'But why go to such lengths at precisely the time when Finbar is severing the knot? She'd put up with him for long enough. Soon she would have been rid of him as a husband through the legal process. Why would she murder him?'

'You didn't see her at the Divorce Registry. I've seldom seen such pure hatred.'

'You're not saying she killed him rather than get divorced?'

Harry brushed the objection aside; he was excited by his latest theory and Jim's doubts served only to strengthen his belief in the likelihood of Sinead's guilt.

'Of course not. Although she'd opposed the divorce all along, I agree that, in itself, is hardly a motive for murder. After all, in my experience, most Catholics who are divorced against their will are able to console themselves with the fact that it's no more than a civil proceeding. No, my guess is that the turning point came when Sinead heard the story about Eileen. As far as she was concerned, Finbar was responsible for a young girl's abortion and death – so she wanted him to suffer too.'

Jim stared at him. 'So what do you propose to do?'

'Talk to Sladdin, I suppose. He may not…'

The phone shrilled and he snatched up the receiver.

'Suzanne, I'm talking with Jim. We don't want to be disturbed until…'

'All right,' said the girl mutinously, 'but I have Kim Lawrence on the line and she did insist it was important.'

Chapter Seventeen

'Kim?' Harry was puzzled, but the chance to speak to Sinead's lawyer was too good to miss. 'Okay, put her through.'

Suzanne muttered something which may have been, 'Make up your mind,' before Kim Lawrence came on the line.

'Harry? Are you there? I wanted to speak to you as soon as I could. Of course, I've heard Finbar Rogan is dead.'

'Murdered,' said Harry, 'although the police haven't said so officially.'

'My God. I can't begin to work out what's going on. I wasn't sure whether you had heard the news about Sinead.'

He tensed, wondering what she was going to say.

'No, tell me.'

Kim gave a weary sigh. 'The police have arrested her.'

Chapter Eighteen

Harry could hardly restrain himself from punching the air in triumph as he absorbed the impact of Kim's news. So – he had guessed right. Finbar's killer was already under lock and key. Justice would be served. Sladdin must have moved with impressive speed.

Giving Jim a thumbs-up sign, he strove to keep his voice calm. 'Already? When did they pick her up?'

'You talk as though you were expecting it,' said Kim Lawrence, sounding nonplussed. 'The police took her in for questioning at two o'clock yesterday.'

He thought either he had misheard or she was mistaken.

'*Two?* Are you sure?'

'Of course! I accompanied her to the police station.'

'So they released her on bail?' The whole scenario was incredible. God, if she'd walked straight out of there and at once murdered her husband, someone would be in deep, deep trouble.

'No,' said Kim Lawrence, 'she was kept in overnight and released on bail this morning. I've just come back from court.'

Harry stared blindly at the telephone, unable to believe what he was being told.

'Are you still there?' asked Kim.

'I don't follow. What's – what's the charge?'

'Criminal damage. The fire and the bomb. Originally there was talk of attempted murder, but they quietly dropped that after they learned someone else had actually done Rogan in that very evening.'

'So – you mean there's no question of her having committed that crime?'

'Of course not.' Kim sounded angry that the possibility had even crossed his mind. 'The present charges are serious enough, but not even a hard case like Sladdin can claim Sinead ran Rogan down when at the estimated time of death he was personally subjecting her to the third degree.'

Chapter Eighteen

Harry swore silently. A few minutes earlier he had thought he had solved the mystery – now he was more confused than ever.

'Can we talk? I mean, now?'

'Yes, if you want to,' Kim said after a pause.

'I'll meet you outside your office in five minutes.'

'Outside? In this weather?'

'This mist isn't anything compared to the fog in my brain.'

She grunted. 'Suit yourself. And perhaps you can tell me a little more about how your client came to die. The police are playing their cards very close to their chest.'

Of course – she was after any information which might help her build her client's defence. Or, more realistically, a plea in mitigation.

'I won't pretend I know much more than you, Kim, but I'd welcome a chat all the same. See you shortly.' He put the phone down and turned to Jim, who had been following the conversation with mounting bewilderment. Quickly, he explained what had happened.

'Look, I have to see Kim. Why don't you go home? You're in no fit state to be out of the house.'

'Are you telling me you're in a fit state to run our business?'

'No need to moan, I know there's a ton of work to do.' A pang of guilt prompted him to add, 'Listen, I'll make you a promise. Let me poke around just for the rest of today and after that you can chain me to the desk. There are a few questions I have to ask one or two people about Finbar's death. I owe him that much.'

'You owe him nothing. He gave you the run-around when he was alive – don't let him do the same now he's dead. Anyway, what do you propose to do about the Graham-Browns?'

'Don't worry, I'll sort out their file. Promise. Things need to come to a head if we're to have any hope of keeping them as clients. By tomorrow I'll be more than ready to leave detecting to the real detectives. Okay?'

Jim gave a resigned shrug. 'That will be the day.'

Harry accompanied his partner to the front door, then raced over to the neat bare garden outside the stone-faced building which housed Kim Lawrence's office. She was waiting for him as promised, a pale and slender figure standing in the shadow of Liverpool Parish Church.

She moved towards him. Long hours spent with Sinead and the police had left her looking tired and defeated.

'So, Harry. Your client's dead.'

He nodded. 'And yours is facing jail. Perhaps we should have put more effort into marriage guidance.'

She smiled and turned up the collar of her raincoat. The air was damp as well as cold.

'I'd sooner have tried to persuade Henry VIII and Anne of Cleves to get back together.'

'Do I take it Sinead didn't shed too many tears when she heard Finbar had been killed?'

'What do you expect? She's no hypocrite and she didn't pretend remorse she could never feel. She never intended him to die, but I think she sees it as a case of just desserts.'

'Does she care less for the lives of people than animals?'

Kim gave him a sharp look. 'Not at all. You forget the dance he led her during their marriage. She's entitled to feel bitter. You've read her affidavit – it's a catalogue of betrayal. I almost wonder that she didn't turn to violence long ago. But I promise you, she wouldn't commit murder. At least I assume it is murder. What exactly happened to him?'

He told her what he knew, then asked, 'Has Sinead told you her motive for launching these attacks on Finbar?'

'She was distraught after hearing about that girl Eileen McCray. You remember, words were exchanged about her at the Divorce Registry?'

'I remember.'

'Apparently Rogan got Eileen pregnant and she died while having an abortion. Sinead found out from the girl's mother only a short time ago; apparently the story had been doing the rounds up at the Irish club, the De Valera. The McCrays had known the Rogans for years and they were devastated. As far as Sinead was concerned, Rogan had gone too far. He'd been careless about wrecking her life, now he'd started destroying others too. She hates the idea of abortion and she felt he deserved to be punished. And then she was presented with an opportunity she felt she couldn't waste.'

'Which was?'

'The animal rights group she belonged to wanted to hit a shop in Williamson Lane. It sells mainly leather goods, but the man who owns it also trades in furs. The idea was to warn him off, maybe put him out of business altogether. When she realised the shop was directly below her husband's studio, she volunteered for the job. It gave her the chance to kill two birds with one stone.'

Harry swore. 'If the fire had really taken hold, she might have killed more than birds.'

'Oh, she never meant Rogan to die. The way she saw it, she was teaching him a lesson. The man was a menace – even you must agree with that.'

Chapter Eighteen

'What did Sinead have to say about the bomb?'

'After the court hearing went so badly, she lost control. She told me she felt provoked beyond endurance.' Kim saw Harry's eyebrows rise. 'I'm not excusing what she did: obviously it was wrong. Even so, I can understand her sense of anger and despair.'

'She could have made herself a murderess.'

Kim became the defence lawyer again. 'I already said, she wanted to give him the fright of his life, not kill him. The bomb had a simple timing device and she was on the scene when it was due to explode, doing her best to make sure no one walked down the side street at the wrong moment.'

'Very public-spirited.'

'There's no need to take that tone! Sinead was misguided, of course, I don't deny it. What she did was a crime. But there are two sides to every story.'

And even if there aren't, thought Harry, *someone like you or I will be paid to create them.* 'I suppose,' he said, 'that she picked up the bomb-making equipment through her connections with FAN.'

Kim nodded. 'It's a small group which splintered off from the mainstream animal lib movement. I've acted for several of its members over the past few years. They favour direct action.'

'Don't tell me – against "legitimate targets", right?' He could not contain his despair at the senselessness of it all. 'Another mob as keen on euphemisms as they are on blowing innocents to bits.'

'That's a ridiculous over-simplification! Activists' methods may be crude and sometimes illegal, but they do have a point. Sinead says all life is sacred – and she's right. I'm a committed supporter of animal rights myself.'

'I might have known it.'

'For Heaven's sake! Are you aware of the terrible things done each day to defenceless creatures in our so-called civilised society? Do you realise that—'

'Okay, okay, okay.' He dismissed her protestations with a sweep of the hand. He cared about animals himself; on another day and in other circumstances he might have agreed with much that she had to say, but right now he wasn't in the mood to debate vivisection. His greater concern was for human life.

'So these characters have their own bomb factory, do they?'

'Naturally, Sinead has refused to implicate any of her fellow activists, although the police put her under tremendous pressure to do so. But, yes, they have gelignite stored somewhere. She did say it had been stolen from a quarry in Wales and she'd been trained in how to use it.'

'How did she know he was carrying on at the Blue Moon?'

'Simple. She waited in her car outside his girlfriend's house that morning and when she saw him set off, she followed. He parked his car off the main road, out of sight. If you know what you're doing, it doesn't take long to affix a bomb to the underside of a vehicle.'

Harry kicked a stone into an empty flower bed: a trivial gesture to relieve the frustration he felt, the sense of impotence when confronted by the brutal absurdities of human behaviour. 'For Christ's sake,' he said. 'Sinead must have been out of her mind.'

'A lot of my clients are. Yours too, I guess. Alone, short of money, they're at the bottom of the heap. Sanity doesn't always stay around for long in those circumstances. I tried to calm her after the court hearing, of course. She talked about revenge, but that's not unusual in the midst of a divorce case. Of course I had no idea what she would do.' Kim's voice faltered. 'You know, I can't help feeling guilty. Irrational, maybe, but I keep thinking I should have realised she wasn't merely letting off steam.'

It occurred to Harry that she needed someone to listen to her whilst she tried to disentangle the knot of her own divided loyalties. In a gentler tone, he said, 'We can't always read our clients' minds. Thank God.'

She sat down on a bench looking out beyond the main road towards the Mersey and he perched on the arm rest beside her. The Liver Building was visible, but the river itself was still wrapped in its grey blanket.

'Sinead says Finbar was the most selfish bastard she'd ever met. And everything I've heard about him tells me she's right.'

'Selfishness isn't a capital offence. If it was, the mortuaries would have standing room only. Of course Finbar had his faults: don't we all? But he didn't deserve to die because of them.'

She said nothing and he contemplated her sombre expression. She wore no make-up and her face was pinched by distress as well as by the cold. It seemed to him that Sinead's arrest had scraped off a layer of Kim's professional outer skin. He had never thought of her as vulnerable before. Stupid of him, really – he knew as well as anyone that a brisk courtroom manner is no less a disguise than a barrister's wig.

'You are certain that Sinead wasn't connected with his murder?'

'Positive. As you would be if you'd seen the surprise on her face when they gave her the news. Even the police are convinced. They didn't object to bail.'

She gazed out at the Titanic Memorial. Euphemists of days gone by had inscribed the stone monument with a dedication to 'Heroes Of The Machine Room' in order to avoid giving passengers boarding ocean liners a direct

Chapter Eighteen

reminder of the risk of tragedy. But Harry understood there was no escaping the reality of death.

'Thanks for your time,' he said.

'What do you intend to do?'

'I'd like to find out who killed Finbar.'

'Isn't that a job for the police? If you interfere, they are sure to disapprove.'

He gave her a crooked grin. 'When did you or I ever let that stop us?'

Chapter Nineteen

Turning into North John Street five minutes later, he saw Baz Gilbert and Penny Newland coming out of the offices of Radio Liverpool, hand in hand.

The disc jockey spotted him crossing the road and waited for him to catch up with them.

'You've heard about Finbar?'

'Melissa called me round last night,' said Harry. 'The police broke the news to her.'

'How did she take it?'

'As you would expect. I don't think it's sunk in yet.'

'She's well rid of him,' said Penny.

Embarrassed by his girlfriend's willingness to speak ill of the dead, Baz said hurriedly, 'As if Melissa hasn't had enough on her plate without this!'

'You mean?' asked Harry.

Again Baz became keen to change the subject. 'Oh, you know, she had a rough time with Finbar – and on top of that, she lost her job.'

Harry sensed the disc jockey had something else in mind. He pressed on. 'No sign of Nick Folley changing his decision and reinstating her?'

'She'll have to crawl to him first,' said Penny.

'And do you think she'll do that?'

Penny shrugged. Harry gathered there was more to be said about the relationship between Melissa and her former boss – but Penny was in no mood to say it. He decided to try another line of attack.

'What about Sophie? Did she seem shocked?'

'She's been very subdued this morning,' said Baz, 'though I suppose that's true of all of us who knew him. Besides, Sophie is another one with problems of her own. I don't think her rift with Nick has healed yet, by any means.'

Chapter Nineteen

'It strikes me Nick is a bad person to cross,' Harry said, trying to sound casual.

'You know what he's like.'

'I know his reputation – but not the man.'

The couple exchanged glances which Harry could not interpret.

'You're probably best keeping it that way,' said Baz.

Baz and Penny were determined, Harry sensed, to keep their own counsel. That didn't surprise him. Both of them took Nick Folley's shilling and he couldn't blame them for not wanting to put their jobs on the line. He would learn more from confronting the man himself.

'Are Nick and Sophie both around today?'

'Why do you ask?' demanded Penny.

Under her keen gaze, he felt himself wavering. Amateur sleuthing was never straightforward; perhaps that was part of its appeal.

'I just wondered if I could have a word with them.'

'Sophie's still in the office,' said Baz, 'but Nick's down in London at the moment.'

'London? When did he go?'

'I heard him say he was taking the train yesterday night, although he's due back shortly. It was a last-minute arrangement – some urgent business cropped up. Suits us, anyway.'

'Why's that?'

'Nick was due to have an expense account lunch at Bellingham's today with one of our major advertisers. We're putting on a show for them tonight, a Hallowe'en party at Empire Hall, and he asked me to step in for him, said I could take Pen along too. That's where we're heading now.'

'Then don't let me keep you. I'll just have a word with Sophie.'

'I don't see what you're trying to achieve,' said Penny. 'You said Melissa asked you round when the police came to see her. What in heaven's name is going on?'

'It's like this,' said Harry, her scrutiny prompting him to candour. 'Finbar's death is unlikely to have been an accident. I'm sure he was run over deliberately.'

'*Murder*?' Baz sounded startled. 'But I thought from the news bulletin…'

'Nothing is certain yet. You could say I'm exceeding my brief, but Finbar was my client and I'd like to learn why he was killed – and who killed him.'

With that, he left the couple staring after him as he hurried up the steps which led to the entrance to the radio station.

'How may I help you?' enquired a young girl at the front desk, forcing herself to tear her eyes from a cheap magazine. She evidently did not remember his previous visit.

'I'd like to speak to Sophie Wilkins,' said Harry, giving his name. 'Tell her it's about our mutual friend.'

'One moment.' The girl spoke into a receiver and raised her eyebrows as she listened to the reply. Fixing a bright, disingenuous smile on her face, she said, 'I'm afraid Miss Wilkins is in conference.'

'I'll wait.'

'She says it will be a very long conference.'

'I'm extremely patient.'

'I don't think she'll have time to—'

'Please tell her I won't keep her long, but I do need to see her. I'm not going away till I've done so.'

Covering her mouth, the girl passed on the message. Leaning over the veneered desk surface, Harry caught the phrase 'looks as if he means business'. Finally she turned back to him. 'Miss Wilkins may be able to give you a couple of minutes after all. She'll come out shortly, but she is very busy and...'

'Fine.'

Harry took a seat next to a tub of greenery. Above his head, a speaker relayed a programme hosted by a DJ whose heyday had been with Radio One in the seventies; he was now reduced to conducting phone-ins interspersed with numbers from the likes of James Taylor and Joni Mitchell. As Harry listened to an attack on the Labour Party's class treachery from an ex-docker with a smoker's cough, Sophie pushed through the double doors which led to the studios. As ever, she was brilliantly dressed, this time in a canary-coloured tracksuit. Yet her eyes seemed dull with fatigue and even her hair had lost its rich shine.

'Thanks for seeing me,' he said quickly. 'Is there somewhere private we can talk?'

She reopened the doors and led him down the corridor into a cramped kitchen.

'This will have to do. I don't have my own office and anyway, I can't give you long. As you ought to realise, I have a great deal of work to organise.'

'I'll get straight to the point. You've heard that Finbar is dead?'

She folded her arms. Harry sensed she was making a conscious effort to be calm and in control.

'We've been broadcasting the news every thirty minutes since we went on the air, so I'm hardly likely to be unaware of it.'

'I believe he was murdered.'

'But the police haven't...'

'The circumstances seem to rule out an accident.'

She plucked at her lower lip. 'Well, it comes as no surprise. After the fire and the bombing, it was obvious someone wanted his blood.'

'This is different. The person who committed the earlier crimes couldn't have run him down last night.'

Sophie screwed her features into a savage frown, clearly trying to decide whether he was shooting a line. Harry felt sure his words came as a shock to her.

'But that's absurd!'

'Not at all. Sinead Rogan had been taken in for questioning about both the arson and the bomb attack at the time Finbar was killed. This morning she was bailed on charges of criminal damage.'

'*What*? I simply don't believe it!'

'Whether you do or not, it's a fact. Assuming Finbar was the victim of a deliberate crime rather than an improbable stroke of bad luck, the police need to find another culprit.'

She cleared her throat nervously. 'Well, there must be plenty of candidates. I never knew a man with such a talent for making enemies.'

'Including yourself, of course.'

'What are you insinuating?'

'Come on, Sophie. Let's be frank.' He could tell her attempt to rein in her emotions was collapsing. 'You didn't part the best of chums, did you? When the police start casting round for possible suspects, they're bound to take a closer look at you. They may arrive with their notebooks any time now, wanting to find out whether you saw Finbar yesterday, where you were last night at the time he was killed...'

'What you say is outrageous,' she said; in her voice he recognised fear rather than the simple rage of the unjustly accused. The last vestiges of her self-confidence had vanished.

'Look, the sooner this whole bloody mess is cleared up, the better – for everyone.'

'How dare you come here and make these slanderous innuendoes? And a lawyer, too! I've a good mind to report you to the Law Society.'

'Join the queue,' he said wearily. 'Listen, Sophie. Anything I can do to help identify who killed Finbar, I will. I'm not saying for a minute that you were involved—'

'You're too kind.'

'—I'm simply pointing out that questions are bound to be asked. You need to be ready for them.'

'Thanks very much. When I need professional advice, I'll contact someone like Windaybanks.'

'Okay, Sophie, have it your way. I didn't come here to pick a fight.'

The truth, if not the whole truth. His motives for turning up here were not disinterested. He had wanted to see at first-hand how she would react to the suggestion that she was in the frame – and he had been rewarded by her hostile response.

'I have to go now,' she said. 'Some of us have work to do.' She turned, but paused to glance back over her shoulder from the doorway.

'I had plenty to keep me occupied yesterday. You know the station's in trouble – I'm working all the hours God sends at present.'

'When did you leave?'

She hesitated and he guessed she was wondering whether he would check on her.

'Five o'clock. Late enough, after my usual dawn start.'

Over the years, he'd encountered many witnesses like Sophie: uncertain how far to spin their stories, more concerned to put themselves in the right than to stick to the truth. He kept quiet, watching her lick her lips.

'And in case you're wondering,' she said, 'after that, Nick and I went to his place. When Finbar Rogan was killed, the two of us were tucked up in bed together. Does that satisfy your curiosity?' She gave him a defiant look, then strode away.

Harry did not attempt to follow; he was satisfied with what he had achieved so far. He'd provoked her into saying too much and into a panicky attempt to allay any suspicion that she had been involved in Finbar's death.

As for the alibi, he was sure she was lying.

Chapter Twenty

Harry re-entered reception, wanting another word with the girl on the desk. She was on the phone; as he waited for attention, a seductive voice from the speakers asked him whether he needed any extra money.

'What about that new car you long for, an extension on your house or the holiday of a lifetime in exotic parts?'

Harry, who would never part company with his MG, lived in a flat and seldom travelled further than the Lake District for a long weekend, had no interest in the soft sell. Even so, his attention was caught by a song performed by a Scouse reincarnation of the Beverley Sisters.

Whatever you choose,
We'll help you get it,
You really can't lose
With Merseycredit.

The promise of an instant no-strings fortune faded as the persuasive man whispered, with a lover's tenderness, that borrowers' homes were at risk if they didn't keep up the repayments, before quoting an APR figure high enough to terrify any listener with a grasp of simple arithmetic.

Harry was no longer paying attention, although he managed to curb his impatience while the receptionist wound up her conversation. She struck him as someone who would not easily be bullied into imparting information, but she might be susceptible to a little flattery.

'Sorry to bother you, I can see you're busy. But I wondered… do Merseycredit often advertise with you?'

She pursed her lips. For a few seconds Harry had a glimpse of her in thirty years' time: a hard-bitten housewife, intent on making her husband's life a misery.

'I dunno. I mean, I never listen to the ads. Does anyone?'

'Come on,' he said, choking back irritation, trying to reorganise his features into an inviting smile, 'this is a commercial radio station. You're at the heart of things, you have the speakers on full blast all day, every day. You must have some idea of whether you do much business with the company.'

'Well,' she said grudgingly, 'I suppose we do. As a matter of fact...'

She paused. Harry guessed her natural disinclination to be helpful was warring with an acute urge to appear in the know.

'Yes?'

'Nick Folley – the boss, that is – was supposed to be meeting Merseycredit today. They're putting on a big Hallowe'en party for their clients and we're broadcasting a special show from the concert room at Empire Hall tonight.'

Harry choked back an exclamation. So Baz and Penny had been setting off to entertain, of all people, Stuart Graham-Brown!

'I thought Nick,' he said, carefully making it clear he was on first name terms with the great man, 'was down in London?'

'Yeah, that's right. Wish I was there, too, that's where all the action is, not in this poxy dump. I'm thinking of looking for a job down there, as a matter of fact. You'd never believe the money they pay! The world would be at my feet.'

She rolled the final phrase off her tongue with relish. Harry guessed she had picked it out of a magazine that fed its readers on unattainable dreams and was tempted to tell her that the streets of the capital were paved not with gold but with cardboard boxes. But he stifled his instinct to defend his home town and simply asked, 'When is he due back?'

She glanced at her watch. 'He told me he'd be back at Lime Street before two, so I could send out a car for him.'

Harry decided to push his luck.

'Any idea when he left last night?'

She gave him a resentful glare. 'Don't ask me! This isn't the British Rail information desk, you know.'

'Sorry. You've been very helpful. One more thing – a man called Finbar Rogan...'

'The Irishman?' The girl's eyes gleamed with the pleasure of knowledge. 'He's dead. Killed last night over at Colonial Dock.'

'Do you remember him phoning yesterday? Might he have spoken to Sophie Wilkins?'

'He didn't *phone*,' smirked the girl. 'He did better than that.'

'You mean he actually came here?'

'Insisted on seeing her,' she confirmed. No doubt about it, she loved being at the centre of events.

Chapter Twenty

'And did Sophie agree to talk to him?'

'Not at first. She had a cob on. In fact she's been a pain in the arse ever since she had a row with Nick the other day.'

'But Sophie and Finbar did meet?'

'When I rang and said he wasn't going to go until he'd spoken to her, she threw a wobbler. But in the end she took him in, same as she did with you. Except this time the raised voices could have been heard in the Liver Building.'

'They quarrelled?'

'I'll say! It was mostly on her side, though. She can be a real cow. Mind you, he smelled like a brewery and had plenty to say for himself.'

'What happened?'

'Nothing, in the end,' said the girl with regret. 'He popped in for a word with the marketing manager's secretary, gave me a wink and was gone.' A claim to fame occurred to her. 'Hey, maybe I was the last person to see him alive!'

'Except for the person who ran him over.'

'Well – yeah.'

He could tell she was entranced by the idea of close contact with sudden death: something to boast about to her friends. Muttering thanks, he hurried out into North John Street, where a taxi driver heading towards the Town Hall caught his windmilling wave.

'Where to, pal?'

'Lime Street.' He hoped to catch Folley on arrival, before Sophie had any chance to forewarn him of her claim that they had spent the previous evening together. The story was surely a spur of the moment invention, a piece of wishful thinking. It also occurred to him that if Sophie lacked an alibi for Finbar's killing – then so might Nick Folley.

Settling down in the back of the cab, Harry wondered if Finbar's abortive one-afternoon stand with Sophie provided her boss with a motive for murder. Folley was not a man to suffer public humiliation in silence, as witness his rush of blood to the head at Empire Hall. Harry recalled Folley's frenzied lunge and the strength of his grip on Finbar's neck. Suppose some unknown chance – or design – had brought the two men together at Colonial Dock the previous evening. Harry could imagine Folley at the wheel of the hire car, seeing Finbar ahead of him in the lamplight, forcing his foot down on the accelerator with the same fury that had moved him to an absurd attempt at a public strangulation.

And yet – what would have taken Finbar to a rendezvous with Nick Folley at Colonial Dock on a cold October night? It was a bleak stretch of water surrounded by disused warehouses, a ghostly relic of Merseyside's maritime past. A place omitted from the tourist guides and described as ripe for development only by those with the most vivid imaginations.

The cab joined a queue of traffic on the climb up Roe Street. At the sight of the cars tailing back from the lights opposite the station, Harry paid and scrambled out into the fume-laden air. He crossed the road, then took the steps to the station entrance hall two at a time. The concourse was teeming with people and he pushed through the crowd to join those staring up at the information board. The next train from Euston was almost due. He wandered over to the paperback stall, where he was amused to notice a doyen of the Liverpool accountancy profession furtively purchasing a girlie magazine, sliding it inside his *Financial Times* with an ease Harry felt sure was born of long practice. Knowing that old rogue, he probably had a scheme for claiming tax relief on his purchase.

As the arrival of the London train was announced, Harry moved towards the gate which led to the platform. He scanned the faces of the returning travellers: students humping rucksacks, back from the bright lights; London businessmen on a flying visit to North West subsidiaries to impose another batch of redundancies; elderly people with bemused expressions, fussing about their tickets and their destinations; a party of burger-munching kids with harassed teachers. And, finally, emerging from the first-class compartment with a smart briefcase under his arm, came Nick Folley.

Folley tossed his ticket towards the collector and sauntered through the barrier. Harry called to him. 'Can I have a word?'

Folley swung round. The expression on his face was one of pleased surprise; perhaps he imagined he had been accosted by a journalist anxious to follow the every move of a prominent celebrity. When he recognised Harry, the smile faded.

'You again.'

'We must stop meeting like this.'

'You were on the London train?'

'No, but Radio Liverpool told me you were and I wanted a word.'

Folley frowned. 'You've been looking for me?'

'I wanted to talk to you about Finbar Rogan.'

Folley sucked in his cheeks. 'I can't imagine anyone I have less wish to discuss.'

'Did you know he's dead?'

Folley put the briefcase down on the ground, with as much care as if it were full of fragile antiques. Was his surprise genuine? Harry could not tell. After all, the man had long experience of performing before the cameras.

'He was killed by a car last night. It was a hit-and-run job.'

'I won't pretend I'm heartbroken,' Folley said slowly. 'Kids driving a stolen vehicle, was it? Didn't he get out of their way in time?'

'I don't think so. I believe he was murdered.'

'Really? Well, you may be right. After all, there had been other attempts, hadn't there? All he was good for was making enemies.'

'The person who set fire to his shop and planted the bomb was already in police custody at the time Finbar died. His wife has confessed to both the earlier crimes.'

'*What?*' Folley could not hide his amazement.

'So anyone who hoped the blame would fall on Sinead Rogan is due for a disappointment.'

'And – what do the police think?'

'No idea. I'm making my own enquiries.'

'Aren't you taking a lot on yourself?'

'I was Finbar's lawyer. And, in a way, his friend.'

Folley snorted his contempt. 'You can't tell me Rogan had any friends – just acquaintances and saloon-bar pick-ups.'

'Jealous?'

For half a second, Harry thought he had struck a nerve; Folley took a step forward and lifted a hand. But then he checked himself and forced his mouth into a humourless parody of the old smile from his television days.

'If you're thinking of Melissa, forget it. I won't deny I was glad to be seen with her at one time of day. But she – well, let's just say in the end she needed me more than I needed her. I dropped her before she started seeing Rogan.'

'And Sophie?'

Two spots of colour came into Folley's cheeks. 'She made a stupid mistake. We all do, from time to time.'

'You weren't so phlegmatic at Empire Hall the other night. You tried to strangle Finbar.'

'For God's sake, don't be so fucking melodramatic. That was *my* stupid mistake, if you insist: something and nothing, over and done with in the space of seconds. I'm working under pressure all the time. Business conditions – they're not easy at present. I've had one or two setbacks lately. That's why I had to dash down to London, if you must know. It's hardly surprising if once in a while I lose my cool.'

'And did you – lose your cool again last night?'

'What?' Folley scowled, then barked a laugh. 'You're not suggesting I was the one who ran him down, are you?'

'Are you denying it? The police are bound to ask the question.'

'Of course I'm denying it, you fool! The whole idea's crazy.'

'So where were you yesterday afternoon and evening, before you set off for London?'

Folley gritted his teeth, as if resolving that the conversation had gone far enough. He picked up his briefcase.

'Mind your own business, Mr Devlin. And now, if you'll excuse me, I'll go and mind mine.'

Chapter Twenty-One

Harry watched Nick Folley stride across the concourse towards a waiting car emblazoned with the name and logo of Radio Liverpool and wondered whether he had been talking to Finbar's murderer.

Why hadn't Folley volunteered Sophie as his alibi? Of course, the obvious and innocent explanation could be the truth: he had no right to cross-examine anyone and Folley might simply have become sick of the questions and decided to co-operate no further. On the other hand – ah, that favourite lawyers' phrase! – perhaps Folley did have something to hide. A glance at the train departure times told him that Folley could have taken an express to London two or three hours after the time when Finbar had met his death. What had Folley been doing before that? Had he been with Sophie – or not?

Harry debated with himself as the travellers jostled by. Melissa had been sacked; Sophie would no doubt refuse to speak to him if he returned to North John Street again. He needed another source of information and his best hope was Baz Gilbert. He decided to make for Bellingham's. Someone else would be there with whom his first meeting was long overdue: Stuart Graham-Brown.

The shock of Finbar's death had pushed Rosemary to the back of his mind – but not out of it. Yet nothing he had learned today made it easier to understand what the Graham-Browns were up to.

The Hallowe'en party sounded like a large-scale public relations exercise rather than a routine knees-up; hiring the concert room at Empire Hall cost serious money. Why would the Graham-Browns go to so much trouble when they were on the point – they hoped – of emigrating? An elaborate bluff? One thing was certain: so far as the house sale was concerned, Stuart had hidden behind his wife for long enough.

Harry didn't have a chauffeur-driven car on hand and the line of people searching for taxis was as long as a Kirkby dole queue, so he took the escalator for the Underground. The Liverpool Loop had long ago been christened the Bermuda Triangle by commuters driven to despair by the cancellation of scheduled services, but for once the metallic voice announcing delays due to a whole host of reasons, ranging from staff shortages to water on the line, was silent. As he arrived on the platform, a train pulled in, and five minutes later he was walking through the misty streets which led from James Street Station to Bellingham's.

The wine bar was owned by a local actor who revelled in Liverpudlian hostility towards central government and he'd named the place after a man who had lived in the city almost two hundred years earlier; the story was told on a plaque inside the door to the bar. John Bellingham felt he'd suffered an injustice at the hands of the Russians; when the authorities failed to put matters right, he'd travelled to London and shot the Prime Minister. In those days there wasn't much scope for defence lawyers and within a week Bellingham had been tried, convicted, sentenced and executed. Would Pearse Cato one day similarly be celebrated? Harry wondered. How long would it take for the memory of senseless brutality to fade, for today's assassins to be regarded with tolerant good humour?

He spotted Baz Gilbert waiting at the bar for service and walked up behind him.

'We meet again.'

'Harry! There's no escaping you. Did you speak to Sophie?'

'Yes. And Nick Folley.'

'He's back, is he?' Baz shook his head. 'Like I said – you shouldn't push your luck with Nick.'

'He didn't lay a hand on me.'

'You don't understand. He's mixed up with some dangerous people.'

'You don't mean Dermot McCray, do you?' Harry asked on the off-chance.

'Who?' Baz's face was a blank.

'An Irishman, a builder. He has connections with Merseycredit as well.'

'The name means nothing to me.'

Harry believed him. 'So who are these dangerous people?'

'Listen, forget I said a word. There are things Nick is mixed up with that I'd rather not know about.'

'And Sophie, is she also mixed up—'

'Hello,' said Penny Newland in his ear. Her voice was sour with disapproval. 'Are you still playing the detective?'

''Fraid so.'

'It won't do any good, you know.'

Chapter Twenty-One

'Neither will your leaving our guests on their own,' said Baz.

She touched his hand. 'Sorry, love, but I've had as much of them as I can take for the time being. They don't seem able to talk about anything other than how rich they are. I've been told at least four times how much tonight's beanfeast is setting them back. In the end, I decided to escape to the loo.'

'It's Stuart Graham-Brown that you're with, isn't it?' asked Harry.

'Yes, and his wife,' said Baz. 'Do you know Stuart?'

So Rosemary was here with her husband. Harry felt suddenly nervous. He took a deep breath, aware the time had come for him to face up to his two clients and find out exactly what game they were playing.

'I've never met him,' he said, 'but somehow I seem to have heard a great deal about him.'

'I'll introduce you if you like,' offered the disc jockey. 'Can I get you a drink first?'

Harry refused, though he had seldom needed one more; this encounter called for a clear mind.

The wine bar was emptying as the last few customers decided they could extend their lunch hours no further. Baz led the way towards a table in the far corner of the room.

Sitting behind it were Stuart Graham-Brown and the hard-faced blonde from Tobacco Court.

Harry didn't understand. Where was Rosemary?

'What's up?' asked Baz. 'Have you seen a ghost?'

'No. But – perhaps I have misidentified one.'

'I don't follow you.'

Harry pointed to Stuart Graham-Brown's companion. 'Tell me her name,' he whispered urgently.

Baz's eyebrows rose. 'I can do better than that, my friend.' He waved to Graham-Brown and the woman and ushered Harry up to their table. 'Let me introduce you,' he said, slipping smoothly into his radio persona. 'This is Harry Devlin, he's a solicitor for his sins. Harry, meet Stuart Graham-Brown of Merseycredit. And this is his partner in business and life – the lovely Rosemary.'

The blonde woman smiled. Close up, Harry could see that she was older than he had realised. The cut of her outfit flattered her figure and although her make-up was liberally applied, the lines round her eyes needed another shot of collagen.

'Good to meet you,' she said. Stuart Graham-Brown nodded. Like his wife, he exuded the confidence that comes with cash in the bank. *They would be the perfect bloody clients,* Harry thought, *if only we acted for them.* Of course, neither had betrayed a flicker of recognition at the mention of his name.

Harry shook hands. Rosemary's grip was strong. She wore even more jewellery than mascara and the cluster of rings on her fingers felt like a rich woman's knuckledusters. He coughed to cover his confusion. For a moment he clutched at the idea that the Graham-Browns might have embarked on an elaborate charade: perhaps his original surmise was right and the blonde was indeed merely Stuart's lover, not his wife. But no sooner had the thought occurred to him than he realised its absurdity. The truth was plain.

'I gather you've hired Baz's services to make your Hallowe'en party go with a swing,' he said in a hollow voice.

'It's going to be a marvellous night for Merseycredit,' said Graham-Brown. 'Come along yourself – we'd be glad to see you. We work mainly with accountants, but it's always good to have a lawyer or two on the team. Never know when I might need your services!' He spoke with the exuberance characteristic of a certain kind of businessman. His manner put Harry in mind of John de Lorean with an East End accent.

'Appropriate dress, mind,' said Rosemary, wagging her finger. 'Hallowe'en costumes are compulsory. The theme is "ghouls just wanna have fun".'

'So the two of you are in partnership together?'

Graham-Brown took his wife's arm. 'We've been together ten years now,' he said. 'I couldn't have made it without Rosemary.'

The complacent tone made Harry want to cringe. But needing to know more, he forced himself into a bonhomie he thought laughably false but which they seemed to take at face value.

'I saw your stand at the exhibition over at Empire Hall the other day. Good to see a local firm doing so well.'

'Glad to make a contribution to the city's economy,' said Graham-Brown. 'Can't claim to be a native, but we relocated from London during the eighties and we've lived in Formby ever since.'

'You feel settled there?' asked Harry, just to make sure.

'Love it. We're at the top end of Crow's Nest Lane, not far from the nature reserve.'

'Pleasant place to bring up children, I should imagine. Do you have any kids?'

'Just one,' said the woman. 'A little girl. Eighteen months.'

'You'll never believe this,' said the proud father, pretending to wince, 'but Rosemary insisted on calling her Rainbow.'

'You have a nanny to look after her, I suppose,' asked Harry, who had rapidly been putting two and two together.

'Yes,' said the real Rosemary. 'I hated the idea of becoming a *hausfrau*. I'd always been a career woman and it was only when that old biological clock started ticking louder that I thought if we were going to have a family, we'd better get a move on. But after she was born, I found counting the minutes between nappy changes and feeding times was no substitute for the kick you get from sealing a deal in the office. So in the end we found a girl, and we've been very fortunate with her, haven't we, Stu?'

'Debbie's very reliable,' confirmed her husband. He winked at the other two men. 'Looks terrific, too.'

'Sounds like the perfect arrangement,' said Baz, not trying too hard to stifle a yawn.

'It suits us,' said Graham-Brown.

Wait till you get home one night and find a strange family sitting in front of your fire and in proud possession of your title deeds, thought Harry. *If that doesn't wipe the smile off your face, nothing will.*

Aloud, he said, 'Pleasure to meet you. And thanks for the invite – I'll do my best to get along. But now I must be off. There's someone I desperately need to see.'

Chapter Twenty-Two

Harry walked back rapidly to Fenwick Court, still trying to absorb the news that the woman he had thought of as Rosemary – the elegant wife of a rich man – was in reality a young Scouse girl on the make. A nanny with crime on her mind, for God's sake!

From his office he retrieved the deeds giving title to Crow's Nest House: the papers which Debbie, as he must now think of her, had seen as the passport to a new life.

'Mrs Graham-Brown must have been on the phone half a dozen times since you left,' Suzanne told him as he headed for the door. 'I said don't blame me, I haven't a clue when he'll be back. I'm only the poor receptionist, no one tells me anything. If you ask me, she's on the point of taking her business elsewhere and then what will Mr Crusoe say?'

'Good riddance, if he has any sense,' said Harry. 'Listen, I may be out for the rest of the afternoon.'

'What if Mrs Graham-Brown…'

Harry rapped the bundle of deeds against the reception desk.

'I'm going to sort her out. Never fear.'

On his way to Formby, he kept cursing his failure to see through Debbie's scam. All the oddities in her behaviour, from their first chance encounter in the waiting room at Fenwick Court, finally made sense: her air of nervous excitement; her desire to use a solicitors' firm not associated with commercial work or Merseycredit; her anxiety to speed the transaction to its end; her refusal to involve her husband and her insistence on contacting Harry rather than waiting for his call or letters. All the pieces fitted only one pattern.

During the day, with Stuart and Rosemary out at Exchange Precinct, she had had the run of the house and, somehow, she'd gained access to the title deeds. The rest was simple, given the eager co-operation of professional advisers equally susceptible to a pretty face and a fat fee.

Chapter Twenty-Two

As he pulled up outside Crow's Nest House, he felt as though he were being watched. *She's bound to be petrified*, he thought. Having to live with the Graham-Browns, knowing she was about to cheat them out of house and home, and suffering the trauma of the Ambroses' default. In a moment of insight, he imagined her tension, her frantic longing to have the whole business over and done.

He strode up the path and rang the bell. She must have been waiting on the other side of the oak door, for she opened it within seconds. He hardly had time to take in her expression of relief before she burst into a torrent of words.

'Harry, it's you! Where have you been? I've been ringing your office every half hour. Your girl didn't have the faintest idea where you were. But thank God you've come. This threat that the Ambroses are going to pull out – they can't do that, can they? I've been beside myself since I saw you this morning. What they're doing is immoral! Surely we must be able to do something to force them to honour their side of the bargain?'

He swallowed hard. 'Do you really think you would be able to honour *your* side of the bargain, Debbie?'

Her jaw dropped as she absorbed the impact of his use of her name. It seemed to hit her like a physical blow knocking the breath out of her, making her gasp for air. Harry stood and watched with his hands in his pockets. On his way over here he had rehearsed phrases of sardonic reproach, but now they seemed irrelevant. Her face had turned the colour of chalk.

'Shall we talk inside?'

She nodded dumbly and led him into the sitting room. Her whole bearing had changed in a matter of seconds; as she sat in the same chair which she had occupied on his earlier visit here, she seemed to have shrunk. No longer was she the lady of the house, entertaining her trusted man of business – she was a servant, a paid help with ideas above her station.

'How much do you know?'

'Enough.'

'Since when?'

'Less than an hour ago. I was introduced to Stuart Graham-Brown and his wife. Rosemary herself.'

'Oh God! What did you tell them?'

'Nothing. I couldn't believe either my eyes or my ears, if you want to know the truth. But all the information I need is only a phone call to Merseycredit away, so I hope you'll make life easier by telling me the whole story.'

She gazed at the ceiling, clearly summoning strength, and ran both hands through her hair.

'I don't know where to begin.'

'Start with yourself,' he suggested. 'Who you are, where you came from...'

She mustered a ragged smile. 'There's not enough material for a *This Is Your Life*. I've never been anywhere or done anything. My name's Debbie Warrington and I'm the eldest kid in a family of eight. I've lived in Liverpool all my life. I like children and I always wanted to be a nanny, but this is the fifth family I've worked for since I left school and I'm ready for something new.'

'In Puerto Banus?'

'Why not? I went there on holiday in the summer, not long after I'd started working here. I'd gone to Marbella with a girlfriend. We were determined to live it up, have a bit of sun and sex. She works in a bacon factory out in Halewood and I'd been dancing attendance on Rainbow, who's a right little madam, so we were dying for a break.' She sighed, as if mourning an irretrievable past. 'In a bar we met these two lads from Liverpool, they've settled permanently in Spain. I think they were in trouble with the law here, but neither of us wanted to ask too many questions. Anyway, Phil, that's my feller, kept telling me about all the money you can make in the south of Spain. He reckoned if I started selling time-shares, there are so many dozy punters, I'd make a fortune.'

And he might be right, Harry thought, remembering the leopardskin lady from Empire Hall.

'Phil was keen for me to stay out there, but I couldn't make the break just like that. I needed to think about it back in England. Anyway, a few more weeks working for the Graham-Browns convinced me I'd be mad to spend the rest of my life flogging my guts out for a pittance. Even a saint could get sick of drying tears and wiping a baby's bum.'

As if on cue, Rainbow began to bleat in her playpen next door. Debbie groaned, half-rose to her feet, then subsided.

'So when did you hit on the idea of selling this house?'

'I'd already decided I wanted out before I went on holiday. Stuart's a crook, if you ask me.'

'You have moral objections to working for him?'

'No need to be sarky. No, but I bet he's up to all sorts of fiddles. What really bugs me is that he acts as if I wasn't there.'

'You resent him for not fancying you?'

'Listen, I'm not looking to be groped by the man of the house! I've had my share of that from so-called respectable husbands and fathers in my other jobs, I can promise you. No, what I hate is that he simply takes no notice. He's a millionaire and I'm just a slave.'

Chapter Twenty-Two

'And Rosemary?'

'What a bitch! You'd think she owns me body and soul. She married Stuart for his money, that's all she cares about. She was his PA before she got her claws into him. But to answer you, I'd already decided I wanted to escape from Merseyside in any case – see a bit of the world while I was still young.'

Someone else who wanted to get away, Harry thought, like the girl on the desk at Radio Liverpool. Why didn't they share his love for the city of their birth? Why couldn't they see beyond the fog and the dirt?

'So I said to myself, give Spain a chance, why don't you? Things might work out with Phil and the timeshares, and if they didn't, I could try something else. I was all set to hand in my notice when that fence at the back blew down in those gales we had a few weeks ago. Stuart wanted to know if he could sue someone – he seems to get off on tax dodges and litigation. So he got the title deeds out of the bureau in his study. I happened to be passing by the door at the time.'

'Convenient. What I can't understand is why the deeds were here. Someone streetwise like Stuart would want the tax relief on a mortgage, so the deeds should be locked up in the safe deposit of some financial institution.'

Debbie shrugged. 'Don't ask me! You're the lawyer. Although I do know there was some stuff about a loan from Merseycredit.'

Mystery solved. It must be cosy for Stuart, borrowing money from his own business. Better than a bank or building society, any day.

'Go on.'

'The key to the bureau was on a ring. Luckily, he keeps it in the pocket of an old coat he hangs in the hall cupboard. When I got the idea about selling the house...'

'Yes, how did that flash of inspiration strike you?'

'I remembered a remark Phil once made, about the money you could make from selling something you didn't have. Much easier than parting with something of your own.'

Phil sounded like a chap who would always keep the lawyers in business. Harry shook his head. 'So the rest was easy. Take the title deeds, find yourself an estate agent and a buyer who wasn't in a chain, offer the place at a cut price to secure a speedy sale, then hey presto!'

'It seems so simple when you put it like that,' she said. 'Believe me, I've died a thousand deaths during the past few weeks. It was no problem coming into town to see you – Mum has a council house down the road in Maghull. She was willing to look after Rainbow with no questions asked. But I could never be certain when the Ambroses or their surveyor came here that bloody

Rosemary wouldn't decide to take an early dart home. I had this nightmare that she would come back and find someone peering under her floorboards or sticking a knife in the putty of her window frames. Thank Christ the woman gets off on working in the city.'

'I see why you said you were ex-directory: to cut out the risk of gaff-blowing phone calls at night, when the owners were at home.'

'Right. I'm not saying there weren't perks. Rosemary has better taste in clothes than in men. She's not much bigger than me, she's got the midriff bulge under control. I loved wearing her things whenever I went into town to see the estate agent or you. At last I knew what it felt like to be rich.' She smiled. 'Believe me, changing your identity gives you a taste of freedom. It's a fresh beginning, a way to put the past behind you and start a new life. But all the same I was scared of putting a foot wrong. The fear of being found out ate away at me. Tell you the truth, I reckoned I was earning my profit.'

'And you were even able to bestow a little largesse, so far as professional fees were concerned.'

She gave him a sly look. 'You must admit, knowing Merseycredit would pay the bill made you willing to give me top priority.'

'That wasn't just because of the costs.'

'Oh?' Her lips parted a little. 'And what other reason could there be?'

He was tempted to explain her resemblance to Liz. But he told himself this was neither the time nor the place. Outside his fantasies, there never would be a right time and place so far as he and Debbie Warrington were concerned.

Before he could decide what to say, a loud thump could be heard from the room with the playpen. It was followed at once by a squeal of dismay.

'Oh God, it's Rainbow! I won't be a minute.'

During her brief absence he mulled over what he should do. He was vaguely conscious that something she had said to him had a deeper significance for him than she had intended, but he could not pin it down. As he heard her coming back, he tossed the deeds envelope on to one of the occasional tables.

'I don't think you're cut out for nannying.'

'I'll have to iron plenty more sleepsuits before I can afford to go to Spain now,' she said. After a pause, she added, 'If I get the chance.'

'Meaning?'

She gazed at him. 'Well, it all depends on you, doesn't it? Whether you shop me or not.'

He pointed to the deeds. 'Put them back in the bureau. Stuart will never know they've gone walkies.'

'What about the Ambroses?'

Chapter Twenty-Two

'No problem. They want out, you want out.'

Of course it was more complicated than that; Stanley Rowe would not easily be persuaded to waive his fee. The mischievous thought occurred to him that Geoffrey Willatt would be delighted to settle for the estate agent's costs if his clients could reclaim the balance of their deposit. Harry saw scope for a little rough justice of a kind likely to cause apoplexy if the Solicitors' Disciplinary Tribunal ever got to hear of it. But perhaps not even he would be quixotic enough to risk his practising certificate for the sake of a neat solution to someone else's problem.

Debbie was staring at him. He could almost believe there was awe in her expression, as if she were a trainee escapologist, taking a masterclass from Houdini.

'Is that it?'

'What else is there? Find another job, why don't you? Write this one off to experience and leave crime to criminals. Sooner or later you'll realise you've been lucky.'

She breathed out and glanced heavenwards. He guessed a silent prayer had been answered.

'Lucky to have been dealing with a human being, for sure. Funny, I used to be desperate to shake the Liverpool dust from my feet. Now I'm not so sure.'

He couldn't help smiling. Perhaps he had achieved something.

'Phil was never going to be the love of a lifetime,' she continued. 'When I was a small girl I used to dream one day I would meet a man I could die for. Well, I've not had much luck in finding him so far.'

'A man you could die for,' repeated Harry slowly. A vague idea began to form in his mind.

She smiled, pleased he was responding to her fantasy. 'Yes, I always wanted that grand passionate affair. One that mattered more than anything else in the world.'

'Be careful,' he said. 'We pay a price for those passionate moments.'

She gave him a quizzical look. 'I suppose I ought to try something new. Perhaps – I might even pick your brains sometime. We could have a drink one evening, if you were willing. What do you say?'

He returned her gaze. Her resemblance to Liz was stronger than ever; Debbie too was a modern Micawber, forever optimistic that something would turn up. He would find it easy to say yes to her. Yet he knew he had to learn to stop believing in ghosts.

'I don't think that would be such a good idea.'

'In that case,' she said ruefully, 'I suppose we'd better say goodbye. I have plenty to do before the Graham-Browns get home.'

'At least it still *is* their home,' he said.

She laughed and led him to the front door. 'Yes. They'll never know what a narrow escape they had. Thanks for everything, Harry. Who knows, we may bump into each other again one day.'

He hesitated as he stepped past her into the cold air of the afternoon. As his cheek brushed her hair he was seized by a fierce urge to put his arms round her, but he conquered it in a split second and did not look back until he was half a dozen paces down the path. She was framed in the doorway, an attractive, naive young woman. Not a ghost at all.

'Take care of yourself,' he said. 'I'll remember you.'

Chapter Twenty-Three

He arrived back at the office on the stroke of five. Despite his lack of sleep, he felt as though he had gained new strength. So much remained unclear to him, but on the drive home from Crow's Nest House, he had made a promise to himself. Before the day was through, he would come face to face with Finbar's killer.

Suzanne was preparing to leave for the day, gathering her bits and pieces together, checking her make-up in a pink pocket mirror. She glanced ostentatiously at her watch as he strode past her and clicked her tongue in reproof.

'You never gave me any idea when you'd be back,' she said. 'I didn't know what to tell your client.'

He swung round and saw Melissa sitting in the corner. She was warmly wrapped in suede coat and cashmere scarf, but he could sense she was trembling.

'Sorry, I didn't realise... Have you been here long?'

'Only a few minutes,' she said. 'Don't worry, it's my fault. I didn't make an appointment. I wanted to talk to you face to face, so I simply turned up on the off-chance you'd be around.'

'Come through,' he said and led her to his room. 'And how are you?'

A shadow crossed her face. 'I saw the police again this morning. They took a statement which confirmed everything I told them last night – about Finbar's coming to see me, our row, the time he left, that sort of thing.'

'You could have called me. I'd have sat in, if you'd wished.'

She twisted a loose thread from one of her gloves between her fingers. 'I was grateful for your help last night, Harry – for rushing round at a moment's notice when I called. You were kind and I didn't appreciate it.'

'Forget it. We were both shocked by Finbar's death.'

'You – you were a good friend to him. Better than he deserved. Which is why you wanted to press me on what happened between us yesterday afternoon, and why I could read your suspicions of me on your face.'

'I was only—'

'And why I came to my senses this morning and saw I was putting you in an impossible position, asking you to help me when, for all you knew, I might have been the person who ran Finbar down.'

Harry could feel his cheeks burning. She was right: foolish to deny it.

'So I decided today I mustn't presume on you any more. I went out and hired another solicitor: Quentin Pike of Windaybanks. I've heard you mention his name in the past, I remember you saying he was good.'

Her logic was impeccable. The previous night he'd been aware, as Sladdin had, of the incongruity of his assisting a woman who might have been responsible for Finbar's death. Yet perversely he felt a stab of rejection; it was as if he had been judged and found wanting, for owing allegiance to a dead man.

'I understand.'

'Judging by your expression, I doubt it. I suppose you think I'm ungrateful. That's why I came here, so I could explain personally, rather than in a note or on the phone.'

'Well… thanks for that. And you've done the right thing. Quentin is a good brief.'

'Yes, he didn't let Sladdin's sidekicks hassle me. They were left in no doubt I was helping them out of public spirit.' She gave him a faint smile. 'He portrayed me as the grieving girlfriend. I almost believed him myself.'

'And how do you really feel?'

She passed her tongue across her lips. 'I'm – I'm too numb to mourn Finbar at the moment. What I'll think when the shock subsides, I simply can't imagine. The last time I saw him alive, I wished him dead.'

'And you tried to make your wish come true.'

'With the scissors? Oh, Harry, I just lashed out! It was a momentary aberration, nothing more. You can't seriously believe I would kill in cold blood?'

The pupils of her eyes were dilated. Because of fear about what his answer may be? He thought not.

'No,' he said. 'All the same, I'm sure his death was not a cool premeditated crime.'

'So who is your prime suspect – other than me?'

'Where do you begin with a man like Finbar? I suppose you could point the finger at Sophie. She says she was with Nick Folley last night. That's untrue, which puts her in the frame – and maybe him as well.'

'You don't – you don't suspect Nick of being driven to murder by jealousy?'

'Who knows?' Harry watched for her reaction. 'He'd already lost you to Finbar, then history repeated itself with Sophie. But there may be some other motive, with roots in the past. Had Finbar known Nick for as long as he'd known Sophie, by any chance?'

'I don't follow you. He hadn't known Sophie long at all, only since I made the mistake of asking Baz to have him on *Pop In*. A matter of days, in other words. Finbar was a fast worker, don't forget.'

Harry knitted his brow. 'I thought he and Sophie went back a long way together?'

'Never. Until this last summer she had a job down south. You surely don't think she picked up that la-di-da accent round here?'

'Has she spent time in Dublin, then?'

'If so, it wasn't on her CV. It passed over my desk when she applied to Radio Liverpool – I was working for Nick at the time, of course. Christ, if I'd guessed what a prize bitch she would turn out to be, I'd have shredded the thing before he ever clapped eyes on it!'

Harry nodded absently, trying to take in what she had told him. If she was right, it turned his ideas upside down. He felt a surge of adrenalin. Instinct told him the solution to the puzzle was almost within his grasp.

She stood up. 'Well, I won't keep you any longer.'

'I'm glad you hired Pike. You did the right thing.'

'No hard feelings, then?'

'Course not. But...'

He hesitated. Even as he spoke he was still trying to untangle the skein of suspicions in his mind.

'Yes?'

He gnawed at his lower lip. *Go for it*, he told himself.

'I do have one last question.'

'Ask away.'

'Melissa,' he said softly, 'where do you get your cocaine?'

She cried out, a sharp yelp of panic mixed with shame. A frail hand flew up to cover her mouth.

'What – what do you mean?'

'Finbar told me you'd been on drugs. I misunderstood at the time, didn't pay much attention. I thought he was talking about treatment you'd had for your nerves. But of course he meant nose candy. I should have recognised the physical symptoms – I've acted for other coke addicts in my time.'

She stared at him, transfixed with dismay, unable to utter a word.

'Please,' he said in his gentlest tone, 'I'd like to help. Not as a lawyer, but as a friend. If you'll only tell me…'

'Help?' At last her tongue was loosened. 'Help? You can't be serious, Harry. No one can help me, the mess I'm in. Do you hear? No one!'

And before he could stop her, she had rushed out through the door. He stood listening to the clatter of her heels along the corridor. Thank God Suzanne had gone. Two women had run out on him inside one day; people would start to talk.

He paced around his office, striving to order his thoughts. What to do now? He wandered through the building, checking that all the staff had left for the day, before walking to the front door, where he could make out no more than the dim outlines of the boarded-up construction site on the opposite side of the courtyard.

The boots of an approaching figure crunched towards him. From the murk emerged a spectral figure, clad in heavy anorak and gauntlets. The man pushed back his hood, revealing carroty hair and prominent rabbit's teeth. Harry recognised him as the landlord's agent, someone with whom he'd exchanged occasional words of greeting since the construction work began.

Good. The chance encounter gave him the chance to test another of the ideas taking shape inside his head. He called out: 'So what happened to McCray's men?'

'What d'you think? They split as soon as they found out they weren't getting paid. The buggers may be Irish, but they're not bloody daft.'

'Money trouble?'

'Too bleeding right. McCray's gone bust.'

Harry nodded. So his latest guess was confirmed; in the end the right answer had been the obvious one. Builders went out of business all the time. And with his own eyes he'd seen McCray haggling with that bespoke-tailored usurer Stuart Graham-Brown.

'When did the news break?'

'First thing this morning. He's been paying the men late, they've been threatening to walk out on the job for long enough. Seems he told them he hoped to put some deal in place last night. It didn't come off and there were no wage packets this morning, so that was that as far as they were concerned.' The rabbity man spat on the ground before adding, 'Can't say I bloody blame 'em either – thought it puts me in a spot. I have to check everything's secure till we get another outfit in to take over the contract. Even on a night like this, stuff walks if you don't keep an eye out.'

Chapter Twenty-Three

Harry leaned forward, conviction that he must talk to the builder growing within him. 'So what's happened to Dermot McCray?'

'Christ knows. Drowning his sorrows, if I know him. He's been at it for months, that's why he's let the business run down.'

'His daughter died, didn't she?'

'Right. He's not been the same bloody feller since.'

'Any idea where he drinks?'

'The De Valera, as a rule. It's that Irish club at the top end of town. The lads used to reckon he spends more time there than he does at home. Why d'you ask?'

'I'd like to have a word with him.'

'Owes you a few bob, does he?' The rabbity face brightened at the prospect of someone else's misfortune. 'You'll get no change out of Dermot McCray. He's a hard bugger at the best of times. You'll be whistling for your cash.'

Harry hurried to his MG. The fog was starting to thicken and as he drove the poor visibility tested concentration to its limits. But his mind kept straying from the road as he tried to decide how to tackle Dermot McCray.

A couple of hundred yards up Islington, he parked on a double yellow line and threaded through an alley clogged with broken bottles and polythene sacks overflowing with noxious rubbish. An amber-eyed cat hissed in warning as he approached the entrance to the De Valera. He banged on the door and was answered by a nattily suited man barely half the size of Mad Max at the Dangerous Liaison.

'If it isn't Harry Devlin!'

'Evening, Liam.'

They had met before, in the Dock Brief; Finbar had done the introductions. Liam Keogh was an amiable, balding man whose fondness for the sound of his own voice combined dangerously with an excessive interest in other people's affairs. He was the friend to whom Finbar had unwisely confided his involvement with Eileen McCray – events had proved that equivalent to taking out a prime-time slot on commercial television. The McCrays had learned the story and before long Sinead had got to hear of it too. Liam's careless talk might easily have cost lives. Yet there was little malice in him and Harry did not doubt the genuineness of his grief when he spoke again.

'Harry, it's grand to see you. But faith, what a bad business about Finbar!'

They exchanged words of reminiscence. Here was someone else who had been fond of Finbar, Harry thought. It wasn't true that everyone his client met had become an enemy. He'd roused strong reactions in people – that was nearer the mark.

'I need to speak to someone and he may be here,' said Harry as soon as an opportunity presented itself. 'I'm not a member, and I'm not after a drink, so I wondered if—'

'We don't stand on ceremony with people we know. Who is it you're after seeing?'

'Dermot McCray.'

Liam's eyebrows shot up. He lowered his voice and with a conspiratorial glance said, 'You know that Finbar and Dermot's daughter...'

'Yes. Is Dermot here?'

Liam took a look at Harry and decided the time was not ripe for casual gossip. 'You're in luck. He showed up not half an hour ago. You'll find him downstairs, supping a pint of Guinness and keeping his own counsel. He's had a lot on his mind since Eileen died. She was the very apple of his eye. And now people say his business is on the skids.'

'Listen, last time McCray and I met, we got off on the wrong foot. Can you keep him from slamming his pint pot in my face while I ask him a few questions?'

Liam tapped his finger against his nose. 'Trust me.' He led Harry down an ill-lit corridor lined with sepia-tinted pictures from the 1916 Rebellion. The decor was a dull dark green; a musty smell hung in the air. Harry sensed this was a place for brooding over old battles, a place where grievances could harden into bigotry and anger corrode into a lust for violence.

Dermot McCray was sitting on a stool at the far end of the bar, nursing his Guinness and contemplating the dreariness of his surroundings without visible emotion.

'Dermot, lad, can I crave a boon? A good friend of mine would welcome a word with you.'

McCray looked at Harry. Scorn tugged at the corners of his mouth. 'You ought to choose your pals with more care, Liam Keogh.'

'Dermot, I gather you and Harry haven't altogether seen eye to eye in the past. But why don't you let the feller buy you another pint and see if you can't both bury the hatchet?'

'Best place for the hatchet is in this sod's back.' McCray drained his glass. 'Anyway, what's it to do with you, Devlin? Your client, that fucking tattooist – he's dead, isn't he?'

'I expect you're celebrating,' said Harry.

'Finest news I've heard in a long while.' But McCray's face betrayed no satisfaction. His eyes were bloodshot, his skin grey. Eileen's death had eaten at him like a cancer; Harry could identify the signs. He suddenly experienced a burst of fellow feeling for the big brutish Irishman.

Chapter Twenty-Three

'I do need to talk to you.'

McCray grunted in derision. 'Come to make another accusation?'

'I want to ask you about Pearse Cato.'

Chapter Twenty-Four

'What's this got to do with Rogan?' asked Dermot McCray ten minutes later.

'It might explain why he was killed,' said Harry. He felt excited but dazed. Every hour that passed was bringing him closer to the truth.

McCray glared at Liam and jerked a thumb towards Harry. 'Your mate's off his head. Thought so the first time I met him. He reckoned I'd tried to murder Rogan.' A sour quirk of the lips. 'Wish I had.'

Liam looked bewildered by the conversation. 'Harry, I haven't a whore's notion of what you're trying to prove, but you're treading on risky ground for sure.'

'The story of my life,' said Harry. He extended his hand to McCray. 'Thanks for your help – I appreciate it. And I apologise for what I said to you at Fenwick Court the other day. I was on the wrong track.'

McCray looked at the hand, then grunted and looked away. 'Rogan killed my Eileen. Same as if he'd shot her between the eyes.'

'He's dead now,' said Harry. 'She's been avenged.'

McCray's face might have been part of Mount Rushmore. He gazed into the depths of his glass as Harry and Liam walked slowly back to the stairs.

'You mind how you go,' said the doorman as they approached the exit. 'Lord knows what you're up to, but whatever it is, I don't like it. You're talking about serious business here.'

'Cato's even colder than Finbar,' said Harry. 'There's nothing to fear from him.'

'You don't understand what you're messing with. If the men in balaclavas killed Finbar…'

'No, they never touched him.'

'What? I thought you were suggesting…'

Harry pulled open the door giving on to the alley. Curls of mist wafted inside the building and the fog outside had thickened.

'I was suggesting nothing, Liam. Thanks for introducing me to McCray. Without you, I'd not have got a word out of him.'

Spreading his arms, Liam waved away gratitude. 'All I ask is, when you do figure out who ran Finbar down, you let me know. I'd like five minutes with the bastard before the police get involved.

Harry stepped out into the murk, edging towards the MG like a blind man deprived of dog and stick. He was glad that at least the fog in his own head was starting to clear.

Once back at his flat, he tossed a pre-cooked meal into the microwave before scouring through his cupboards and wardrobe.

As if in preparation for a jumble sale, he gathered together oddments of clothing he should have thrown out years ago: a black three-piece suit which had scarcely fitted in his days as a trainee lawyer, when he was ten years younger and did not have a beer gut; a graduation gown borrowed from a fellow Polytechnic student who had not wanted its return; an old bow tie, souvenir of Harry's one and only attendance at a Law Society Dinner; a plain white shirt which testified to his lack of expertise with an iron.

Having eaten, he changed into the outfit he had assembled. Then, after slicking back his hair with the pungent lotion a distant relative had given him one long-forgotten Christmas, he stood in front of the bedroom mirror and experimented with a lascivious smile.

A charity shop Dracula leered back at him. He lacked the aristocratic mien of the Transylvanian count, but at least the dramas of the past twenty-four hours had drained all colour from his cheeks, obviating the need for make-up. A pity he didn't have sharper teeth or longer nails.

On his way out of the flat he noticed a screwed-up ball of paper lurking in a corner of the living room. Curious, he smoothed it out. What he saw on the sheet startled him for a moment, before he realised that it reinforced the idea which had already established itself in his mind: the idea which offered an explanation for Finbar's fate.

He walked the short distance through the gloom to Empire Hall. A couple of petite Scouse girls dressed as hobgoblins were on the main door, checking invitations and collecting coats and scarves.

'Rosemary and Stuart Graham-Brown invited me.'

'Of course we did,' cackled a warty-faced witch standing in the entrance lobby. Harry took a couple of startled seconds to penetrate the crone's disguise. 'Hello, Rosemary.'

'How marvellous you've been able to come,' said his hostess, reverting to her usual tone and doffing her impossibly tall steeple hat in welcome. 'A good many of our guests are already inside, but a few fainthearts have cried off because of the weather. Thanks for making the effort.'

'I only live around the corner.'

Not that it mattered, he thought. He would have battled through fog all night long for the chance of catching up with Finbar's killer.

'Let's go through.' She took his arm and guided him into the concert room. A grey phantom shimmered towards them, bearing a tray of drinks.

'Will you have a drop of punch?' she asked. He recognised the voice of the girl from Merseycredit's exhibition stand. 'Or do you only drink blood?'

'I had a bite before I came out,' he said.

As Rosemary laughed, he surveyed his surroundings. This evening the lights were low in Empire Hall. Black cats cut out of cardboard prowled along the walls; broad-winged bats and ravens swooped down from the ceiling. The demonic faces of hollowed-out pumpkins with lighted candles inside grinned at him from every nook and cranny. Already the place was filling with representatives of the city's financial services sector, disguised with unconscious irony as an unholy gathering of demons. As yet there was no sign of the person Harry sought.

Misreading his mind, Rosemary said, 'Hallowe'en is such a fascinating time, don't you agree?' She cackled again. 'The day when the souls of the dead revisit their homes. A time to placate the supernatural powers.'

'I'd never have suspected you of an interest in pagan rites.'

'What else is consumer credit? Don't tell Stuart I said so, mind. Ah, talk of the devil…'

A hideous monster from the bowels of hell put a clawed hand on Rosemary's rump, then pulled off his weirdly misshapen head to reveal the grey hair and charm-laden smile of Stuart Graham-Brown.

'Grand to see you, Harry. Is my wife looking after you?' He squeezed Rosemary's shoulder. 'You seem to have cheered up, darling. This afternoon you were breathing fire and brimstone, weren't you?'

'Practising for tonight?' asked Harry.

'No, no,' said Graham-Brown. 'You remember at lunchtime we boasted about our nanny? When we arrived home this evening, to check all was well with Rainbow before coming over here, we found Debbie with her bags packed and an immediate notice of resignation in her hand. I was livid. Told her she was in breach of contract.'

'And how did she react to that?'

Chapter Twenty-Four

'Said she had the best lawyer in Liverpool and would see me in court. Stupid little bitch – as if I would believe for a minute that she could afford Maher and Malcolm's fees! Anyway, you won't mind if we circulate?'

Stuart was wearing a dog collar and a lead which Rosemary grasped between forefinger and thumb. With a hiss of pleasure, she led her husband away to meet a group of newly-arrived guests.

As Harry finished his drink someone behind him whispered, 'You'd better take care when the eats are brought round. They're covered with garlic.'

He spun round and came face to face with Sophie Wilkins. A white dress clung to her with a sensuality which mocked its virginal high neck and she was carrying a posy of dried flowers. A huge ersatz diamond ring glinted from the third finger of her left hand.

'The undead can never be too careful,' he assured her. 'You can bet I won't be crossing the Mersey tonight.'

She giggled and he guessed she had been making free with the punch. Drink had washed away the hostility she had shown earlier in the day.

'Have you guessed who I am?'

'Bride of Frankenstein?'

She clapped her hands. 'Well done! You really are a detective!'

'Dare I ask who Frankenstein is?'

'One guess.'

'Nick Folley? Thought as much. Is he here?'

'Somewhere around. But what brings you to this jamboree?'

'I came to find out the truth about Finbar's death.'

'Don't you ever give up?'

'Life's too short for giving up.'

She sighed. The drinks passed by again and she helped herself from the tray. As she moved closer to him, he could feel her warm breath on his face.

'I lied to you about last night.'

'I know you didn't spend it with Nick.'

'You see, he had work to finish before he caught the London train. I left him to it, went home alone.'

'Why did you lie?'

'You had no right to ask! You're not the police. I'd been shocked by the news, I couldn't think straight. I didn't want Finbar's lawyer to start accusing me of murder.'

'So you no longer have an alibi – and Finbar called to see you yesterday afternoon. I hear you didn't part the best of pals. Perhaps you followed him to the Colonial Dock and seized the chance to run him down.'

His suggestion sobered her. 'Not even you can believe that.'

'So what did happen?'

'He turned up without warning. He'd had a few drinks and Melissa had shown him the door less than half an hour earlier. He had the nerve to say he'd enjoyed my company at the Blue Moon and hoped we could get it together again. So I gave it to him straight, told him I wouldn't be seen dead in bed with him again. An unfortunate choice of words, in the circumstances...'

'How did he react?'

'In his usual win-a-few, lose-a-few way. As if he simply had to turn over another page of his little red book.'

'And how did you spend the evening?'

'At home. Alone – I took a bottle of gin to bed with me rather than a man. Sorry, no proof – except in the alcohol.'

She put her glass and the flowers down on the floor and stood facing him with her hands on her hips, challenging him to call her a liar. He didn't much like Sophie Wilkins, but the misery in her expression touched him. He had to feel sorry for a woman so desperate for Frankenstein as to want to be his bride.

Rosemary Graham-Brown had found a microphone to welcome guests; she was promising them a night to remember. The phrase reminded Harry of the *Titanic*, which had sailed proudly from Liverpool to death and disaster.

'We're honoured that Radio Liverpool will be broadcasting live from here later tonight as we celebrate Hallowe'en in a very special way with that enormously popular disc jockey – Mr Baz Gilbert!'

As applause broke out, Sophie shook her head. 'A guy with Baz's talent reduced to this kind of crap! God, how demeaning.'

'People say he's been unlucky, and I'm beginning to believe it. But why did he never make it into the big time?'

'Who knows? He looks the part and he certainly has more talent than half the kids on Radio One these days. I suppose he's simply been in the wrong place at the wrong time. Perhaps it runs in the family.'

'How do you mean?'

'Haven't you heard about his brother John? It's a tragic story. They were identical twins: very close, by all accounts. John was in the Army.'

Harry cast his mind back to a conversation at the Russian Convoy and his appearance on *Pop In*.

'I remember – he has a photograph in the studio.'

'Right. John was on a tour of duty in Belfast when terrorists killed him. They lured the poor kid to one of their strongholds and tortured him before blowing his head off.'

Ireland again, thought Harry. *Whichever way I turn, I find myself looking across the Irish Sea.*

There were two questions he must ask. The first was one he'd kept forgetting to put to the Radio Liverpool crowd. To begin with, he'd had no more than idle curiosity about the answer; now he thought it crucial to the secret of Finbar's death.

'Can you cast your mind back to the morning Finbar appeared on *Pop In*?'

Sophie looked baffled. 'Will I ever forget it? I'd never met him until then. God, if only I hadn't been there that day!'

'He caused a fuss, didn't he, over his choice of music?'

'That's right,' she said. 'He kept changing his mind about his favourite song. It sticks out in my mind, because he was behaving so oddly.'

'What did he do?'

'He'd opted at first for a track by the Dubliners – lively Irish stuff. After he got in the studio he suddenly decided he wanted something different. By Val Doonican, of all people! Not my idea of Finbar's taste at all.'

'And the song?'

'An old one, called "Elusive Butterfly". I sent Tracey out in a panic to check our library and we didn't have it. So he laughed as if he was enjoying a huge joke and said he'd settle for an old Number One by Frank Ifield.'

'I might have known,' said Harry. '"I Remember You".'

Chapter Twenty-Five

'I don't understand,' said Sophie, when she had answered his second question.

Harry had anticipated her reply. No doubt was left in his mind that at last he knew the truth.

'You don't need to.'

'Surely you can't imagine that...'

'Never mind my imagination.' He spoke more harshly than he had intended. Sophie had confirmed his suspicions, but that afforded him no pleasure. All he wanted was to bring matters to an end.

'I must be getting back to Baz,' she said. 'Oh – here's Nick!'

Nick Folley approached them, blowing a kiss at Sophie, giving Harry a dismissive nod. His elaborate make-up failed to disguise the self-satisfaction of his features; he gave no hint of the loneliness and misery of Mary Shelley's monster.

Harry tensed. Folley's arrival gave him a chance to put another of his ideas to the test. He recalled that Frankenstein inspired loathing in anyone who saw it: in that, at least, he saw a point of resemblance between Folley and the creature created from the bones of charnel houses.

'Doing any business tonight?' asked Harry, not bothering to hide his contempt.

'You never make much sense to me, Mr Devlin. What kind of business would I be doing?'

'I suppose this kind of event is ideal for trade. Plenty of rich people looking for kicks.'

'What in God's name are you talking about?'

'Cocaine,' said Harry softly. 'Easy money for a man with the right contacts. No wonder people reckon you have the Midas touch. Even if your media ventures run into trouble, there's always a market for drugs in your crowd.

Chapter Twenty-Five

Does Graham-Brown help you launder the cash?'

Folley gave him a hard unblinking stare: a form of cover whilst he thought fast. Harry pressed on.

'When I appeared on *Pop In*, I heard the news about the haul made by Customs and Excise. Was that why you had to slip down to London last night: to pick up alternative supplies so you could be sure of keeping your customers satisfied?'

'You're off your head,' said Folley.

'Nick...' began Sophie.

'Shut it!'

She made as if to voice a protest, then changed her mind and slunk away, dejected. Had she been aware exactly how her lover had made his fortune? Somehow, Harry doubted it.

'What I hate about it all,' he said, 'is the way you treat people. Take Melissa. You make her dependent, then you cast her aside – you even sack her, so—'

Folley leaned forward, his hands on the lapels of Harry's jacket. 'What has Melissa said?'

Harry remembered the man's uncontrollable temper. On another occasion he would have welcomed the chance to hit him, to strike a blow on behalf of lives ruined by addiction. But not tonight. He had so much yet to do.

He squirmed out of Folley's grasp. 'She hasn't betrayed you yet, though God knows why. I hope she'll change her mind.'

With that, he headed off through a group of fiends and phantoms, towards the makeshift studio rigged up on the stage. A glance over his shoulder confirmed that Folley was not in pursuit. Ahead of him, the bearded engineer from *Pop In* was testing for sound levels, whilst Rosemary Graham-Brown chatted to a man with the head of a wolf.

'Baz!' he called. 'I'd like a word.'

The disc jockey pulled off his savage mask, his mouth stretched in a smile that his eyes did not share.

'Doesn't he make a good lycanthrope?' asked Rosemary, with a witch's glee. 'We ought to beware, of course – the werewolf is cursed by a horror that turns him into a murderous beast against his will.'

Baz raised his eyebrows in weary amusement. 'Harry! We must stop meeting like this.'

'I know you're busy, but can you spare me a minute? I'd like to talk in private.'

After a second's hesitation, Baz shrugged. 'Okay. But I don't have long.'

Harry led him to the fire exit at the far end of the room and lifted the bar. It gave onto a space floored with concrete at the foot of an emergency staircase: a cold and gloomy place, with one barred window barely letting through the dull glow from a riverside lamp outside. The echoing of their footsteps contrasted oddly with the muffled noise coming from the other side of the door; the antics of the party-goers seemed suddenly absurd.

Baz leaned against the wall, nonchalant. 'So what's all this about?'

'Your twin. John.'

Baz gnawed at his lower lip. 'What possible interest can you have in my brother?'

'He was killed by Irish terrorists, isn't that right? And specifically, I would guess, by a man called Pearse Cato.'

Baz straightened and clenched his fist. Even mention of the name seemed to anger him.

'So people say. No one was ever convicted and the victim's family is never told exactly who tore them apart. But you're right – the powers-that-be, as well as the media, always reckoned Cato was responsible.'

'You know he died a couple of years ago?'

A bitter smile twisted Baz's lips. 'The news I'd prayed for ever since John was murdered. I wish I could meet the men who gunned him down, simply to shake them by the hand.'

'You wanted vengeance?'

'Who wouldn't? I loved John. There's a special bond between twins. We went our separate ways, of course. He joined the Army, all I wanted was to work in the music business. Even so, we stayed close – never rivals, simply the best of friends.'

'What do you know about his death?'

Baz shut his eyes. Harry wished he had not needed to put the question, forcing recollection of the past. He guessed that the memory of John Gilbert's murder was never far from the disc jockey's thoughts.

'He was shot through the head. Not before Cato had hurt him cruelly. It was all so cowardly, so sick. How any human being can—'

Baz broke off. His eyes were open again and filling with tears. 'What is it to you? John's dead, Cato's dead: we're talking about history.'

'Don't they say old sins cast long shadows?'

'I don't know what you're talking about.'

Harry sucked in his cheeks. He'd reached the point of no return.

'Finbar Rogan came from the same street as Pearse Cato. Were you aware of that?'

Chapter Twenty-Five

Baz stared at him. 'No. Not at all. But – what of it? Finbar was many things, by all accounts, but you're surely not telling me he was a terrorist.'

'No, but...'

Something inside Baz seemed to break. His face grew tight and ugly, as if he were wearing the wicked mask again. He seized Harry's wrist in a painful grip and spoke in a croaky whisper. 'Christ knows why you're raking over the old embers, but I don't like it. Take my advice, Harry Devlin – keep your nose out.'

'Darling, you're wanted!'

The soft urgent voice of Penny Newland startled both men. She stood behind them, framed in the doorway. At the sight of her, Baz released his hold. Harry rubbed his wrist; when he looked at the girl, she turned crimson.

'You're due on soon,' she told her boyfriend. 'Sophie wants you behind the mike. Come on. I'll stay here for a bit – I need to talk to Harry.'

As Baz moved back towards the party, Harry looked straight at the girl; something in his expression seemed to hypnotise her. Baz brushed her neck with his lips, but she remained motionless.

As soon as her boyfriend had disappeared, Harry nodded at Penny. 'Over here,' he mouthed.

As if in a trance, she shut the door behind her and walked towards him, her high heels clicking on the concrete. She too was clad as a vampire, all in black with flowing cape, minidress and patterned stockings. The whiteness of her complexion contrasted with the scarlet of her lips and talons. Beneath the neck of her cape he caught a glimpse of ivory shoulders.

She stopped within touching distance of him. 'What do you want of me?'

'I think you know.'

'You tell me.'

She folded her arms, as if determined to test her will against his.

His whole body tingled with excitement and fear. He sensed that during the next few minutes, the course of a human life would change.

'Let's start with how John Gilbert died.'

She was standing in shadow. It was too dark to read her expression.

'Now then,' she said in her soft Irish accent, 'what more is there to say about John Gilbert's death?'

He ran his tongue over his lips. Any man would find her attractive, he thought: the thick dark hair, the almost perfect features, the bare white skin and the body-hugging dress. Penny Newland was an exciting woman.

'I believe there's a link with the killing of Finbar Rogan.'

'And what might that link be?'

He leaned forward. She took a couple of steps back, pinning herself in a corner by the bottom of the stairs. Advancing, he felt her shrink away from him.

'You,' he said. 'Finbar remembered you.'

She closed her eyes, seeming to hold her breath for a long moment before answering.

'And I… I could never forget him. Hard though I tried, it simply wasn't possible.'

She breathed out and bowed her head. It seemed to him that she had come to a decision.

'You see, Harry, he left his mark on me.'

As he watched in silence, she fiddled with the strings knotted at her neck and the cape slipped silently to the floor. Taking the narrow straps of her dress in the crook of each forefinger, she eased them downwards. With the straps off her shoulders, she began to peel the velvet from her, pausing only when her large dark nipples were exposed. His mouth was dry and when at last he spoke, his voice was hoarse.

'The elusive butterflies.'

And he ran the tips of his fingers over the exquisite insects that, long ago, Finbar Rogan had tattooed on the breasts of the woman who would one day run him down.

Chapter Twenty-Six

She closed her eyes and breathed deeply. The tattooed breasts rose and fell. The butterflies were beautiful; Harry contemplated his dead client's artistry with something close to wonder. After a little while she pulled the dress up again, concealing the final clue he had sought. Opening her eyes slowly, she spoke in the softest of whispers.

'When I saw you lead Baz out here, I knew you'd discovered my secret. I was afraid you would. From the moment I met you, I could tell you were determined, that you never let go.'

'I don't know the whole story, though I've worked out a great deal.'

'And the police?'

'I haven't told them about you.'

'They'll find out before long, won't they? Someone caught sight of me last night. God – last night! It feels like a lifetime ago.'

'Who saw you?'

'A courting couple. They came driving up as I stood over Finbar's body. Why I needed to check he was dead, I can't explain; I'd not only run him down, but reversed back and forward over his body to make sure. I could… I could feel him beneath my wheels.'

She shuddered. Harry could sense her re-living the moment when she snuffed out a life.

'Anyway, this car trapped me in its headlights. I was temporarily blinded, but then I made out a girl in the passenger seat, staring at me. She turned to the driver and he put his foot down and accelerated out of sight. They had plenty of time to get an idea of my appearance. I expect they'll come forward, once they hear the police appeal for witnesses.'

'Not necessarily. They may have something to hide.'

'Don't we all? For a short while last night, I thought I could trust Finbar to take his pound of flesh, then leave me in peace. Stupid of me. And soon everyone will know.'

'That you were Pearse Cato's lover?'

Penny shivered. 'He was an evil man.'

'So how did you get mixed up with him?'

'I was only a kid from a village in County Limerick: a seventeen-year-old virgin by the name of Edna Doyle. I'd not been able to find work near home, so I decided to try my luck in Dublin – the big city. In the end, I took a job in a bar near Trinity College. I was so naive. I didn't realise it was a haven for men with more of a thirst for blood than for booze. And that's where I met Pearse Cato.'

'He picked you up?'

'Oh, he made it clear from day one he was doing me a favour. I was nothing – a colleen from the countryside – while he was a big shot. In more ways than one, though I didn't learn for a while how handy he was with an Armalite. He had other women, he was too vain to bother to conceal the truth. I was a possession. He even had me branded as his personal property.'

'The butterflies?'

'Yes. He said tattoos on women turned him on, but I think it was something more than that. He wanted my body to bear his insignia permanently, so that although one day he would tire of me, I would never be free of him.'

A tremor ran through her body. He wanted to put his arms round her, but knew it would be the wrong thing to do.

'I'll never forget the pain. I thought it would never end and I screamed in agony – it was like an injection coupled with a dentist's drill. But even worse was watching my body being disfigured forever on a psychopath's whim.'

Harry flinched. He could almost feel the tip of the needle entering his own skin. So much for the romance of carrying your life history on your flesh.

'And you got to know Finbar?'

'Yes. He twitched at the mention of Cato's name – no shame in that, most people did. He'd grown up in the same street, he knew what Cato was capable of. I could tell he fancied me, but he didn't dare do anything about it. If Cato had found anyone messing around with me, he'd have gone berserk. A word out of place could cost a man his kneecaps. Try to take Cato's woman and he'd have you begging for a swift end.' She touched the place where her cheek was marked. 'This scar is the legacy of a small disagreement we had. I had the temerity to argue with him about the armed struggle. He soon put me right.'

Nausea swamped Harry. 'How could you stand living with him?'

'Strange what you can get used to when you have no choice. Cato wasn't a man you jilted. I once heard of a girl who did exactly that, before I met him.

Chapter Twenty-Six

One night, a couple of masked men jumped out on her as she was walking home. They threw acid in her face and ruined it, as well as blinding her in one eye. Then they crippled her new feller for good measure.'

'So how did you get away?'

'He wanted me to do something, to stay in Belfast with a friend of his called Fitz. I was to go with Fitz's sister one night to a bar in a Prot area. British soldiers used to frequent the place, you see. We were supposed to chat up a couple of them, let them think they were in for an easy lay. We had to invite them home, then lead them instead to Fitz's flat.'

'And?'

'Cato never told me more than he thought I needed to know. All the same, you didn't need to be a genius to guess what would happen to the Brits. He was ordering me to lead them to their deaths.'

'And did you?'

'No!'

Her denial was passionate and he did not doubt its truth. Next door he could hear Baz chatting to the audience. The party was in full swing.

'So you disobeyed Cato?'

'I pretended to be sick, feigned bad stomach pains. I managed to convince the doctor I was dying and he rushed me into hospital. Cato didn't visit me. He'd wanted his killings to coincide with some bloody Republican anniversary or other. He left for the North, to make sure someone would die on schedule, whether I did his dirty work or not.' She winced at the recollection. 'First chance I got, I discharged myself from hospital, headed for Dun Laoghaire. I'd taken a case with me and I'd packed all the clothes and money I could lay my hands on – precious little it amounted to. I caught the ferry to Holyhead and hitched all the way to Liverpool. I reckoned it was time to begin again.'

'So you became Penny Newland?'

She contrived a faint smile. 'Because I found a bedsitter in Penny Lane. Could have been worse – I might have become Miss Upper-Parliament, if I'd lived a couple of roads away.' The smile faded. 'I had to bury the past. If Pearse Cato had ever caught up with me, I'd have been dead meat. And as soon as I got off the boat I couldn't miss the story in the papers, about the murder of a young soldier over in Northern Ireland. He was called John Gilbert. The surname meant nothing to me then, of course.'

'When did you get into local radio?'

'At first, I tried what I knew best, working behind a bar. I served pints morning, noon and night till I'd saved enough to take a secretarial course so I could find myself a better job. A year ago I fetched up at Radio Liverpool and met Baz. The rest you know.' She paused. 'Or do you? Exactly what was it brought you here?'

A long trail, he thought. Debbie, of all people, had given him a clue; she'd spoken of the kind of man a woman could die for. Might a man who engendered such strength of passion also be one that a woman could kill for? He'd been thinking idly – perhaps enviously – of the devotion Penny showed at every turn to Baz. When Melissa told him Finbar's acquaintance with Sophie did not in fact date back over the years, he had puzzled over the identity of the girl whom Finbar had hoped to meet at the Danger, after running into her again on the day of the fire. The day of his appearance on *Pop In*.

Could it have been Penny? She had an Irish accent and in the theatre bar Baz had implied that she'd dropped into the studio – in the way people often did – whilst Finbar was on the air. Harry recalled Finbar having a private word with Penny during the exhibition; he'd hinted he knew her. And Harry recalled what Debbie had said about changing her identity, making a new start. A new start – in a new land?

So he'd checked with Dermot McCray, who made gruff reference to rumours that Finbar had once tattooed the breasts of Pearse Cato's girlfriend and that when she'd run out on the terrorist, he'd vowed to kill her. But she had disappeared for good.

Harry remembered Finbar mentioning a butterfly tattoo whilst he'd dozed in the flat on the night of the exhibition. Try as he might, he couldn't recall details, but once back from the De Valera, he'd uncrumpled the picture Finbar had swiftly sketched to illustrate a story: something about a girl he had an interest in.

When Sophie told him about the song Finbar had chosen on impulse just before going on air, he had hardly needed to confirm that Penny Newland was the marketing manager's secretary whom Finbar had, according to the receptionist at Radio Liverpool, spoken to on the last afternoon of his life. No prizes for guessing that he'd tried his luck with her. But at last that luck had run out.

'Finbar brought me,' he said, finally. 'I felt I owed it to him, to understand why he was killed.'

Penny gazed at him steadily. 'He was a selfish man. Not wicked, like Pearse Cato – I don't claim that I rid the world of a monster, whereas I'd have been glad to fire the bullets that blew out Cato's brains. When I heard the news he was dead, I could scarcely contain my joy. I thought I'd succeeded in destroying my own past.'

Chapter Twenty-Six

'Your path and Finbar's never crossed in Liverpool?'

'Not once. I'd been told Melissa had a new man, but she and I never had much to do with each other. She sat at her desk outside the MD's office and I was downstairs, so I didn't hear the new boyfriend's name and it never crossed my mind it might be Finbar Rogan. I hadn't even heard he'd moved over to England; as far as I knew he was still plying his trade back in Dublin. That's not to say I'd been able to put him out of my mind. After all, I carried his handiwork around with me every day of my life.'

'Didn't Baz ask questions about the butterflies?'

'He's always loved them – poor fool. So perhaps something good did come out of my time with Cato, after all.'

'I suppose it was simply bad luck so far as you were concerned. You dropped in to *Pop In* and, lo and behold, who should be there goggling at you but Finbar Rogan.'

'We knew each other at once. I couldn't believe my eyes. He was too crafty to greet me when Baz and Sophie were there, so he talked about a song called "Elusive Butterfly" and finally plumped for "I Remember You".'

'To leave you in no doubt he knew who you were.'

'When he gave me a ring later that day, he was in high good humour. He seemed to think that having tattooed me gave him some claim over my body. He asked me to meet him at a dive, but though I tried giving him the cold shoulder, it didn't work.' She sighed. 'I was so afraid that if I antagonised him, he'd let it slip that I'd once been the lover of the man who had killed Baz's brother.'

'Did you know about the connection before you became involved with Baz?'

'It cropped up during my earliest days at Radio Liverpool. There had been some outrage in Northern Ireland and Baz seemed very moody when the news was broadcast. Someone said his twin brother had been murdered by a terrorist gunman. The surname rang a bell, so I checked the old newspaper files – and there it was, in black and white, like something out of a nightmare. John Gilbert was Baz's twin. I couldn't believe it.'

'Yet you still got together with Baz?'

'Yes. You'll think this is the stupidity of a callow Irish girl, but I felt somehow it was *meant*. Already by then I fancied him like mad, though he'd never asked me out – at the time, he was getting over a relationship with a girl from a group which used to tour the clubs. John's murder brought us closer together, if anything. Call it fate, if you like. After all, we'd both been victims of Pearse Cato.'

'Why not come clean?'

'Are you serious? It would have finished any chance I had with him. Who wants to sleep with a terrorist's tart? And more than that – I'd done nothing to stop Cato killing John. I could have called the security forces, I've asked myself a thousand times since why I didn't. The truth was, I was scared. It was as much as I could do to pluck up the courage to run away.'

'You could have explained.'

'Baz would never have understood. Believe me, I know him. He was – and is – so bitter about Cato, I knew I'd be tainted for ever in his eyes if he found out the truth. No, it was all the more important for me to keep my identity as Penny Newland if I wanted to win him. And I did. Anyway, in the end Baz started taking notice of me and for a time everything was wonderful.'

'Until Finbar arrived on the scene.'

'He simply would not take no for an answer. The blarney didn't cut any ice with me, but I couldn't shake him off. For God's sake, someone was trying to murder him: the fire, the bomb in the car. And yet he still had only one thing on his mind.'

'He wanted to sleep with you?'

'Well, he dressed it up a little, but I wasn't born yesterday. I grew up a lot during my time in Dublin, and Liverpool was my finishing school in self-preservation. I didn't find it difficult to resist him. But yesterday he came to see me and said he was going to make me an offer I couldn't refuse. He said he'd finished with Melissa and Sophie and would I like to go out with him for a couple of hours in the evening. To talk about old times, he said – there's a euphemism, if ever you heard one!'

'And you agreed?'

'Not at once. I tried to give him the brush off. Looking back, maybe I sounded too cold. Anyway, he dug his heels in and gave a veiled hint that if I didn't say yes, the world and his wife would find out about my background. He knew about John – either Melissa or Sophie must have told him – and he could see Baz was my weak spot. I wouldn't dare do anything which might let the cat out of the bag.'

'Where did you arrange to meet?'

'Outside the Adelphi. He'd hired a car and he'd said he would take me out to some swish place in Crosby. Needless to say, we never made it.' She bowed her head and lapsed into silence. Harry said nothing. He sensed that, in her own good time, she would bring the story to its conclusion.

'He parked up at Colonial Dock,' she said at last. 'I didn't have much choice but to get in the back of the car with him – I'll spare you the details. Anyway, after a while he decided he needed a pee. He pulled himself off me and got out of the car. I saw him stagger thirty yards down the road, then start pissing into a grid. I thought how much I wished him dead. All the time he'd been on top of me, I'd been worrying, what if this isn't the end, but just the beginning? He had a hold over me. All right, most of the time he was harmless enough – but every now and then, when his girlfriend of the day let him down and walked out of the door, he'd remember me. The woman who never would dare to say no.' She sighed, a long low sound. 'You can imagine the rest. I hauled myself into the front of the car. His key was in the ignition and I started the engine the moment he straightened up and turned back to re-join me. Sweet Jesus, I don't think he even bothered to zip his fly!'

Her eyes were unfocused as she remembered. 'I can still see his look as I accelerated towards him. Disbelief was written all over his face. He stood frozen in the road, he didn't even try to dive out of the way. So I hit him.'

'Then drove over him again to make sure.'

She spread her arms, in defensive response to the bitterness in his tone. 'So, Harry Devlin, what will you do? Tell the police? Turn me in?'

'You have a case for claiming it was manslaughter. Find yourself a slick defence lawyer – this city's full of them, we get enough practice. You might only be looking at a couple of years' probation.'

'That doesn't sound like justice. I killed a man.'

'According to you, he as good as asked for it.'

She stepped towards him and a splash of light from the lamps outside fell across her face. He could see in her expression how she was haunted by the past, tormented by what she had done.

'Don't you understand? When I was with Cato, I had enough of death and deceit to last a dozen lifetimes. I thought it hadn't corrupted me, but I was wrong. Killing's got into my blood and no Liverpool lawyer can suck it out.' She laughed, a sharp scornful sound. 'Not even if he's another vampire.'

'So you'll go to the police?' He swallowed, knowing he had to act. He couldn't let her walk free, like Debbie. After all, a man had died. 'If you don't, I must.'

'Of course you must. But right now, I need time to think – face up to things, if you like. Do you mind?'

'I'm not one for making citizen's arrests. Do all the thinking you need.'

She touched his hand before walking towards a door which led out to the river. For a moment she paused with her hand on the metal bar, as if she meant to say something else. But then she stepped into the foggy night and he sensed he would never speak to her again.

Chapter Twenty-Seven

'Did Penny do it deliberately?' asked Jim Crusoe, five days later.

'Oh, she meant to kill Finbar, all right,' said Harry, 'although I'm sure it was a spur of the moment—'

'No, no,' his partner interrupted. 'I was talking about her own death.'

The swollen body of Edna Doyle, also known as Penny Newland, had been washed up at Botanic Dock on the morning of All Saints' Day. A homeless teenager, sleeping rough in the ruins of a disused boatyard, had discovered the corpse. No one could tell how she had come to drown.

'The post mortem confirmed she was alive when she went into the Mersey. There's no question of murder and it may be she lost her footing soon after leaving me. Conditions were treacherous on Hallowe'en. Quite apart from the fog, there were patches of ice on the ground and vandals had made a gap in the walkway railing.'

'Do you seriously believe… hey, look at that!'

Jim was distracted by the first flowering of the fireworks against the night sky. The slivers of silver shone in the dark with a brilliance that shamed the stars.

They were at a Guy Fawkes celebration in Sefton Park. Heather and the kids were a couple of yards away, munching treacle toffee and parkin. For the Crusoes this was a major event in the family calendar and Jim, back in the office again, had urged Harry to join them. Harry could see his partner was bursting with curiosity about the case and he felt talking about it might help him get the whole mess into perspective. Besides, he had reasons of his own to avoid being alone on November 5th.

'You were asking if I thought she fell by chance? I doubt it, but I can't be sure and neither can Sladdin. Either way, nothing will ever be proved.'

'You've talked with the police?'

'At length. Any doubt they had about Penny's guilt evaporated when the witnesses from Colonial Dock turned up: a contract manager from a computer company and his secretary. He'd been hoping his hardware would be compatible with her software, but after seeing Penny drive back and forth over Finbar's body, they didn't feel in the mood for love any longer. Penny's fingerprints were on the car and the fact she didn't wear gloves or even wipe the vehicle tends to confirm she hadn't planned to kill him and panicked when she realised what she had done.'

'Presumably she could have got off lightly with a good brief?'

'People often do. Even some of my own clients.'

'How has Baz reacted?'

'How do you imagine? In the space of forty-eight hours he lost both his job and his girlfriend.'

The Bank That Cares had put Radio Liverpool into receivership, pulling the plug within hours of Nick Folley's arrest for suspected drugs offences. The station had been losing money hand over fist; only the bankers' belief that Folley had the acumen to turn the business around had kept it going so long. As soon as they learned the main source of his income, panic set in.

It seemed the Drugs Squad had been keeping an eye on Folley for months. But evidence had been lacking until the day after the party, when Harry had finally persuaded Melissa to seek long-term treatment for her habit and tell the police all she knew about her former boss's dealings in coke. The Graham-Browns, too, were now helping with enquiries.

Released on bail, Folley had called a press conference. You had to admire his nerve, if nothing else. Sophie Wilkins had been by his side; he'd introduced her to the media as his fiancée and next day the papers had been full of pictures of the glamorous woman willing to stand by her man through thin as well as thick. There could be no sterner test of true love, said Folley.

Questioned about the folding of his company, he had blamed the economic climate and the fickleness of financial institutions. He said he pleaded guilty to having faith in local radio and the good people of Liverpool. The drugs business he described as a stitch-up. He vowed to bounce back.

In closing, he'd paid a special tribute to a junior employee whose death had – he said with a catch in his voice – overshadowed his own personal misfortunes. He hinted that Penny Newland had slipped and fallen into the river while taking a breather from the Hallowe'en broadcast because her mind was distracted by anxiety for the station in which she, like her boss, believed with all her heart.

'Does Baz know the truth?' asked Jim.

'That she killed Finbar for the love of him? No, and the odds are he never will. The inquest is bound to be tricky, but most coroners are discreet. Besides, there's every chance of a verdict of accidental death.'

'And how do you feel about your client, now you've discovered how he treated Penny Newland?'

'I never pretended he was an angel. Dermot McCray put his finger on it when I spoke to him in the De Valera. He said Finbar had always been the same, playing with women like a small kid messing about with his toys. He kept forgetting people are flesh and blood. McCray was thinking of his daughter, but he might as well have meant Sinead or Sophie, Melissa or Penny. The day had to come when the toys grew tired of being flung out of the cot.'

A roar of approval from the crowd greeted the latest rockets to climb towards the moon and dissolve in a spectacular cloudburst of red, white and blue. Harry could not quell the memory of a Guy Fawkes Night in the past, when he'd gone to watch the display at Albert Dock and there met the darkhaired Polish girl who would later become his wife. On each anniversary of that first encounter he found himself replaying old moves, like a defeated chess master, trying to see precisely where the game had begun to slip out of his grasp. With each year that passed he saw more clearly that the outcome had been ordained long before the day he actually lost his queen. They had, from the first, been ill-matched.

Jim's wife and children squelched through the mud towards them; Harry noticed Heather clasping Jim's hand in a gesture of security and shared affection. It made him feel superfluous.

'I'll take a look at the bonfire,' he said.

He walked towards the huge pile of rubbish which was already well ablaze. Young boys and girls jigged and shrieked in front of it: primitives celebrating an ancient rite. A middle-aged woman was collecting for charity and he thrust his hands in his pocket to find some change. As well as the coins he brought out a dog-eared piece of paper. As the woman stuck a badge on his lapel to record him as a giver, he re-read the note he had received that very afternoon.

Harry

I changed my mind and decided to go to Spain after all. I called Phil on the phone – reverse charge! – and he offered to pay my fare out. He's making a killing over there, he says. So, I thought, why not give it a try?

    I'd still like to see you again, to say goodbye properly and thanks for everything. I'm leaving next Saturday. Give me a ring. My mum's number is in the book.

Debbie

Chapter Twenty-Seven

The flames writhed before him like exotic dancers feigning ecstasy. The last fire he had seen had been in Williamson Lane; its vigour was still vivid in his mind. He could still hear Finbar gasping that the heat was a foretaste of hell. Where was the Irishman now?

He moved closer and gazed into the bonfire. Patterns formed and reformed in the blaze. For a second it seemed to him that he saw there the outlines of a familiar face. It belonged not to the girl who had passed herself off as Rosemary Graham-Brown, but to his murdered wife. He squeezed his eyes shut with so much force it hurt.

In this new darkness he could not escape images of violence and death. Before coming out tonight, he'd caught the six o'clock news: in Armagh a man, said to be an army informer, had been gunned down in his own front room, before the eyes of his wife and daughter. Meanwhile FAN! had claimed responsibility for an explosion at a cottage owned by a scientist known for performing experiments on live animals. In interview, a spokesperson for the group stroked a puppy and said he would decline to utter facile words of condemnation. It would not be principled to do so, he explained, when he could understand the frustrations of those who carried out the attack.

Harry thought too about Finbar Rogan. And about Eileen and Sinead and Penny. He'd started by searching for a culprit, but had found only victims.

Opening his eyes, he hurled the note from Debbie into the bonfire. Memories were as treacherous as passions. Maybe there was no escaping them, but he suddenly knew he must break with the past.

The blaze was dying. Its fury was spent and little remained but the dull glow of the embers. The piece of paper lodged on the spike of a scorched twig, where it curled, browned and crumpled, and he watched until nothing was left.

By that time, the face in the flames had disappeared.

Yesterday's Papers – Preview

Book four of the Harry Devlin series

Chapter One

'Mr Devlin, I would like to talk to you about a murder.'

Harry Devlin stopped in his tracks on his way out of the law courts. For a fantastic moment he thought the man who had hurried to catch him up and lay a hand on his shoulder was an arresting officer.

Twisting his neck to see his assailant, Harry found himself staring not at one of Liverpool's finest but at a scrawny old man in a soup-stained bow tie and a shiny blue suit. Although he was wheezing with the exertion, his bony grip was surprisingly fierce, as if he feared Harry was about to take flight. The thick lenses of his spectacles magnified the shape and size of his eyes and made them seem not quite human.

Harry guessed the fellow was one of the city's courthouse cranks who sat in the public galleries each morning and afternoon, watching scenes from other people's lives distorted by the fairground mirrors of litigation. Most lawyers disdained the spectators as voyeurs, brushing by them in the corridors and on the stairs, but sometimes Harry would pause in passing to exchange a casual word. He could not resist feeling sympathy for anyone whose life was so barren that this place became a second home.

'Want to make a confession?' he asked and gestured towards a man in an overcoat striding past them towards the exit. 'The detective sergeant there specialises in them. Don't worry, he doesn't need much. Just give him your name and he'll invent the rest.'

The man released his hold and bared crooked teeth in a conspiratorial smile. His shoulders were stooped, his wrinkled skin the colour of parchment. In one claw-like hand he was carrying a battered black document case and his breath seemed to Harry to have the whiff of mildewed books.

'It is your help I need, Mr Devlin. No-one else will do.'

He enunciated each syllable with pedantic care, as if English was not his native tongue. But it was the urgency of his tone that quickened Harry's interest.

'Are you in some kind of trouble?'

'No, no. You misunderstand. The murder I am speaking of occurred almost thirty years ago. Nonetheless, I believe you are able – if you will pardon the phrase – to assist me with my enquiries.'

'Thirty years ago?' Harry shook his head. 'I sometimes screamed blue murder as a babe in arms, but I never committed it. Sorry I can't help, Mr...'

'Miller, my name is Ernest Miller. Let me explain. I am looking into one of this city's most notorious crimes. You will have heard of the case, I'm sure. The newspapers, in their melodramatic way, dubbed it the Sefton Park Strangling.'

'It rings a bell.' Harry sifted through old memories. 'Wasn't it a young girl who was killed, the daughter of a well-known man?'

'Yes, the case attracted a great deal of publicity in its day. Carole Jeffries, the victim, was only sixteen years old. More importantly, to secure her lasting fame in death, she was a pretty girl with a good figure and a taste for short skirts.'

'And I seem to remember the murderer was a neighbour of hers?'

'A young man named Edwin Smith who lived nearby was arrested, it is true. Before long he confessed to having strangled Carole, but twenty-four hours before his trial was due to open, he tried to anticipate his fate by hanging himself. In that, as in so much else during his short life, he failed. A warder arrived in time to cut him down and save him for the gallows. Even so, the day of reckoning was postponed. Although the court proceedings were expected to be a formality, the authorities were reluctant to hang a man with an injured neck.'

'The executioner preferred more of a challenge?'

'I see you indulge in black humour, Mr Devlin. The best kind, I quite agree. But I think you miss the point. In those days – we are talking of 1964, you will recall – the campaign to abolish capital punishment was intensifying. The establishment dreaded a newsworthy incident.'

'Such as?'

Miller's tongue appeared between his teeth. 'They feared that a mistake might be made. If undue pressure were applied on the scaffold, there was a risk that the neck might snap and Smith would lose his head. Imagine, Mr Devlin, how the media would have feasted on that.'

Miller's eyes sparkled as he spoke, causing Harry to feel as cold as if he had stepped naked into the wintry streets outside, but something made him ask, 'So what happened?'

'The trial took place at the end of November and Smith was duly sentenced to death. However, as you will know, the law required three Sundays to pass before such a verdict could be carried out – and in the meantime the House of Commons voted to abolish capital punishment. As it happened, no hangings took place after the August of that year. Smith could certainly have expected a reprieve.'

'A lucky man.'

'Not so lucky as you may think,' said Ernest Miller. 'Having escaped the noose, Smith finally managed to kill himself in jail. Once again the authorities were careless – as they so often seem to be. He slashed his own throat on a jag of glass one night and severed the jugular vein.'

Harry bit his lip. His imagination was vivid – he had never quite decided whether that was an asset in a solicitor, or a fatal flaw – and Miller's words made his skin prickle. He could not help seeing in his mind's eye the sickening scene: the blood-soaked remains of a human being stretched across the concrete floor of a silent and unforgiving prison cell.

Gritting his teeth, he said, 'So where do I come in?'

'Smith's solicitor was Cyril Tweats.'

No wonder he was found guilty, Harry said to himself, the thought easing his tension. But all he said aloud was, 'I see.'

'You begin to appreciate my interest? I gather Mr Tweats retired recently and your firm took over his practice. Which is why I wanted to take a little of your time to talk about Carole's killing.'

'I don't quite...'

'I wonder,' said Miller. 'Your case has been adjourned until tomorrow morning. Perhaps you might allow me to buy you a drink and give you an idea of the information I am seeking. And if, at the end of half an hour, you decide I am wasting your time, well, no hard feelings. What do you say?'

Harry hesitated. He knew how much work in the office awaited his return; if he missed the last post, the following morning the sight of a mound of unsigned correspondence would reproach him like the grubby face of a neglected child. Besides, he had been repelled by the impression of pleasure Miller had given in lingering over the phrase *He slashed his own throat on a jag of glass one night and severed the jugular vein*. It was easy to visualise him salivating as he waited for a judge to don the black cap.

He glanced back over his shoulder towards the ground-floor lobby. The judicial roulette wheel had stopped spinning for the day, leaving losers to sulk in their cells whilst winners walked free to celebrate in style. His clients, Kevin and Jeannie Walter, had already disappeared, whisked off to the city's priciest restaurant by minders from the newspaper which had spent so much money to buy their story. He had last seen their barrister, Patrick Vaulkhard, in the robing room, taunting his opposite number about cover-ups and corruption. One of the bent coppers in the case was hanging around at the bottom of the open-tread staircase, waiting for his colleagues. With his hands in his pockets and his eyes fixed on the floor, he seemed deep in thought. If he had any sense, he was making plans for an early retirement.

Harry found himself recoiling from the prospect of ending the day back behind his desk. He was not by nature indolent, but a long afternoon in court had left him in a Philip Larkin mood: why should he let the toad of work squat on *his* life? The letters could wait: a drink would do him good. In any case, surely no harm could come from a brief conversation, however unappealing his companion?

He began to move towards the revolving door. 'Why not?'

'Splendid. I am most grateful for your co-operation.'

Outside a raw wind nipped at Harry's cheeks and knuckles. On the far side of Derby Square, harsh lights from the office blocks burned in the dirty darkness. Queuing commuters stamped their feet and tried to keep warm as they waited at bus stops for the procession of maroon double-deckers with bronchitic engines moving in sombre ritual along James Street. The snow of early morning had turned to slush, treacherous underfoot. Harry's shoes slid as he crossed the road at speed, trying to dodge the spray thrown up by a passing juggernaut.

At the corner of North John Street he waited for his companion to catch up. When at last he made it through the traffic to the safety of the pavement, Miller bent his head. 'Not – not as young as I was,' he panted.

'None of us are.'

Miller's breath was coming in shallow gasps and he seemed unsteady on his feet. The legacy, Harry guessed, of too many days, weeks and months spent in cramped surroundings, poring over faded type and living life at second hand.

He gave him a minute to recover before asking, 'So what is your interest in the Sefton Park murder?'

'I live on my own, Mr Devlin. My wife died ten years ago; I have no family and few outside interests. Since finishing work, I find I have a lot of time on my hands, and I need to occupy myself somehow. Crime has always fascinated me. Now I like to indulge my curiosity. The Sefton case is a superb example of its kind. It has all the classic ingredients.'

Miller lowered his voice, as if afraid that homeward bound shoppers might overhear, and ticked the items off on his fingers. 'A good-looking girl, forward for her years. A famous father and a pop musician boyfriend. A sudden brutal slaying – and a mystery. Police investigations carried out under the remorseless spotlight of the press and television. A suspect hounded without pity and brusquely condemned. And, above all, a grave injustice.'

His eyes gleamed and Harry again felt a chill of distaste. But he could not resist putting the question for which, he had no doubt, Miller was waiting.

'Who suffered the injustice?'

Miller studied Harry's expression before nodding, as if satisfied by what he found there.

'I spent much of today listening to your case from the back of the court. You must be happy with the progress your counsel made. The judge made it plain he is unsympathetic to the police, and no wonder. Your client, Mr Walter, was convicted of a crime he did not commit. He must be hoping for massive compensation.'

'We'll have to wait and see.'

'From all I have heard, you care about justice, Mr Devlin.'

If there was a hint of irony in the words, Harry was content to ignore it. Life as a lawyer in Liverpool had taught him to grow a thick skin. 'It's a rare commodity,' he agreed. 'Worth seeking out.'

'Forgive me for saying so, but I suspect most lawyers care more about their fees. However, let that pass. I would value your co-operation, since you have access to the files of Edwin Smith's solicitor. It is too late for Smith, but you may yet help me to prove he suffered a grievous wrong.'

'Did he protest his innocence at the trial?'

'On the contrary, he pleaded guilty.'

'Yet you're suggesting the confession was false?'

Miller cleared his throat. The strange shining eyes belied his deliberate manner. He was like a small boy, Harry thought, brimming with private knowledge and unable to restrain his excitement at making a disclosure.

'I am. And that is, for me, the fascination of the murder of Carole Jeffries. I do not pretend to have embarked on any moral crusade. I cannot even claim to share your devotion to seeing justice done. But I find murder irresistible – and perfect murder most of all.'

'No-one ever described the Sefton Park Strangling as a perfect murder.'

'You miss the point, Mr Devlin. If you accept that Smith was innocent, the conclusion is unavoidable.'

Miller showed his crooked teeth again.

'The true culprit escaped scot-free.'

The Harry Devlin Series

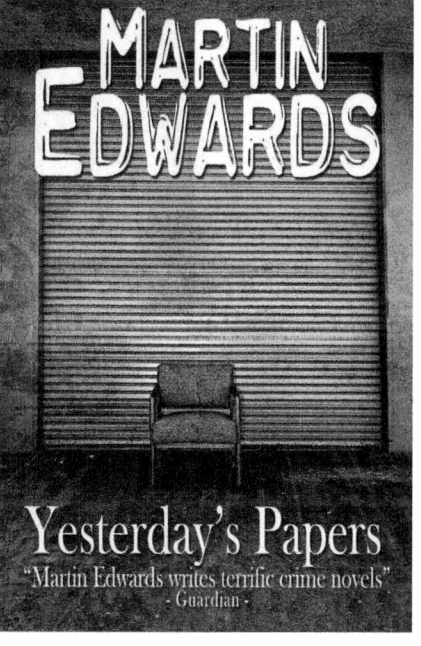

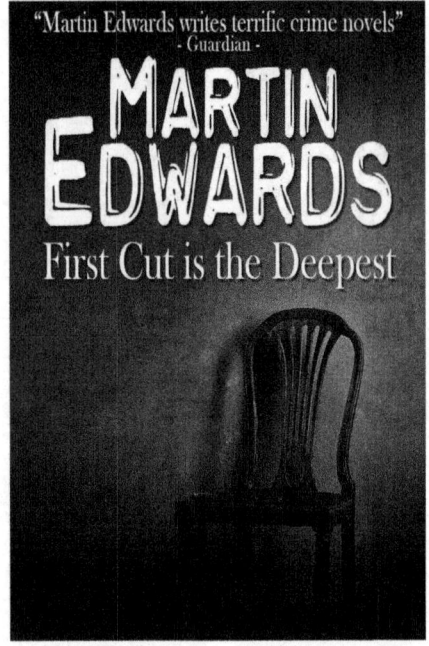

Printed in Great Britain
by Amazon